uprising

....

HEATHER SUNSERI

Sun Publishing
VERSAILLES, KENTUCKY

Heather Sunseri/Sun Publishing
PO Box 1264
Versailles, Kentucky 40383
www.heathersunseri.com

Publisher's Note: This is a work of fiction. Names, characters, places, and incidents are a product of the author's imagination. Locales and public names are sometimes used for atmospheric purposes. Any resemblance to actual people, living or dead, or to businesses, companies, events, institutions, or locales is completely coincidental.

Book Layout ©2014 BookDesignTemplates.com
Cover design by Mike Sunseri
Edited by David Gatewood

Ordering Information:
Quantity sales. Special discounts are available on quantity purchases by corporations, associations, and others. For details, contact the "Special Sales Department" at the address above.

UPRISING/ Heather Sunseri. -- 1st ed.
ISBN 978-1-943165-07-0

To healthcare workers on the front lines of fighting infectious diseases across the globe. I salute you.

chapter one

Cricket

A thin line separates life from death. One misstep. One wrong choice. Will today be the day the fever comes?

It was a long way down.

Sitting on the stone railing of the Biltmore Estate's third-floor balcony, my tattered winter coat pulled tightly around me, I stretched out my legs in front of me. The distance to the crumbling patio below wasn't nearly as intimidating as the chasm between the people of New Caelum and those of us who had spent the past six years building a life in the wreckage of a society nearly destroyed by a devastating virus.

Westlin Layne—my West—second-in-command of New Caelum, a city of people who took it upon themselves to be the chosen vehicles for mankind's survival, was still asleep beside the campfire that had dwindled to just a few remaining embers. His disheveled brown hair peeked out from under the down comforter he'd brought with him from the city when he came to rescue me.

I scoffed internally at the idea that saving me was even possible, but I also loved that West *wanted* to save me. To save the world, really.

His hand reached out from beneath the cover. He patted the ground beside him. When he didn't find what—or whom— he was searching for, his eyes sprang open. He sat up and turned left and right until he spotted me. His shoulders fell forward with relief.

I offered a slight reassuring smile. I knew he was terrified I would run. And I did nothing to reassure him. I would never lie to him. And I wouldn't promise to stay in one place forever. Unlike him, I didn't believe our country was stable enough to merge our two worlds. Too much had happened.

He was delusional to think he could bridge New Caelum with the outside by one day opening up the doors of the city, letting citizens who hadn't felt the wind on their faces in over six years walk out again into the broken outside. Besides, he had no evidence that anyone on the outside was even receptive to such an idea. I chalked that up to elite arrogance. He'd been brainwashed by a city of people who instinctively believed that *their* way was the best way for the entire country's survival— and that their timing for reconnecting two very different groups of people was the right timing.

West meant well. If I didn't believe that his motivations were pure and from a loving place in his heart, I would have pushed him away already.

He shuffled over to me. After rubbing sleep from his eyes, he grabbed my chin and directed my face toward his. He leaned in and placed a kiss on my lips. "Good morning," he whispered. He slid his hand around to the back of my neck, his fingers cool.

I blinked up at him. He wasn't just craving to touch me; he was checking my temperature. Over the past twenty-four hours, we'd already had several arguments about how often he was asking me how I was feeling.

"I feel fine."

"I didn't ask."

"I know." My lips twitched.

He guided me off the ledge and into his arms. My winter coat was unzipped and hung open. He slipped his hands around to my back and under my sweater, letting his cool palm meet the warm skin along my spine. I squirmed and let out a squeal, but he only held tighter as he laughed into the crook of my neck.

"West, your hands are freezing!"

"This is what you get for leaving me all alone over there." He brought my body even closer while his hands continued to roam my back.

After I finally relaxed into his hold—and his hands warmed—I leaned my cheek into his chest and breathed in the lingering smell of burning wood from last night's campfire. He rested his chin on the top of my head.

"It's a pretty morning," he said.

"Mm-hm," I agreed.

"What do you want to do today?"

I tensed under his hold, and I knew he noticed because he shifted his arms to make sure I couldn't draw away. West had allowed me to spend the past two days inside this dilapidated mansion, hiding from the community of people I'd spent the past six years with. He'd even left one of his guards with me when he ventured to the hospital to check on Ryder, Key, and Dylan.

There had been little change in their conditions as of last night. They were still suffering from the Samael Strain, the virus that had destroyed our nation. The virus that New Caelum had reintroduced into the world last week.

He was first to draw back when I didn't answer. "Cricket, you are not going to get sick and die, but you can't hide out up here on this ledge threatening to jump if you come down with a fever."

"I would never—"

He pressed a finger to my lips. "Are you telling me you haven't considered—not even for a second—the idea of throwing yourself off this balcony if you were to catch Bad Sam again?"

It was easy for him to stand confident. He was immune to the Samael Strain. I turned and stared toward the forest in the distance. He kissed the back of my head. My silence probably told him everything he needed to know.

It wasn't that I wanted to kill myself. Not even close. No matter how hard life had been in the early days of surviving in a broken world, I'd never been suicidal. But I was not afraid to die, either. And just the thought of suffering through Bad Sam again—or making people who loved me watch me suffer—was enough to allow some of my darkest demons to resurface.

West pulled away abruptly and paced with his hands behind his neck. "I could kill Justin," he said through gritted teeth. He pinned me with his hazel eyes. The golden specks of his irises flared with a fiery anger. "I still might if you get even the slightest headache or rise in temperature."

Justin Rhodes, vice president to New Caelum until a few days ago, purposely exposed me to the virus when he sliced an opening in the hazmat suit I'd worn while treating West's sister, Willow. He knew that the antibodies my body produced after surviving Bad Sam had weakened over the past six years. Killing me when he had the chance would have been more merciful than giving me that debilitating disease a second time.

Now I would have to either wait out the entire incubation period of twenty-one days—or return to New Caelum to test my blood for the presence of the virus. I'd have gone to Caine Quinton—doctor to Boone Blackston, my home off and on for the last six years—but he was only capable of testing for the Samael Strain after symptoms were present, which could happen anywhere from now until three weeks from now.

At least Justin Rhodes wasn't doing much better. He was locked inside a windowless room awaiting trial for the crime of betraying his city.

I was glad the city seemed intent on punishing the people responsible for bringing life back to a viral killer thought to be long extinct, but none of them knew what it was like to suffer through that dreadful illness like I did. I was the only one in history to have ever survived it. And I wasn't sure I could do it again.

I placed a gentle hand on West's cheek. "I will face whatever comes. I would never intentionally take my own life." That much I could promise. "And you will be brave and not do anything that will get you in trouble with your city."

"I can't even believe we're having this conversation."

"I can. It's a horrible disease. I wouldn't wish the pain of Bad Sam on anyone. Not even Justin. But I also understand your anger." I understood because I had lived with an anger toward the city of New Caelum for so many years that I'd sometimes forgotten exactly who or what I was angry about.

"Well, I can wish it upon Justin. We don't even know the extent of what he's done yet."

West was right. We didn't know how many of the scouts he'd sent out from New Caelum had been infected with the Samael Strain. Or if those scouts had made it to other settlements. We only knew that Ryder and Key had been infected, and that almost immediately after leaving the city, they had developed symptoms. Soon after that, Dylan developed symptoms as well. We also knew that at least two additional scouts had been infected, but that the New Caelum guards shot and killed them when they attempted to return to their beloved city.

"Will you promise me one more thing?" West pleaded. "Will you promise me you'll tell me if you feel the slightest bit... *off*?"

I slid my arms around his body and hugged him. "You know I'm not capable of promising that." I couldn't even promise we'd be together when—*if*—I developed symptoms.

He sighed, but didn't argue further.

I stared at my backpack, which lay on the ground beside the fire. In it was a vial of a protein compound developed by Dr. Hempel inside New Caelum. It was thought to be capable of repairing my deteriorating antibodies while supercharging my immune system for fighting infection. Dr. Hempel had hoped he could pair the protein compound with my antibodies and treat the patients sick with Bad Sam inside New Caelum, but everyone who had received the experimental medication had died shortly after the injection.

Instead of using Dr. Hempel's compound, I had injected myself two days ago with a dose of medicine made from my own antibodies—a concoction created by Caine—and blood-stone, crushed into a fine powder. I gave the same treatment to the others who were now fighting for their lives. The bloodstone had probably saved my life the first time I almost died from the disease, but I couldn't be sure that this treatment was enough to keep me from becoming ill. It might save me from dying, but what I wanted was a guarantee that I wouldn't develop the painful symptoms of the virus.

I was still tempted to inject myself with Dr. Hempel's protein compound. If it worked the way it was supposed to, my antibodies would strengthen, and maybe—just maybe—I wouldn't get sick at all.

Or I could die like the little girl inside New Caelum.

~~~~~

Two guards followed West and me to the hospital near Boone Blackston: Shiloh, who had helped Dax and me escape New Caelum only a few days ago, and Derek, who hadn't said much since he had accompanied West the day he found me on the balcony of the estate. Both wore beige and dark brown now, instead of the red Shiloh had worn when I first met her or the light gray of New Caelum government guards, a position she was recently promoted to. And their clothing was looser, more relaxed than the tailored uniforms worn inside the city—a better choice while outside the city. Still, I wondered silently why they wore the drab color of New Caelum's lowest sector.

As we got closer to the hospital, a truck came around a corner.

I tightened my grip on West's hand. I immediately recognized the large army truck as one of New Caelum's vehicles, like the one West traveled in the first night he ventured outside the city with Ryder and Key, his best friends, who were now crippled with Bad Sam.

"It's okay," he said. "They're here to help."

"What do you mean?"

Two men dressed in emergency sector red sat in the front cab.

"They're here to take Ryder and Key back to New Caelum." He stepped in front of me. "And Dylan, if Dax and Nina will allow it."

I pulled my hand from his grasp. "I wouldn't even allow that."

"They'll get better care inside the city. You know this."

I backed away. My eyes darted from West to Shiloh and Derek to the men in the truck awaiting orders from West. "Your doctors killed the only person they treated inside New Caelum."

"We have more supplies and medicines. Caine has to be running low on what he needs."

Dr. Caine Quinton had helped save my life the first time I nearly died from the Samael Strain, when he helped me escape New Caelum and start a life outside the city. But that was six years ago, when we were still flush with resources.

I swiped at a strand of hair that blew into my eye. "I don't know, West."

"Let's go talk to Caine and your friends." He reached his hand toward me. "Who knows? Maybe they've improved greatly since I checked last night."

I stared at his outstretched hand. "I can't go in there with you."

"Why not?" He lowered his arm.

"You know why."

He sighed. "Cricket, you're not sick. You have no symptoms, so you're not contagious even if you have the virus. Your friends need you. I need you to convince Dax to let me help his brother."

I admired his willingness to help Dylan, but there was no way Dax was going to allow West, or any other city person, near his brother.

"You can't be sure that I'm not infected. Bad Sam is too deadly to take any chances." I hugged my coat tighter. The air had gotten gradually colder every day for the past month, and though I typically fought through the pains of falling temperatures, my heavy coat felt like a thin windbreaker. "And Dax is not immune. The less I expose him to the possibility, the better."

Derek shifted beside Shiloh, while Shiloh remained perfectly still. Though neither of them had gotten very close to me, they had to be nervous to be around me.

I tilted my head back and looked up at the window of the floor where I knew two of West's best friends and one of mine lay recovering from the Samael Strain. They were fighting for their lives, and Dax, Caine, and Nina were watching and praying, helpless to do much else. I was sure that Caine was keeping them hydrated, but, like West said, his resources had to be dwindling. I had done everything I could to bring back a treatment I thought might help them. But could New Caelum do more for them at this point?

It was ironic that I'd had the ingredients all along—the treatment Caine had concocted using my antibodies along with the healing properties of the bloodstones my parents had brought back from Africa. It had taken being inside New Caelum on the roof with West to jog my memory of what my parents had said about the bloodstones.

However, we wouldn't have needed the treatment at all had people inside New Caelum not infected some of their own citizens and sent them outside the New Caelum walls to infect others. And for what? Just to frighten their citizens into believing New Caelum was the only safe place to live?

West grabbed one of my arms and pulled me closer to him. "We'll take this one minute at a time until you're convinced that you're safe from Bad Sam. For starters, let's move the patients back to New Caelum. While we're there, we'll test your blood for any sign of the virus."

I drew back. "I'm not going back."

West narrowed his eyes. "Christina, be reasonable." He only said my real name—the name he'd known me by six years ago—when he was frustrated.

"I *am* being reasonable. *Your* people exposed me—*and* all of them"—I gestured to the windows several stories up—"to civilization's worst nightmare. So you'll just have to find it in your heart to forgive me if I'm not ready to trust the people inside your elite sanctuary high up on that stupid hill."

chapter two

West

I stormed away from Cricket in a huff. She had just stood there with her arms crossed, staring, as Shiloh, Derek, and I, along with two of my city's emergency personnel, suited up in protective gear and struggled to attach our Tasers and PulsePoints to belts outside our hazmat suits.

"She is so stubborn," I blurted as I pulled the door to the hospital open and let it slam against an outer railing. With the others beside me, I began the climb to Ryder, Key, and Dylan, hoping their conditions were improving.

Though I hadn't been seeking a response, Shiloh said, "Can you blame her for being cautious? I know you only want to help Dylan, but he wouldn't have the virus if..." Shiloh's voice trailed off.

"No, I guess I can't blame her." But I was going to have to convince Cricket, and a lot of other people, that not all of New Caelum's leaders were corrupt like Justin and Dr. Pooley.

"We're going to have to send people out to find our last set of scouts," I said. "I need to know if Justin is responsible for sending more of the virus to other settlements."

"I'll work on it as soon as we return to the city," Shiloh said.

I sensed something was wrong the moment I set foot on the last set of stairs. A mixture of sobs and loud yelling rang out from above. I traded panicked looks with my three companions. Drawing our Tasers from our belts, we proceeded slowly up the steps.

We walked into the outer chamber of the infectious disease units—a hallway that separated the well from the sick—and were immediately drawn to the commotion in one of the rooms. Covered in protective gear, Caine knelt above one of the patients and was administering CPR.

My heart picked up speed. I couldn't see who it was, and a million thoughts passed through my mind at once. The thought of losing Ryder, my best friend, sent my heart rate into overdrive. Or my best friend could be losing Key, the love of his life. Or... if that was Dylan—an outsider infected because of a corrupt leader of New Caelum—the chain of events his death could trigger were unfathomable. The sounds around me suddenly seemed to be coming from a long tunnel.

Cricket's best friend Nina watched her father from several feet away. Through the hazmat mask, I could see that her face was stained with tears and snot. Her muffled cries echoed off the walls of the chamber. Dax, Dylan's twin brother, was outside the room, gripping a chair so hard that his knuckles were white. Zara, the tough guard from Boone Blackston, had an arm around Dax's shoulder. Neither was in a hazmat suit, and though they should technically be protected outside the infectious units, I didn't understand why they would take the risk.

Continuing to scan the area, I found confirmation of my hopes *and* fears. Ryder and Key were each lying in separate beds in the same closed-off room. They faced each other, their arms stretched out so that they could hold hands. Key's back was to Caine, but Ryder looked on with a knowing look of terror.

Finally, Caine sat back on his heels and angled his head backward to stare up at the ceiling. He climbed down off the bed and approached his daughter. He moved slowly at first, but then he took two quick steps and caught Nina in his arms as she collapsed. Though she'd already been crying heavily, this time when her sobs rang out, I knew she'd lost Dylan.

chapter three

Cricket

C all it a sixth sense. Maybe a window was open near the floor where my friends were inside the hospital. But I could have sworn I had heard Nina cry out. I took off in a sprint, tearing through the dark hospital lobby and up the stairs until I stood in the doorway leading to the infectious unit.

As I stepped out of the stairwell, I spotted Dax fifty feet down the hall. One second he was gripping a metal chair, the next he was hurling it against the wall behind him and releasing a furious roar that I would never forget.

I scanned the scene. Caine was rocking Nina in his arms as she sobbed uncontrollably on the floor behind one of the glass windows. They both wore hazmat suits. Beside them was a hospital bed. My heart raced as I recognized the skeleton of a man, overrun by a disease that had disfigured his body. My friend, Dax's twin brother, Nina's true love...

Dylan was dead.

Dax's chest rose and fell in quick breaths. His hands formed fists at his side. His head turned slowly toward me. His face shifted from ghostly pale to deep crimson in a matter of seconds. And nothing would have prepared me for what happened next.

He darted at me. His hands circled my neck and he slammed me to the ground, knocking every last trace of air from my lungs. "This is your fault!" he screamed. "Yours and that asshole of a boyfriend that you lied about!"

Almost as quickly as Dax took me to the ground, West pulled him off and shoved him toward Derek. Derek was inches from tasing Dax in his rib cage.

"No! Don't!" I choked. I jumped to my feet, my fingers massaging my neck where Dax had closed off my air supply. My heart sank to my stomach as I took in the rage radiating off Dax as he struggled in Derek's hold.

Derek stopped and looked to West. West shook his head, silently ordering him to stand down.

"Don't hurt him." I stretched my fingers wide. I wanted to go to Dax. To comfort him. But every ounce of his anger, frustration, and grief was aimed directly at me.

"Go ahead. Taser me until I'm unconscious." Dax stared straight at me, his eyes a fiery amber. "No sting from your boyfriend's weapon will ever hurt me as much as you killing my brother."

I flinched at his harsh words, but I knew he was right. I had failed Dylan. Whatever I had injected him with hadn't saved his life; it had killed him instead.

"It's not her fault," West said, his breathing uneven. "She's fought like hell to save him, risking her own life."

"You forget. I saw her inside New Caelum playing house with you."

West stepped forward, but I raised my hand to stop him. "Don't."

West stopped, relaxing his hand holding the Taser.

"Dax, I am so sorry." Tears slid down my face. Tears for the friend I'd just lost, and tears for my best friends—for Dax and for Nina—who were left behind to grieve.

"I want you out of here. I can't even look at you right now." Dax shrugged out of Derek's grasp. Derek relented but stayed close.

"Come on, man," West pleaded with Dax. "This is not her fault. You're making a big mistake."

Dax turned on West. "It's not her fault alone. Your city did this." He stuck out his chest and stepped closer to West. His uncovered face was inches from West's mask. With both hands he shoved West against the wall.

Derek and Shiloh both tensed, but West called them off with a shake of the head. He adjusted the mask of his suit, then pushed himself back to his feet.

"You need to get your friends and go back to your hole of a city," Dax said. "If it's the last thing I do, I will make sure New Caelum pays for what they've done."

"Fine. We're going," West assured him. "But we are not the enemy, Dax. The people who caused this are already locked up and will be dealt with harshly."

Dax laughed. "Right. Whatever you're doing to them is not enough." When his eyes found mine again, they looked like they were made of glass. I could tell he was fighting back the sadness that threatened to overcome his anger. I wanted to hug him, to hold him through his grief.

He looked like he wanted to say something more to me, but instead he turned and walked over to Caine and a distraught Nina, who had just emerged from the decontamination chamber, having rid themselves of their protective gear. Dax put his arm around Nina and steered her away from us, to the opposite end of the hallway. Nina didn't once make eye contact with me. She, too, must blame me for Dylan's death.

I swallowed against the painful obstruction in my throat.

West tried to put an arm around me, but I ducked away from him. His touch would surely start an avalanche of emotions I wasn't ready to face. "They're right," I said. "I failed. Whatever I did wasn't enough to save Dylan. You need to get Ryder and Key and return to New Caelum."

He nodded. "You're right. I need to get Ryder and Key home. And we can make sure you're virus-free."

I swiped at a tear that had escaped. "I'm not coming with you."

West's jaw tightened. Many heartbeats passed before he asked: "Where will you go?"

"I'll go back to the mansion for now."

"Don't do this, Cricket. You need..." He stopped speaking when I held up a hand.

I squeezed the bridge of my nose. "I need to think. I want to be alone for a while." There was nothing New Caelum could do for me that I couldn't do for myself right now.

West grabbed my elbow and gently pulled me into the stairwell. Once there, he lifted his mask off. "I'm going to take Ryder and Key back to the city, then I'm coming back for you." He slid his hand into my hair at the nape of my neck. "And you and I are going to talk about what happens next."

I narrowed my eyes. "What do you think could possibly happen next?" He was refusing to acknowledge that I might be dying. If the treatment didn't save Dylan, there were obviously no guarantees.

"I want you by my side. And I want to be by yours. Together, we can—"

"We can what, West?" I sucked in a breath and tried not to let it out in the form of a frustrated sigh. "You think we're going to bridge our two worlds?" I rotated my shoulders back. Sick or not... "I am *never* going to live inside your cruel city." My words came out much harsher than West deserved.

He put a finger on my lips. "This discussion is not over. Too much has happened between us." Leaning in, he kissed my forehead. "I'm sorry about your friend."

I hugged him, then, and I feared it was for the last time.

chapter four

West

Thankfully, Nina, Dax, and Zara left the hospital, leaving only Caine to supervise as my people and I prepared to move Ryder and Key back to the city.

"I'm sorry about Dylan," I said to Caine, afraid he might punch me. We were all covered in protective wear, but I could tell by Caine's flushed cheeks and bloodshot eyes that he was not only exhausted—understandable, as he'd been giving three patients around-the-clock care for the past week—but overcome with grief.

"I am, too," he said, his tone surprisingly calm. "And... about earlier. Dax will realize that this isn't Cricket's fault." He took a deep breath, then placed a gloved hand on my forearm. "How is she?"

"Why didn't you ask her?"

Caine had just stood and watched while Dax attacked Cricket. They both knew that something had happened to Cricket while she was inside New Caelum. And they knew she was no longer immune to contracting Bad Sam.

"I've practically raised these kids," Caine said. "All of them—Cricket, Dylan, and Dax. I love them like they're my very own. Cricket is like a daughter to me. But I'm not sure Nina will ever experience heartbreak worse that what she's feeling right now. Dax either. Cricket is strong..."

I flinched backward from Caine. "Are you kidding me? Because Cricket's strong, she deserves to suffer alone? She might be facing this deadly virus for a second time. She loved Dylan, too. *And* she cares for Nina and Dax like they're family. But what? She deserves to suffer alone because of her association with me?" I couldn't help how loud my voice had gotten. My guards were close. They both had hands on their weapons.

Caine didn't answer. He turned and gathered up two hazmat suits, which he handed to me. "For Ryder and Key," he said. "It's time you took your friends home. I'd like to report back to my town that the threat of Bad Sam has been removed. The sooner the better." The chill in his voice was like a slap to the face.

"Are you honestly turning your back on Cricket?"

He grabbed a handful of my hazmat suit. "I will never turn my back on her. You think because you're in love with her you're now an expert in what's best for her?"

The way he put air quotes around my love for Cricket with his free hand had me tightening my hold on the gear I held.

"She'll never live with you in that city of yours. She hates everything New Caelum stands for."

"I can make her happy. We can take care of her if she gets sick."

"I will take care of her. If she gets sick, she'll come to *me*."

I thought about that for a moment. So far, Cricket had shown no sign of wanting Caine's help. Or mine, for that matter. "I hope so," I finally said. But I already knew there would be no way I'd let her suffer Bad Sam outside the walls of New Caelum. We had a much better facility to help her survive, and I would not let her die.

~~~~~

"Hi, Key," I said softly through my mask when I entered the hospital room. Ryder had drifted back to sleep. "How are you feeling?"

"Much like a person mauled by a shark and then thrown up on a beach in 110-degree, 90 percent humidity."

I smiled. "That good, huh?"

Beads of sweat formed across her forehead, a sign that her fever was trying to break. She turned her head toward Ryder. "Is he going to survive this?"

She didn't ask if *she* was going to live. I wasn't sure if it was because she was more concerned for Ryder, or whether she thought she might be out of the woods.

"I'm going to do everything I can to ensure that you both fully recover." I set one of the suits aside. "Now, let's get you in this suit and get you home."

Only Shiloh had come in with me; we had decided that the fewer people inside the room where Ryder and Key had been suffering, the better. Shiloh and I helped Key get into her protective gear, then we turned our attention to a near comatose Ryder. He was much weaker than Key, but neither was in good condition. They had both lost so much weight. Their cheeks were hollowed out. Sores covered their bodies. And I was only going by the parts that were exposed before we dressed them in the protective suits.

"Gonna have to fatten this one up again," I said, trying to make light of a horribly tense situation. Key acknowledged the poor joke with a weak smile.

Once we had them both dressed, we moved them to stretchers to make it easier to transport them to the truck waiting downstairs.

Ryder called out in his sleep. "No. Don't take her from me. Key..."

"Ryder, it's me, West. We're not taking Key from you. You're both going home."

"No," he answered, but his mumbles were so incoherent, I couldn't decipher anything else.

Shiloh and I carried Key while two men in red hazmats carried Ryder. Derek walked behind us with a weapon drawn. He appeared uneasy as we loaded the patients in the truck.

My thoughts turned to Cricket. I was tempted to drive straight to the Biltmore Estate before heading home and force Cricket to return with me. But for now, I'd trust her need to be alone.

chapter five

Cricket

I ducked behind a pile of metal next to the hospital, the remnants of old cars stripped for parts, and watched West and his guards load Ryder and Key into the bed of the truck just a few yards away. It would be a miserably cold ride, but it was the safest way to transport two people ripe with disease. West covered each with a mound of blankets, then sat beside them, preparing to make the long ride to the city in the cold.

Derek and Shiloh closed the gate to the truck bed. Just as they turned to head toward the front cab, West called out to Shiloh. She stopped. A couple of seconds passed before she climbed up on the bumper of the truck to face West.

"I'm sorry to ask this of you," he said, "but I need you to return to the estate and stay with Cricket."

My body tensed as I watched for Shiloh's reaction. What New Caelum citizen in their right mind would want to stay outside the city to protect a stubborn girl who may or may not be dying from a highly contagious virus?

"Of course," Shiloh said. "I'll call you later tonight."

"Thank you."

I was tempted to step from behind my hiding spot to refuse Shiloh's protection, but I didn't want to argue with West further. Shiloh would discover my wish to be left alone soon enough.

Though Shiloh's hazmat suit covered her from head to toe, I knew that beneath that suit was a stunning girl, just slightly taller than me, and a year or two older, with short black hair. She was pixie-cute, though I was pretty sure she could wrestle any one of us to the ground, including her male counterparts. And she was obviously truly dedicated to West to agree to guard me instead of returning to the warmth and comfort of New Caelum.

"I'll just have the guys drop me off near the Biltmore," she said to West. She looked away for a second, but then looked back at him. "Do you know how many scouts they sent out with Bad Sam in their blood?"

"Four scouts are unaccounted for. I don't know if they were sick. So you'll need to watch out for signs of the disease."

Shiloh nodded. She hopped down and then climbed into the cab of the truck. The truck pulled away, and I watched as the taillights faded into the distance.

I didn't have much time.

~~~~~

After West and his guards were out of sight, I returned to the top floor of the hospital. I took the long way around to the lab where days ago I had left some supplies and my PulsePoint. I tucked the communication device and a few other items in my backpack, then placed additional supplies inside the refrigerated medicine case, along with dry ice to keep them cold.

Next I reached for some tools for drawing blood. After awkwardly tying a rubber strap around my upper arm, I managed to stick a needle with an attached vial directly into a vein and extract a sample of blood. When the vial was filled, I removed the needle, untied the strap, and taped gauze where the needle had been. I discarded the needle, but hung on to the vial.

I exited the lab and made my way back down the hall, stopping in front of the window into Dylan's room. I could see clearly just how badly Bad Sam had tortured my friend's body. The sheet that covered his legs and torso was soaked through with blood—it had come, I knew, from the sores that formed from a hemorrhagic fever. And his face was nearly unrecognizable due to dehydration and rapid weight loss.

A door hit the wall behind me, and I spun to find Caine holding a folded white sheet in his hands.

"What are you doing back here?" Caine asked.

I looked at my feet then back at him. "Dylan was *my* friend, too. I wanted to say goodbye." I held out my hand and uncurled my fingers to reveal the vial of blood I had just extracted from my arm. "And I wanted to leave you this."

Caine stepped toward me. "Yours?"

I nodded.

"Are you showing symptoms?"

"No. But West will be back. Give it to him. He can take it back to New Caelum. They can test it even when symptoms aren't present."

Caine took the vial from me and pulled me into his arms. He smoothed my hair out behind me, and I succumbed to my own grief. My shoulders shook, and tears fell. "It's going to be okay," Caine said. "Dax is going to realize that you did everything you could."

It didn't matter. I hadn't done enough. And now I couldn't even hug my friends and share in their grief. How would they ever forgive me?

I pulled away from Caine. "Why did Dylan die, when Ryder and Key seem to be improving?"

Caine placed his hands on the ledge beneath the observation window and stared at Dylan's body through the glass. "His heart just stopped. His body didn't fight the infection the way the others are. But without an autopsy, I can't give a complete answer."

"Are you going to do one?"

He nodded. "If it will help us gain more insight into what worked and what didn't..." He drew in a deep breath, then let it out slowly. "Willow, Ryder, and Key all seem to be improving. In small ways so far, but improving nonetheless. So the question becomes: What do the residents of New Caelum have that Dylan didn't?"

"Perhaps it was just a tragic coincidence that the one outsider was the one whose heart couldn't hang on long enough."

"Dylan was an extremely healthy young man. I'm not buying that."

A shiver passed through me. Even the air inside the hospital was turning colder. "I better get going," I said.

Caine grabbed my arm. "You going to be okay?"

I attempted a smile. "Yeah. I need to stay away while I wait out the incubation period." I wouldn't break the trust that Boone Blackston was built upon. If we suspected a case of Bad

Sam, we would do whatever it took to keep it from spreading. "Please tell Nina and Dax that I love them very much."

"I'm sorry that it has to be this way."

"Yeah, me too. I know that I'm not contagious yet, but..."

"You'll let me know if you become sick? You know I'll take care of you."

I hugged Caine one last time, then practically flew down the stairs and away from the hospital.

chapter six

West

"What do you mean she's not there? Where did she go?" I screamed at Shiloh through my Pulse-Point, but I knew as well as she did that Cricket could be anywhere. And if she didn't want to be found, it would be near impossible to do so.

I stood in the reception area outside the isolation chambers where nurses had been caring for Willow ever since she came down with Bad Sam. Ryder and Key had been placed in private rooms adjacent to Willow's, but they had been separated from each other, which was driving Key crazy.

Willow's vitals were improving, and her brain activity was strong, but she was still in a coma. The doctors said that her body would continue to heal and fight infection while she slept, and that, for now, it actually wasn't a bad thing for her to remain in a coma.

I would have to take their word for it.

"West, what do you want me to do?" Shiloh prompted after waiting patiently for direction.

I sighed. "I'm sending a truck out for you."

As soon as I ended the call with Shiloh, the door behind me opened. Mom entered, dressed in a fitted black dress and a double strand of large, lustrous pearls. "West, honey, I'm so happy to have you home."

I grabbed her elbows as I leaned in and kissed her cheek. "Mother. You look much stronger."

"Of course. Now that I have Justin out of my life, I *am* stronger, and the city is going to be stronger than ever with you by my side." Justin had been Mother's vice president. He had thought that by sending Bad Sam into the outer settlements, the citizens of New Caelum would decide to remain inside the city and continue to need strong leadership. He had been working to take Mother down and become president himself, but his plan backfired.

I faced the isolation rooms again. Ryder had yet to wake up. "I don't know what I'll do if Ryder doesn't make it."

"He will. Now, come. The council has gathered to discuss the state of New Caelum. They're waiting for us." She turned and headed back the way she had come in.

I followed. It was my job to know what was going on inside my city. After former Vice President Justin Rhodes and former Councilman Dr. Pooley had been exposed for injecting the scouts with Bad Sam and sending them out into the settlements, the council had named me the new vice president.

And it was time I started acting like a leader.

~~~~~

The council had gathered in the large conference room in the government sector. I recognized six members, including Mrs. Canary, who kissed both of my cheeks when I entered. "Thank you for bringing my Ryder home."

"You're welcome. I'm sorry I couldn't tell you more about your son as it was happening."

She patted my arm. "It's okay. I understand city business as much as anyone at this table." Her eyes darkened before she whispered, "Justin will pay for what he has done."

I nodded, then turned to the others. "The council has shrunk quite a bit since we last met."

Mr. Gatewood tapped his chin with steepled fingers. "Unfortunately, we have been unable to verify the innocence of several council members. Some have been proven guilty and locked up, while others have only been removed from the council temporarily, while we continue to investigate the situation."

"The guilty will reveal themselves," my mother said. She was all business as she handed out folders to everyone. "Let's get started." She looked at me and gestured to the far end of the table. "West, have a seat."

I did as I was ordered, sitting at the foot of the long table, and she took her own seat at the head. She picked up her PulsePoint and began pressing buttons. A screen lowered from the ceiling along one wall. Mother sat her PulsePoint in the middle of the table and pointed at the screen. The image of Dr. Hempel appeared. He was sitting in a hospital bed.

"Dr. Hempel? You're awake," I said.

Dr. Hempel's lips lifted in a small smile. "I'm alive," he said weakly. "Thanks to whatever I was injected with." He paused every few words to take a breath, obviously still weak from the lingering illness. We could only assume that Dr. Hempel had somehow broken preventive protocol and had exposed himself to the disease while dealing with samples of the live Samael

Strain and working with Cricket's antibodies to come up with a cure for Willow.

"Dr. Hempel, please share with West and the council what you told me," Mother said.

"The antibodies from the sole survivor are gone from the lab."

"The antibodies are gone?" I stood and leaned into the table. "Did Cricket take the antibodies with her when she left?" Why would she have done that?

"No. The antibodies were here when Christina left, according to my nurses. But they're gone now."

"And you trust these nurses?" I asked.

His voice took on a severe tone. "With my life."

I scanned the faces around the table. "What do we make of this?"

"That's not all." Mom pointed to the screen again.

"The vials of live Samael Strain are also gone from the lab."

I sat. My fingers pressed hard into the solid wood table in front of me; the skin behind my nails turned white. "Are you saying what I think you're saying?"

"That someone inside our city has in their possession the most deadly weapon known to man?" my mom said. "Yes." She sat back in her chair, her arms crossed while she tapped manicured fingernails against her elbow. "A single vial could unleash the deadly virus on every citizen of New Caelum."

"Who would want to do such a thing? And why? Wouldn't they be killing themselves in the process?" *Unless they're immune,* I thought, answering my own question.

"One more thing," Dr. Hempel said. His voice was getting more hoarse the more he spoke. "Christina left no evidence of what she actually concocted to treat your sister or me."

I squeezed the bridge of my nose, then sat back in my chair. Vials of a deadly virus had been stolen from the labs, and New Caelum was no closer to knowing how to treat or cure the disease. And even if we did know what cured the disease, we no longer had any of Cricket's antibodies.

"How long until we can harvest antibodies from current survivors?" I directed the question to Dr. Hempel.

"There are no 'survivors' yet. Current patients will have to test negative for all traces of the Samael Strain before they can be considered as such. Second, not only was Christina Black rare for surviving the Samael Strain, she was also a universal blood donor, which meant her antibodies could be used to develop a treatment capable of helping almost anyone who contracted the virus. So far, that treatment seems to be working on those currently sick with the virus."

Except for one.

"But," Dr. Hempel continued, "those currently sick all have more rare blood types. Even if we currently had access to their antibodies, they would only be useful to others of the same blood type."

"Meaning Christina's antibodies are still our only hope for a universal cure."

"Until we can conduct more studies with the protein compound Dr. Pooley and I had been working on."

"We will continue to investigate the theft of these substances," Mother said. "Dr. Hempel, thank you for keeping us informed. We wish you a speedy and full recovery."

Dr. Hempel nodded, and Mother shut off the videoconference. The screen retreated back into the ceiling.

"Moving on..." Mother said. "As you all know, the Founders' Day Gala is fast approaching." The Founders' Day Gala, held on the anniversary of the day that New Caelum was officially closed off from the rest of the world, kicked off a week of celebration. Many used the week as a time for spiritual awakening and renewal, a time to be grateful and to celebrate hope of another year, while others just spent the week partying. At the end of the celebration period, the city came together for the biggest celebration of them all—the Renaissance Ball. I typically attended the gala and the ball, if only because my mother required me to.

"In preparation for the event, there is something I would like for you all to review." Mother held up a black folder adorned with the shiny gold seal of New Caelum. It was identical to the folders she had placed in front of me and all the council members. "You have in front of you an excerpt from the original... vision statement, if you will... that we had for New Caelum before our wonderful city even formed. Please read it now."

I opened my folder and pulled out a single piece of paper, which was also embossed with the New Caelum seal. The others around the table did the same. Lowering my eyes, I read:

All young government officials will marry and reproduce when they reach the age of eighteen or when they take office, whichever comes first. They will set an example for rebuilding society and encourage all citizens of New Caelum to do the same.

My pulse sped up, and heat spread down my neck. I shifted as I broke out in a cold sweat. "What is this?" I stared down the long conference room table into my mother's eyes. She had blindsided me, and she knew it.

"West, you will be formally named vice president of New Caelum during a ceremony at the Founders' Day Gala on Saturday night. We told the citizens of our city that you plan to marry—"

Christina. It was supposed to be Christina. "Yes, but Mother... You know—"

She raised a hand, silencing me. "Your constituents don't have a preference with regard to whom you marry." Meaning she didn't care that Christina was no longer inside New Caelum and had no plans to return. "But they do wish to see this city continue to grow. This city's plan was always to have leadership that combined experience"—she pointed to herself—"with youth. New Caelum needs leaders who are young, fresh, and poised to lead another generation into existence. And the founders of New Caelum believed that in order for our city—our country—to recover from the Samael Strain, these young leaders would need to reproduce and provide a strong foundation for future generations."

"So," I said, "not only do you wish me to choose a wife, you want me to knock her up?"

"Don't be crass, West." Mother stuffed the vision statement back inside the folder. "But yes. You are nineteen, a year late by my calculations. The city has been lenient with you. But you are now a leader of New Caelum. This city expects you to act like it."

"By getting married."

41

"Yes. After you are sworn in as vice president, Annalise Gatewood will be formally presented to you as your match at the gala, and the two of you will be married at this year's Renaissance Ball."

Annalise Gatewood? I wanted to scream, but her father was mere feet away from me. "A week? That's how long you're giving Annalise and me to accept this ridiculous plan?" Surely not even Annalise would agree to this.

Councilman Gatewood held up a hand. "There are others who have been groomed to lead, and who would gladly step into your role," he said. A clear threat.

I had to find a way out of this matching. No freaking way was I going to marry Councilman Gatewood's daughter.

Mr. Herod, a council representative from the education sector—a historian—cast a sideways glance at Mrs. Canary. No one seemed to notice except me. I looked back toward my mother, then to Mr. Gatewood. "I have never shied away from my responsibilities. I won't start now."

chapter seven

Cricket

It was dark, and Boone Blackston was quiet when I approached the gate. I pulled my coat tighter around me and braced for a fight with Zara to get inside the walls of the settlement—my home.

The closer I got, the faster my heart raced. I was not at risk for exposing anyone inside Boone Blackston to Bad Sam since I was exhibiting no symptoms. But with deadly viruses, most people were overly cautious. No one would want me around, knowing that I was possibly infected, but I needed some of my things—mainly a box of memorabilia inside Caine's apartment. Since he was at the hospital outside the settlement's walls, I hoped I could sneak in and out unnoticed.

Placing a gloved hand on the wrought iron gate, I slowly pushed it open. I was surprised when no one—meaning Zara—stopped me.

A chill moved down my spine, and I trembled as I shuffled along the dirt and broken concrete road toward the building where Caine lived. A rodent scurried behind an old, rusted mailbox that hadn't been used in six years.

When I reached Caine's building, a dim light flickered in the window. I descended the stairs to the basement apartment and knocked lightly on the door. Silence was followed by the sounds of hushed voices. Footsteps approached the door, and I took several steps back.

When the door swung open, Zara stood in the doorway. She narrowed her eyes and gave me a once-over. "It's not a good time, Cricket."

"I'm not here to cause trouble. I just need a box of my things. It's on top of Caine's bookshelf."

Zara glanced back over her shoulder. I couldn't see what she was looking at or who else was even there.

After a few seconds, Nina appeared, holding the box I needed. Her eyes and face were red and tear-stained. My heart suddenly felt too big for my chest. "Nina," I whispered. "I... I don't know what to say."

She obviously didn't either, because she thrust the box into my hands and then disappeared back inside, further crushing my heart.

It was the perfect opportunity for Zara to twist the imaginary knife sticking out of my chest, but instead her face fell. She opened her mouth to say something, but must have thought better of it and remained silent.

"Take care of them," I said.

Zara nodded and started to go back inside. But then she turned to face me again. "Dylan's death was not your fault. They just don't understand your connection with West and with New Caelum. Or why it took you so long to make it back out of New Caelum with a treatment. Dax is telling a story about how you were dressed in beautiful clothing and engaged to marry the next president of the city."

"But that's not how it happened."

"I know. I think he even knows it, but he's hurting."

"Just take care of them, okay?"

"I will. And Cricket? I have my PulsePoint. It's on at all times."

I nodded in understanding.

~~~~~

Even in the dark, I knew the way. My childhood home was only four miles from Boone Blackston and less than two miles from the start of a seven-mile forest trail that led to New Caelum. And I was accustomed to traveling in the dark. For years, I'd been escaping Boone Blackston when I needed time alone.

But my old childhood home was not one of my typical destinations. For one, the house held way too many memories—happy memories—which now only drudged up a suffocating sadness when viewed against today's reality. For another, the house was too far away from New Caelum, and in recent years, I'd often camped up in the mountains in order to keep an eye on the happenings inside the outer walls of New Caelum. That's how I'd first discovered that the Samael Strain had returned—when I saw that their incinerators were running at all hours of the night.

But now, I wanted to distance myself from New Caelum—and from West. I was on a mission to find my parents' hidden supply of bloodstones in the hope that they would help me come up with a way to obliterate Bad Sam forever. And I didn't want the people close to West ruining it.

My parents and I had lived on a small piece of land on the outskirts of Asheville. The farmland around the house was overgrown with trees and weeds, but because winter had come early this year, enough of the overgrowth had died back for me to make out the gravel driveway leading to the house. The night was quiet but for the breeze that rustled the grass and tree limbs and the sound of my feet shuffling over gravel.

So I immediately stopped in my tracks when a long, high-pitched howl—the sound of an animal enraged—cut through the tall weeds and bare trees to my left. The muscles in my arms and neck tensed as I stared in the direction the sound had come from. I had no idea what kind of animal would have made such a noise, but I knew I had no weapon to protect myself. And if it was rabid or, just as bad, starving, I could very well become its midnight snack.

I picked up my pace and stayed on the grassy edge of the drive to make my footsteps quieter.

I heard the sound of the animal again—closer this time—and I ducked down, trying to make myself as small as possible. I was still thirty yards from the front porch, and I still needed to dig out my key. As silently as possible, I set my backpack in front of me. I unzipped the main pouch, cringing at the sound it made. I reached in and lifted out the box of memorabilia like it was a bomb about to blow.

The animal cried out a third time. I was certain now that the animal was either extremely ill or injured.

I removed the house key from the box and returned the box to the backpack. Without zipping the bag, I began stepping lightly toward the house again. I was still twenty yards away when I heard the animal again. But this time it was not a wailing from beside me—it was a low, deep growl vibrating behind me.

I didn't turn to look; I took off in a sprint. I raced up the wooden porch steps, staying to the outer edge, remembering how the middle of the steps had shown signs of rot the last time I'd been there. I dropped my pack and jerked open the outer storm door. Fiddling with the keychain in my hand, I struggled to fit the key in the lock.

My hands shook at the sound of snarling growls and snapping teeth. I fumbled the key—and dropped it.

Bile rose in my throat. I had broken out in a full sweat, and my heart raced so fast I thought I would pass out. As I bent down to snatch up the key, I saw the animal. It was now lunging toward the porch at a full sprint.

I grabbed the key, jammed it in the lock, and turned it. But the door was stuck, warped from years of moisture and lack of use.

I heard a crash behind me as the crazed beast hit the porch steps. Why was I still standing? It should have sunk its teeth into my flesh by now. I lowered my shoulder and rammed it into the door. It burst open, and I fell through, landing on the dusty floor inside. I scrambled to my feet and turned to face my pursuer.

It was a German shepherd, his thick coat caked with detritus and blood. He had fallen through the rotten stairs leading to the front porch, and was now fighting and clawing his way through the splintered wood. I slammed the door shut just as he heaved himself onto the front porch.

His body crashed against the door, but it held. I collapsed to the floor. Lying on my back, I placed both hands over my wildly beating heart.

The dog pawed and scraped at the door, trying to dig his way into the house. For twenty minutes I just lay there, listening to the animal that had almost cut my already short life even shorter. And though the noise quieted after a time, the vision of the dog's canines ripping through my flesh inhabited my dreams as I fell into a restless sleep.

chapter eight

West

When I awoke, I immediately thought of Cricket. I should never have left her alone out there. But she'd given me no choice. I'd fallen for a headstrong outsider who needed time to process the current state of things.

I sat up, placing my feet flat on the carpeted floor, and rubbed my temples.

The distant sound of Mother's voice reminded me I was never alone. I'd grown up around a city of people, and had rarely experienced quiet. Somewhere in the noise of my upbringing, I had landed myself in a position of power. And with that power came responsibility. According to Mother, that responsibility included not only leadership, but producing offspring for the next generation.

I pulled a black T-shirt over my head, slipped on some charcoal gray flannel dress pants—the uniform of a government elite inside New Caelum—and exited my bedroom to face my mother.

"Well, he better start talking, or he'll never see the light of day again," Mother was saying. She looked up when she heard my approach. "I'll call you back." She ended her call.

"Good morning, West. How did you sleep?" She poured hot water into a porcelain cup and steeped a tea bag.

"I've slept better. Who were you talking to?"

She waved a hand while taking a sip of tea. "Oh, no one."

"Mother, why did you make me vice president if you were going to keep secrets from me?"

"Don't be overdramatic, West. I was simply speaking with Mr. Gatewood. We think Justin might know who stole the vials and antibodies from the labs."

"Of course Justin would know. He was probably behind the theft."

"Come. Have a seat and tell me how Christina is doing."

I walked over to the teacart and grabbed one of Mother's delicate teacups, but instead of hot water and a tea bag, I poured coffee. Black. I immediately took a big sip, letting the hot liquid coat the back of my throat and make a beeline to my bloodstream. I started to sit down next to Mother, but the sound of my PulsePoint stopped me. I'd received a message from Shiloh:

Incident in the quarantine unit. Someone attacked Key. She'll live, but you should come.

"Everything okay?" Mother asked.

I didn't know why, but I hesitated to tell Mother the truth. "Yeah. It's nothing. Shiloh is having a problem with some of the guards who are unsure of their duties since Justin is now out of the picture."

"Well, you'd better take care of it. We'll talk after."

~~~~~

"What happened?" I asked before the door had even closed.

Shiloh nodded toward a nurse sitting next to a computer station outside the infection units. Her legs bobbed up and down. She fidgeted with her fingers in her lap.

"You were the nurse that was on duty when Christina Black brought a treatment in for my sister," I said.

"Yes," she answered hesitantly, probably wondering why I was bringing that up now.

"Janet, right?"

She nodded.

I wanted to question her about the cure Christina administered, but it wasn't the time. I gave my head a small shake. "What happened to Key?"

Janet stood and wrung her hands. "I was supposed to start my shift at seven a.m. When I arrived, no one was at the nurses' station or inside the infected rooms—that I could see— besides the patients themselves." She nodded at the chambers behind me.

"So what did you do?"

"The lights to the patients' rooms were dark, which is normal at that time of the morning. I first looked through the glass and saw that your sister appeared to be sleeping calmly. Then I walked over to the computer station and looked at the patients' vital readings. Willow's readings were normal, but Ryder's were crazy. His heart rate was way too high. His blood pressure had gone through the roof. And when I looked through the glass, he was convulsing on the floor."

I walked to the window of Ryder's room. "He appears to be sleeping soundly now."

"I gave him a sedative."

"And Key? The message said she was attacked."

"Like I said, Ryder was on the floor, so I flipped on his light, which partially lit up Key's unit beside his. That's when I saw him." Janet's voice cracked. "A man in a black hazmat suit was smothering Key with a pillow. When the light went on, he stopped and immediately crossed through the decontamination chamber."

"There's only one way out of here, so..."

"I hit the alarm, and the guards came in and took the man away."

"Well? Who was it?" Seemed like a stupid plan on the perpetrator's part.

"It was one of Justin's guards. He said he was just following orders and refused to say anything else."

I ran a hand across my unshaven chin. Before long, we'd run out of room to house the criminals piling up in our jails.

While I was here, I wanted to go in and visit with Key, Ryder, and my sister. I made my way to the room with protective gear and proceeded to suit up. Shiloh and the nurse followed.

"What should we do with the man who did this?" Shiloh asked.

I thought about it for a minute. "Who else knows about this?"

"Only Janet, me, and the guards who were on duty. And now you," Shiloh said.

"Call the guards and have them place him in a cell in the dungeon jail."

Shiloh glanced nervously at Janet, then back at me. "Those haven't been opened in years."

"Well, our city jail is starting to fill up. And this crime is a bit more hideous than normal, don't you think? Throw him in solitary. He's going to tell us who ordered him to hurt Key, and why. Call Derek, and have him interrogate the perpetrator first. Justin hasn't had any visitors besides city leaders, so if the former vice president is issuing orders, it's through one of them."

Shiloh nodded. "Yes, sir."

~~~~~

I pulled a chair over and sat beside Key's hospital bed. As I lifted her hand in mine, her eyes fluttered open. "Hi," I said.

"Ryder?"

"He's fine. Sleeping." I pushed her hair off her forehead. "Did the man who attacked you say anything?"

"No, nothing. Why did he try to kill me, West?"

"I'm going to find out."

If the old movies and television shows I'd been allowed to watch as a kid were any indication, people usually killed for money or information. And since our city didn't run on riches, this man had to have been after information—but he hadn't tried to ask Key anything. So perhaps his intent was to *destroy* information. What could Key possibly know that was so valuable, someone was willing to risk his freedom to destroy it?

"Key, what do you remember about being sick?" This was the first time I'd had a conversation with her since she'd developed the fever.

"I remember being in a warehouse, and that nice girl gave me some water. I was so thirsty. What was her name? It was a bug or something."

I chuckled softly. "Cricket."

"That's right. Oh, no. Did she get sick? She shouldn't have gotten that close."

"You didn't make her sick. But I am wondering how you and Ryder were exposed to the virus."

Key stared up at the ceiling. "I don't know. I was always so careful when dealing with the virus. But even if I hadn't been, that wouldn't explain..." She stared up at me, panic in her eyes. "Did I get Ryder sick?" She slammed her head back against the pillow. Tears fell from her eyes and streamed into her hair. "I almost killed him, didn't I?"

"Stop." I squeezed her hand, which was dwarfed inside my gloved grasp. "We don't know how Ryder got sick. He may have already been sick when he left the city. He was simply slower to show symptoms."

"I felt so invincible only a month ago. I was promoted to my last year of nursing and was going to study medicine with Dr. Pooley. I was on my way to gaining doctor status. They'd even started vaccinating me so I could study other infectious diseases. I was going to be on the team to study a vaccine for Bad Sam. Then I was matched to the love of my—"

"Wait," I interrupted. "Back up. What kind of vaccinations?"

"They vaccinate all nurses and doctors who are selected to work in the infectious disease lab. Dr. Hempel said it would build up our immunity to any disease we might inadvertently expose ourselves to."

I was so busy processing what she was telling me that I didn't even realize how tightly I was squeezing her hand.

"West." She wiggled her hand beneath my grip.

I released it. "I'm sorry. It's just that..." I stood and paced. I thought about how solid Key's and Ryder's relationship was. I went back to her, leaned over her, and looked directly into her eyes through my hazmat mask. "Key, it's just me. I need you to be honest with me. I promise there will be no repercussions to what I'm about to ask. Did you give Ryder these same injections?"

Key didn't dare look away. Fear swarmed deep within her dark brown eyes. Though she had no idea I had now taken the job of vice president of New Caelum, she knew I was being groomed to work under my mother high up in government. She also knew that breaking protocol within the medical sector could result in her losing her ability to practice medicine—even resulting in her being cast into the lowest sector of New Caelum.

"I'm concerned for Ryder," she said. "I don't want him to be punished for something I did."

"You may have saved both of your lives. But I need to know what you did."

Hesitantly, she let her head dip into the slightest of nods. "I only gave him one of the injections—one thought to fight infection. I was told it was part of some protein compound developed by Dr. Hempel. Dr. Pooley said it was being used to develop a vaccine for Bad Sam." She grabbed my arm with both hands. Given how weak she was yesterday, I was surprised at the strength in her grip. "I was scared, West. Dr. Pooley was experimenting with some really dangerous stuff, including Bad

Sam. One wrong move, and I would have been exposed. And he said that the protein compound only worked if a patient received it prior to being exposed to the virus. Receiving the injection after exposure would kill you."

Cricket had been right. They had been experimenting on human subjects by infecting them with the virus. But so far, they hadn't saved a single patient without Christina's antibodies. Or the bloodstone.

That's why they infected Willow and set everything in motion for my mother to reveal where Christina had been hiding all these years.

"Cricket doesn't know," I said, mostly to myself.

"What? Cricket doesn't know what?"

I didn't have time to explain to Key that Cricket was Christina. I had to find Cricket before she injected herself with the protein compound. If what Key was saying was accurate, and if Cricket had the Samael Strain and injected herself with the protein compound, she would die.

~~~~~

I hadn't even had breakfast yet, and I was suiting up in my second hazmat suit for the day. If what Key had told me about the protein compound was true, she may have saved her and Ryder's lives.

I needed Dr. Hempel to tell me everything about this compound he'd invented. How had it helped Key and Ryder? And would it truly kill someone already infected with the virus?

Once I had my hands double gloved and my hood secured, I entered Dr. Hempel's room. "Good morning, Dr. Hempel."

He was sitting up in bed. A nurse dressed in powder blue was taking his blood pressure and his temperature. "Good morning, West. To what do I owe the pleasure of both your and your mother's company this morning?"

"Mother was here?"

"Yes. Just left." He folded his hands in his lap.

"Why was she here?"

"Oh, just city business."

"City business, huh? Well, since I'm the new vice president, she can fill me in this afternoon when I meet with her."

"That's right. Congratulations on becoming vice president."

"Thank you."

"And I hear you are to be matched at the Founders' Day Gala coming up."

"That's what they tell me." I sat in the chair beside his bed. "Dr. Hempel, do you think you could tell me more about the injections of protein compound that the people of the medical sector have been receiving?"

Dr. Hempel glanced nervously at the nurse. Her hands shook slightly as she pushed a syringe into Dr. Hempel's IV line.

"Do you need anything else at the moment, doctor?" the nurse asked.

"No. I'm fine." We both watched as the nurse left the room and entered the decontamination chamber. "They've been fussing over me all morning," Dr. Hempel said. "And they must be adding new nurses constantly these days. I've never even seen that one before."

"So, the protein compound?"

"Yes, I thought it was going to be the key to a Bad Sam vaccine, because of how it helps with heart conditions."

"Heart conditions?"

"Yes. Our studies determined that the main cause of death with Bad Sam is heart failure." He paused to take in a deep breath. He closed his eyes briefly before continuing. "After the virus takes root, infection develops and moves throughout the body, eventually attacking the heart. We hoped this compound would help people at least survive the illness, much like Christina Black did. Still, we needed Christina and her antibodies to develop a true vaccine. And after testing the compound, we discovered a problem with..."

Dr. Hempel suddenly stopped talking and his eyes grew large.

"A problem?" I prompted. My eyebrows lifted, and I gestured rather impatiently with my hand for him to continue.

Dr. Hempel's head fell back against the pillow. He raised his arms and bent them both awkwardly at the elbow and the wrist. His eyes rolled back in his head. He appeared to be having a seizure or a stroke of some kind.

"Dr. Hempel?" I reached for the call button and screamed into the speaker. "Nurse!"

A white foam formed at his mouth, and I realized Dr. Hempel had been poisoned. Almost as quickly as the fit had started, his body went limp. His head rested awkwardly, cocked sideways, and his eyes were glassy and without life.

I backed away from the bed, slowly at first, but then I turned and fled the room.

Once I had decontaminated with a triple dose of the disinfectant shower and redressed, I flew from the hospital sector and began private-messaging Shiloh.

Find Derek. Meet me in...

uprising

Where could I meet them where no one would hear or sus-
pect anything? I needed to act normal until I could do what
needed to be done. I couldn't risk being pulled in for a long,
drawn-out questioning about Dr. Hempel's death.

... *Meet me in the garden cafe.*

I'd meet them in a public place.

~~~~~

Beads of sweat formed across my forehead and streamed
along my temple. I ordered a coffee and a bagel and found a
seat in the middle of the cafe. It was nearing ten a.m., so the
cafe wasn't as crowded as it usually was earlier in the morning.

A couple of women with toddlers sat by a window that
overlooked New Caelum's garden of fruit trees. Five historians
wearing orange sat at a large table in the back. A couple of
young female gardeners dressed in green purchased cappucci-
nos to go. They giggled as they passed, barely noticing me.

I used a napkin to wipe my brow. After a few sips of coffee,
Shiloh entered the cafe, followed by Derek.

"What's wrong with you?" she asked, taking the chair beside me. "You're as pale as that napkin."

Ignoring Shiloh, I asked Derek, "What did you learn from
our prisoner?"

He shook his head. "He's not talking, but..."

"But what?"

Derek glanced around the cafe before answering. "Councilman Gatewood stopped the guards on their way to the lower
sector and instructed them to place the prisoner in the government sector with all the other prisoners. He told them the
dungeon jail was off-limits."

59

"Off-limits, huh? Fine. Whatever." I had more serious issues to deal with. "Do either of you know anything about a protein compound that some people working in the medical sector are getting?"

They traded a glance, then shook their heads. I repeatedly stretched my fingers straight and curled them into my palms.

"What is this about, West? You're starting to scare me." Shiloh kept her voice barely above a whisper. "Does this have anything to do with the attack on Key?"

"I'm not sure, but Dr. Hempel is dead," I said. My voice was so low that they both had to lean in to hear me.

"What? How?" Shiloh asked.

"Best I can tell, he was poisoned."

Derek's head popped up. He eyed the cafe entrance behind me. "Don't look now, but your mother just walked in. With Annalise Gatewood."

Shit. I sat back in my chair and belted out a laugh. Derek smiled and Shiloh chuckled. Derek did a better job of pretending that we were just three coworkers having a breakfast meeting than Shiloh or I did.

"What's so funny?" Mother asked when she approached our table. "Shouldn't you three be working?"

"Oh, Mother, we *are* working." I nodded to Annalise Gatewood, the daughter of Councilman Gatewood. "Annalise." Annalise had recently been training to shift from the emergency sector she was born into and the government sector where she wished to work. She wore a red and black dress that was cut low enough in the front to show more than a hint of cleavage. I'd have to be dead not to notice, but Annalise didn't interest me in the least. Never had.

60

I also couldn't help but notice the jeweled necklace she wore around her neck. Though the necklace was comprised of onyx and ruby, there were enough bright blue sapphires in the necklace to hint at her desire to be matched. Colors meant everything inside New Caelum, and the addition of royal blue to her outfit was not lost on me. She, too, knew of the city's plan for us. I refused to acknowledge it right then.

"Mother, we were just getting ready to discuss the various sectors in need of extra patrolling. With the change in leadership and so many representatives of the council removed from office, some sectors are getting a little... restless." I took a drink of my coffee, wishing I had ordered water instead.

Mother stared at me like she was debating something as boring as redecorating the city. After several beats, she linked arms with Annalise. "Annalise was just telling me about the dress she plans to wear to the Founders' Day Gala Saturday night."

"Are you sure that it's wise to hold the gala Saturday? Don't you think we should put that off until Willow is better? Or until we know that this latest *flu* outbreak is under control?" I couldn't mention Bad Sam; I had no idea what Annalise's father had shared with her.

"Nonsense." Mother waved a hand and pulled Annalise closer. "Willow would want our city to recover quickly from this... unfortunate ordeal. I've already ordered your tuxedo to be pressed."

Annalise's brightly covered lips pulled back to reveal unnaturally white teeth, straightened to perfection. "Besides, Westlin," she said, "I've been promised your first dance. You wouldn't want to disappoint me, would you?" Her lips came together in a playful pout.

I didn't dare glance toward Shiloh, but I was certain her eyes were rolling to the ceiling.

What was Mother doing? She was serious about moving forward with the gala and my matching. All I could think was: surely she didn't want grandchildren from *this* girl. Or did she really want to sit across from Annalise during every holiday dinner?

"Fine, Mother. Now, unless you or Annalise would like to discuss the trouble we're having in the lower sectors with curfew..." I gestured toward Shiloh and Derek, who were waiting patiently for this unfortunate conversation to end.

"No, carry on. I have a busy day ahead of me. Annalise and I were just grabbing herbal teas to go."

As Mother and Annalise walked arm in arm to the counter to order their tea, I closed my eyes and cringed inwardly at the thought of having to endure a matching with anyone other than Cricket—even if Annalise and I were only a short-term matching while I figured out a way to be with my true soul mate. Because there was no way in hell I'd ever go through with marrying Annalise.

I turned to find Shiloh's mouth open slightly and her eyebrows raised. "When were you going to tell us that Annalise Gatewood was the frontrunner to becoming the new vice president's first lady?"

I angled my head while making sure Mother and Annalise were out of earshot. "I think we have more important things to discuss."

"Like how your mom didn't even mention Dr. Hempel's passing yet?" Derek asked.

I held a finger to my lips. I needed time before Mother and the other council members went crazy over losing another city doctor. "I'm sure she doesn't know. Which is why I need to act fast."

The three of us waved when Mother and Annalise finally exited the cafe.

I turned back to my two trusted guards. "I need the two of you to do something for me."

"You know we'll do anything," Derek said. "Say the word."

"Derek, I need you to cover for Shiloh and me. I need to leave the city, and I want Shiloh to come with me. We'll be back tomorrow."

"West, we can't leave." Shiloh looked around the cafe. "You know they're not going to keep allowing you to pass in and out of the city."

"I don't need your permission, Shiloh, but I need your help. Are you in or out?"

"Fine," she breathed. "In."

"Derek, I also need you to guard my sister, Ryder, and Key. Gather our most trusted guards and assign them to help. Don't let anything happen to them. I hope to have answers by the time I return."

"And when will that be?" Shiloh asked.

"Hopefully tomorrow. Before Saturday night's gala at the latest."

chapter nine

Cricket

The desperate sounds of the dog outside my door mercifully faded just before daybreak. I passed in and out of sleep until I finally woke to the bright sun shining directly in my face through the leaded glass window over the grand doorway. I was lying on my back on the dirty hardwood floors inside my childhood home, having collapsed from the adrenaline rush of escaping the crazed dog in the middle of the night.

I rolled over and pushed myself to my feet. My body ached from exhaustion and anxiety. I made my way to a living room window that looked out onto the front porch. Pushing back the sheer lace curtain, I surveyed the damage. The steps leading to the porch were broken and splintered down the middle. And the dog was still there. He lay between the steps and the door, on his side with his back to me, his chest rising and falling. He was bleeding, possibly from falling through the rotted steps, but some of the blood was older, dried and black.

I crossed the foyer to the dining room and peered out a mirroring window. When I saw the dog's face, I took in a sharp breath. His face was bloody with what looked like open sores.

Pus oozed from wounds, possibly the result of another animal attack. Or maybe he was sick.

I let the curtain drop back into place, releasing a puff of dust, and stepped away from the window. I'd have to find a way to lure the dog away from the house later. I knew one thing: I didn't want to be the reason he died, but if it came down to him or me, there would be only one winner.

The house looked just as I remembered it: formal living and dining rooms in the front of the house, a large kitchen and sitting room in the back. All the furniture was covered in white sheets, something my mom had done before their last trip to Africa—before she and my dad sent me to live with President Layne inside New Caelum. This was before New Caelum closed its doors to the outside and before it looked like the Samael Strain would kill everyone it touched. I didn't understand the severity of the situation at the time. I was only twelve.

Beyond the sitting room was my father's office. Mom called Dad's office "the cave" because it was lined with dark wood paneling and rich mahogany bookshelves, and it was the one place where Dad could just be himself. The rest of the house was light and airy and painted shades of sunny yellow and pale blues. A modest staircase in the foyer led to the second floor, which consisted of three bedrooms and a full bath.

The Victorian farmhouse was the home of my parents' dreams—a home to raise a family in and to grow old together.

Now the air was thick with dust and carried a musty odor, evidence of it having been closed up for years.

I carried my backpack to the kitchen and unloaded the supplies I'd brought with me. I left the cooler of antibodies, viruses, and other substances closed, hoping to keep them cool for as long as possible. I'd get the refrigerator working as soon as I got the solar panels hooked up again and generated enough electricity to run the necessary appliances. I also had access to water from a well behind the house, but in order to get water pumped into the house, I'd have to venture outside—where the German shepherd kept vigil.

After setting everything out on the kitchen table, I stared at the PulsePoint for ten minutes while debating whether to call West. He deserved to know I was okay. I hadn't meant to hurt him, only to put space between us while we figured life out.

And there was the danger that I was sick and dying. Again.

I couldn't argue against his claim that I'd have a better chance of surviving Bad Sam inside New Caelum, but I wouldn't even be wondering if I had the virus had it not been for the corruption inside that city. New Caelum was responsible for the resurgence of the disease.

So for now, I would take my chances on the outside.

I fingered a syringe and needle in a protective packaging and stared at the protein compound Dr. Hempel had created. I had never gotten the chance to ask him if he thought that compound would strengthen the antibodies already inside my bloodstream. He and Caine both informed me that my antibodies had weakened. I had even seen a slide of the broken cells with my own eyes. And Dr. Hempel had shown me what happened when those antibodies were treated with the manufactured protein compound.

I twirled the package through my fingers like a miniature baton, mentally debating whether to inject myself with the substance. All I knew for sure was that the concoction, along with my strong antibodies, had killed a little girl inside New Caelum.

Yet there were moments when I remembered the pain and high fever from Bad Sam, and in those moments I wanted to just rip open the packages and inject myself with Dr. Hempel's compound. The risk of getting Bad Sam again was far more frightening than the risk of dying from the experimental drug.

West knew this about me. It was probably why he thought I was suicidal.

And what if the compound worked? What if it rejuvenated the antibodies running through my blood and made me resistant to developing the symptoms of Bad Sam? Was it worth the risk?

Yes, I decided. It was.

I picked up the syringe and had my hand on the bag that held the compound when the sound of distant voices interrupted me. I pushed away from the table and eased up to the kitchen window, where a patterned cafe curtain hung. I pushed it back and spotted two men just twenty yards away. I let it drop immediately, my heart leaping into my throat. One of the men had been looking straight at the house, and his eyes had shifted directly to mine when I moved the curtain.

"Dude, someone's in there," I heard him say.

"Where?" his companion asked.

"Inside the house, stupid."

"Crap," I whispered. I darted from the kitchen to the living room and grabbed a poker from beside the fireplace. I had no idea if these guys were dangerous or not, but it didn't take a genius to know that a girl alone in the woods, miles from any

uprising

settlement, and facing two men she'd never met, was a bad combination.

By the sounds of their voices, they were walking toward the back of the house. I knew the back door was locked, but I didn't want them breaking a window. I was already quite fortunate that the house had withstood six years of neglect and remained sealed from the outside elements.

I grabbed my coat and made my way to my father's office, where another door led out to the side of the house. Before going outside, I opened Dad's top desk drawer, where he had always kept a revolver. I verified that it was loaded, then tucked it in the waistband of my pants at the small of my back—only to be used if absolutely necessary.

After smoothing my hair so that it hung against the scars on my cheek, I slid out the side door, down two steps, and followed the path stones to the back of the house. Silently, I approached the men from behind. They were peering through the windows in the back door. Before I could say anything, one of them jabbed an elbow through one of the panes, shattering the glass.

"Why did you have to do that?" I asked.

They spun around, spooked by my voice. I held the poker loosely at my side, not looking for a fight, but ready to defend myself if necessary.

They traded looks before stepping down off the porch. They weren't men, just boys. The older one, seventeen or eighteen if I had to guess, held his hands out to his sides as if to prove he was unarmed. He wore a thick flannel shirt with plenty of layers underneath and had some sort of pack on his back with something sticking out of it. "We're just passing through. We saw you at the window."

"So, you just thought you'd break in? Did you try knocking first?"

"I knocked. You didn't answer."

His friend, who looked to be several years younger, a kid even, stuffed his hands in his jeans pockets. The sleeves of his army green barn jacket were tattered, but the coat looked heavy enough for the weather. Neither of them appeared to be armed. Or at least they hadn't drawn any weapons yet.

"Are you here by yourself?" the one with the backpack asked while scanning the property behind me. He stepped to the side of the porch and reached down to grab something. That's when I recognized the crossbow, and the things sticking out of his pack as arrows.

I tightened the grip on my poker and slid my other hand around to rest on the revolver. "No," I lied. "One of my friends is resting, and my other two friends are out hunting. I expect them back any minute." *With their giant shotguns*, I lied silently to myself.

They both nodded. A grin played with the corners of the kid's lips. He bent down and picked up his own backpack, sliding his hand into a side pouch.

"Before this gets out of hand, why don't the two of you tell me what you want?"

The kid pulled out a hand-rolled cigarette and a lighter. "Tell 'er, Steve." He stuck the cigarette in his mouth and lit it while leaning a hip against the porch railing. If the front porch steps were any indication of the condition of other wooden surfaces around the house, I was actually surprised the railing held his weight.

"I don't see the harm," the younger one continued, "especially since I'm pretty sure you're lying about having friends returning."

My hand began to sweat. I wanted to rub it on my pants. I didn't bother to confirm or deny his suspicion.

"We're on our way to New Caelum," the older one said. "We've been instructed to spy on the outer walls."

"Why?" I asked.

The kid pushed off the railing and, after taking a drag on his cigarette, stepped closer to me. He was shorter than me but not by much. I opened and closed my fingers around the handle of the revolver behind me, but didn't step backward. *Don't show fear.*

"Have you seen anyone sick recently?" Smoke escaped his mouth as he spoke.

"What do you mean by sick?" I played dumb.

The kid cocked his head. "As in with Bad Sam." After taking another drag, he dropped the cigarette to the ground in front of me and used his boot to extinguish the sparks. He was a gutsy kid. I'd give him that.

"Bad Sam? Are you guys crazy?" I forced a bit of shakiness to enter my voice. Most people would be terrified at the pure mention of Bad Sam. "That virus is long gone. It's been six years."

"Afraid not," Steve said. The kid backed up a step, and I released a breath. "A couple of city boys ventured into our settlement a week or so ago. Two days later, they both collapsed with fever. Our resident doctor—a veterinarian, actually—insisted it was the Samael Strain."

"Did they die?" I asked, genuine alarm in my voice this time. "Has it spread?"

They traded uneasy glances again. Steve then smiled, and the coldest of chills traveled the length of my already cold body. "Oh yeah, they're dead. So are two other New Caelum residents who invaded another settlement south of us." He narrowed his gaze. A frown tugged at his lips. "And yes, it spread, which I think is exactly what the city expected, and wanted, to happen."

The other settlements had to have been at a disadvantage. They didn't have a paranoid crazy person—me—watching for signs of Bad Sam the way I'd been. Thanks to the virus being absent for six years, they'd probably let their guard down.

"So, you're planning to go to New Caelum to do what, exactly?"

"We're just going to see how many guards are lining their walls. Leaders from six settlements west of here have joined together to plan an assault against New Caelum. As far as they're concerned, the city has declared war on the outer settlements. If you're smart, you'll return with us to our settlement when we go." Steve chuckled. "Your friends, if they exist, are welcome to come, too. Speaking of which..." He turned and looked at the house. "You mind if we come in for a bit and warm up? Maybe your friends will be back before we have to leave. We can invite them ourselves. You got a fire built in there?" He gestured to my poker.

"Actually, no, I don't. Sorry."

"This cold weather, and you don't have a fire built?"

I hadn't gotten around to it, yet. But I had no intention of telling these two that I had just gotten here, or where I had come from.

"We could help you with that."

"That won't be necessary." I looked around, trying to hide my nervousness at them coming inside my house. If they saw my collection of medical supplies, they might jump to the wrong conclusions, or they could discover that I knew more about Bad Sam than I'd let on. Bad Sam tended to make people a little jumpy—for obvious reasons. "You boys sound like you have business to take care of, and I don't want to keep you from it."

"Why, blondie, you sound like you don't want to invite us into your home. That's not very hospitable of you. Whatever happened to good ol' southern manners?"

I shrugged. "Guess I'm just not feeling all that hospitable at the moment." A distant sound I didn't recognize perked up my ears. When I heard the low growl again, the little hairs on the back of my neck stood at attention, and I knew exactly whom the growl belonged to. "I think it's time you both get going." I pulled the revolver from my waistband.

"Whoa." The kid backed away, his hands lifted to the sides. "No need to get all violent."

"It's not for you, unless you threaten me."

The German shepherd growled louder this time.

Steve turned. "What was that?"

I cringed. I was going to have to let them come into my house. Or watch them get eaten by a diseased animal.

"That's a friend of mine. He's not feeling very well today." I began backing away toward the side of the house and the door

I had exited. "Looks like you're going to get to come inside after all."

The sound of the German shepherd came again, from the opposite side of the house. The dog came around the corner, bloody and baring his teeth. A low reverberation thundered from his chest.

"What the hell is that?" Steve asked. He pulled an arrow from his pack.

The shepherd rocked on his feet, continuing to snarl. I backed up several more steps. Steve struggled with the cross-bow. Suddenly the dog leapt. I turned and ran, and the young boy followed me.

Just before disappearing around the corner of the house, I looked back. Steve had landed an arrow in the chest of the wild beast, but it hadn't stopped it. The dog plowed into Steve, knocking him to the ground with a thud. Steve groaned, and the dog pinned him to the ground, snarling. I raised my re-volver and shot the dog square in the chest, but not before he'd sunk his teeth into Steve's neck, tearing out a huge chunk of flesh.

The kid stood, paralyzed. Gurgling noises erupted from Steve's neck, and the dog lay motionless across his body. Steve convulsed one last time, and I closed my eyes in a silent prayer.

"Let's go." I physically turned the kid and shoved him gen-tly forward until we were safely inside the house.

chapter ten

....

West

Thick gray clouds rolled overhead as Shiloh and I approached the settlement of Boone Blackston. It was nearing midday, and Shiloh and I had searched for Cricket everywhere I thought she might have sought shelter, including the run-down Biltmore Estate. I didn't think she would risk camping in the mountains, not with temperatures dropping below twenty degrees Fahrenheit at night.

Even though Cricket and I had had limited time together, I knew I couldn't force her to live inside New Caelum with me. But the thought of her out there—cold, sick, or alone—made it impossible to concentrate. How could I possibly lead a city of scared citizens to the next chapter of their lives if I was constantly worried about Cricket? I needed her beside me.

But for now, my only objective was to save her life. I had to find her before she injected the protein compound into her blood.

A parade of people were walking through the gates of Boone Blackston. No one noticed Shiloh and me at first. But then I locked eyes with Dax. Cricket's friend, Nina, walked beside him. Anger flashed across his face, and his jaw hardened.

He looked like he might come at me with fists flying. But instead he leaned in and whispered something to Nina. Her head lifted, her eyes searching. She changed direction, and, dodging a couple of kids in the line of people, she made her way toward us, bringing Dax with her.

"What are you doing here?" she demanded, shoving me backward with both hands. Her face was red, and she breathed heavily as she appeared to fight back tears. "Surely you know you're not welcome!"

Dax's fingers were curled into fists, his knuckles white. A vein pulsed in his neck, and his eyes were bloodshot.

Shiloh had a hand on her Taser. She took a step forward, and I motioned for her to stand down. "I know. I'm sorry," I said. I knew my apology was just empty words to them. Then it dawned on me why so many people were exiting the Boone Blackston gate: I was interrupting Dylan's funeral procession. "I know that my apology is not enough, but..."

Nina scanned the area behind us. "Where's Cricket? She could at least pay her last respects to our friend. Why isn't she with you?"

I narrowed my eyes. After Dax had practically choked Cricket to death, I'd assumed she was lying low somewhere, but I'd hoped she'd at least stayed close by. "Have you seen her at all?"

"No," Nina answered. Worry crept into the lines across her forehead.

"We assumed she left with you," Dax said, with something close to regret or concern in his voice. Better late than never, I guessed.

"I took Ryder and Key back to New Caelum. She refused to come with me."

"That sounds like her." Nina cast a panicked glance toward Dax. "You think she's at the Biltmore somewhere?"

"We went there first," I said. "I saw no sign of her."

Nina dropped Dax's hand and wrapped her arms around herself in a hug. "We pushed her away. We accused her of something terrible. Something that was *your* city's fault." Her eyes burned into mine, but then softened into something more urgent and pleading. "Dax said she was no longer immune to Bad Sam. Did your city expose her to the virus? Is that why she disappeared after she brought us a treatment?"

"No. She looked fine the other day," Dax said. "The likelihood of her contracting the virus was slim. Caine agreed. She just turned her back on us, is all."

Nina turned on Dax. She raised her hands and shoved him backward, even harder than she had pushed me. "You're just pissed she didn't tell you about West. You're angry about Dylan, and you blame Cricket. Only..." She let out a sob. "Cricket didn't give Dylan Bad Sam. *That city* did." She spat out "that city" like it was an evil curse. And I couldn't disagree with her, though I hoped I could eventually redeem the city I hoped to run. "Cricket risked her life to find and bring back a treatment."

"Well, it didn't work," Dax argued. "Not for Dylan. It only cured the privileged elite."

"That wasn't Cricket's fault." Nina was crying now. "And now you've pushed her away. And I let her go." She buried her face in her hands. "What have I done?"

Dax opened his mouth to say something, but immediately closed it. His shoulders slumped forward. When he finally looked at me again, his hands were in tight fists. "Your city is responsible for killing my brother *and* for sending that disease back out into the world. When I've buried my brother, I will find Cricket. I'm not about to tell *you* where she might be."

I'd been calm, even nice, up until that moment. Now I reached out and grabbed two handfuls of Dax's coat and brought him close so that our eyes were level with each other. "I'm sorry about your brother. I am, whether you believe me or not. I can't waste time caring any more than that right now. Cricket is in trouble. She was exposed to the same disease that just killed your brother. No one knows the pain of that disease the way Cricket knows it. She has all but admitted she doesn't have the mental or physical capabilities of surviving Bad Sam a second time. She has the medicine that saved Ryder's and Key's lives, but if *she* takes it, it will kill her. She doesn't know this. I have to find her before it's too late." I shoved him backward. His chest rose and fell in short bursts.

"She probably went to her childhood home," Nina said. She wrung her hands nervously.

We all looked at her. "How do you know?" Dax asked.

"I'm sure that's why she came for that box of stuff last night. The key was inside. She hasn't been back to that home in years, but I know that's where she would go."

"Do you know where it is?" I asked."

....

chapter eleven

Cricket

"**W**hat's your name?" I asked the kid. I laid Dad's revolver on the corner of the desk.

He sat in my dad's desk chair, staring at the floor. His eyes were glossed over. A chill started at the top of my shoulders and moved down my arms and spine until goose bumps formed on my legs. The house was cold, but the kid and I probably suffered from a bit of shock as well.

"Cade." His eyes found mine. "Is he really dead?"

I nodded. "I'm sorry."

Cade looked down again. There were no tears; he just looked numb. "He was like a brother and a father to me. Is that weird? He was only five years older than me. And we had only known each other a little while. But he looked out for me after my father died last year."

I kneeled in front of the chair, careful not to touch him despite knowing I wasn't contagious without symptoms of Bad Sam. "No, that's not weird." We all tended to look for fathers, mothers, siblings in the people left behind. I'd found a father in Caine, a sister in Nina. I'd tried to shut myself off from others, yet still I'd found love from those surviving around me. Even when I hesitated to acknowledge it.

"How old are you?" I asked.

"Twelve."

I offered him a weak smile. "Well, Cade, how 'bout we build a fire? You can stay with me until we figure something out."

Cade followed me into the living room. I found a metal hook beside the fireplace. After struggling with it for five minutes, I felt a burst of cool air from the opening of the flue. Old yellowed newspapers and kindling lay in a nearby basket, and a couple of logs were in a copper container on the hearth. I crumpled up the newspaper and layered small twigs atop them inside the fireplace. I found some matches and proceeded to light the newspaper on fire. Flames erupted and consumed the small space before slowing. By the time the flames appeared to be going out, some twigs had caught fire. I threw a couple of larger pieces of kindling on top.

I had started many fires while camping in the forest, but it was much easier to light a fire with the right kind of kindling and starter supplies than out in the damp woods. I remembered watching my dad start fires in this fireplace dozens of times. As I stared at the flames and inhaled the scent of wood burning, I lost myself in the fleeting memories of my parents inside this house.

"Do you live here alone?" Cade asked.

"In this house?" I stood and looked around as if seeing the house for the first time since I'd entered last night. "No. I spent several years of my life here before..." I let my voice die off, not really knowing how much I wanted to tell this stranger.

Even if he was just a kid, I didn't know him or where he'd come from.

"How did you get those scars on your face?"

I lifted my hand and let my fingers linger against the textured skin. "That's a long story for another time, maybe. Why don't you tell me more about what's going on in the settlements you came from." I motioned to one of the wingback chairs. A sheet covered it. Cade sat on top of it, and a puff of dust exploded on contact.

"Two guys showed up at Morgan Creek over a week ago. They convinced Father O'Malley, one of the leaders of our settlement, that they'd been thrown out of the city just because they said they were tired of living like prisoners."

"Your settlement leader is a father? As in a Catholic priest?" I took a seat on a sheet-covered ottoman.

Cade nodded.

"Go on."

"The two city boys seemed harmless enough at first. They had these electronic devices with them, but we couldn't get them to turn on. And the only weapons they carried were these Tasers that stung like hell, but didn't do any long-term damage."

My spine tightened slightly. I knew all too well how badly a Taser hurt. "What do you mean, their electronic devices wouldn't turn on? Were they broken? And these men didn't know why they wouldn't work?" I had to be careful. I didn't want Cade to think I knew anything about the PulsePoints.

"Well..." Cade paused. "They both got sick."

"With Bad Sam."

He nodded.

And I knew: the devices couldn't be operated without their original owners' fingerprints to power them. "How did your people react?" The little hairs on the back of my neck stood as fear moved through me.

"We have rules to follow. But word spread fast. I was with Steve when we heard. Not ten minutes later, we heard gunshots. Two of them. The city burned the bodies and everything that came with them that couldn't be decontaminated."

I closed my eyes. The leaders of Cade's settlement had executed two men who'd probably had no idea they'd been sent like suicide bombers to deliver a virus. "Didn't Morgan Creek have a way of handling illness?"

"They do. They're just not a big fan of New Caelum sending a deadly virus into our homes."

I couldn't argue with that.

"Steve said the leaders of the settlements saw the act as a declaration of war. Did the virus spread at all?"

"Yes. And everyone who has gotten sick has died."

"Steve also said leaders of the settlements sent you to spy on New Caelum?"

"Leaders from other settlements came the day after the two city guys died. They were pissed. No one knew why New Caelum would send these guys out into our world after all this time, so they decided to send some of our own people to scout the city walls."

"And they sent you and Steve?" I asked, a little surprised they would send someone as young as Cade.

"No. Steve wanted to go, but his father wouldn't allow it. Instead, he formed a group of his own trusted men."

"Who is Steve's father?"

"He's the governor of six settlements west of here."

My eyes widened. "Steve's father is Governor Jackson?" I had heard rumors about Governor Jackson. Those stories were some of the reasons I had never ventured close to the settlements that spread through Tennessee, Georgia, Alabama, and Mississippi.

"Yep. And he forbid Steve from leaving Morgan Creek." Cade planted his face in his hands. "I have to tell the governor that Steve is dead. He's gonna blame me. He'll banish me for sure." He reached out and grabbed my arm. "Will you come back to the settlement with me? You can tell them what happened. They'll believe you."

I pulled my arm away from Cade, stood, and backed away from him. "I can't go to your settlement." I'd never risk getting caught up in Governor Jackson's totalitarian rule. I'd be better off inside New Caelum. And I surely wasn't entering those settlements now, when I could very well be facing my own bout of Bad Sam.

How was I going to get rid of this kid? "You said you and Steve weren't actually sent out by the settlements to spy on New Caelum? But Governor Jackson did send people?"

Cade nodded. "He sent a few. But he's also gathering and training a huge group from the settlements to surround the entire wall of New Caelum. They want revenge."

"We're going to need to find the small group your settlement sent out. You need to return home with them."

Cade stood. "I don't need help finding my way back."

"Oh yeah? And what are you going to do when you run into another feral animal looking for his next dinner?"

Cade sat back down, probably remembering the same vision I was struggling to erase from my mind: the constant footage of a wild dog ripping Steve's throat out.

At the sound of a motor, Cade and I traded panicked looks. I crossed the room in five quick steps and peeked out the front window. It was a city truck. I looked closer. *West.* "Great," I whispered.

"You know them?" Cade asked. "That's a city truck." His head turned slowly toward me. I could feel his intense gaze, though I refused to make eye contact with him. "That's why you're not a part of some settlement. You're one of them, aren't you?" He backed away slowly. When I failed to reassure him that I wasn't a city girl, he turned and took off in a full sprint.

"Where are you going?" I chased after him. When I reached my dad's office, the door leading outside was wide open, and Dad's gun was gone."

chapter twelve

······································

West

After driving as fast as possible up the overgrown dirt and gravel road, I cut off the engine in front of a sizable farmhouse. Victorian. Probably a wonderful home to have grown up in. A large biohazard symbol was painted on the front door, a symbol universally used to inform people that the Samael Strain had infected the structure in some way, and that it was dangerous to enter.

"Smart girl," I whispered to myself.

Shiloh placed a hand on my arm, stopping me from exiting the truck. "That's just for show, right?"

"Would you enter a house if you stumbled upon that symbol?"

"No way." Her eyes widened, and she shook her head.

"That's why it's there. To keep people out." I was fairly certain, due to the fact that it didn't look like fresh paint. Still, my pulse sped up slightly, and I fought off the notion that she might have developed a fever since yesterday.

As I had raced to Cricket's childhood home, I had refused to consider that I might be too late. Cricket had given herself the same treatment she had given the others, with the hope that it would prevent her from developing Bad Sam at all. And she had chosen not to inject the protein compound into her bloodstream after the little girl inside New Caelum had died. She should be fine.

But I had no guarantee that the pressure hadn't gotten to her.

Now that I was here, I was terrified to enter the house. It looked quiet. What if she had changed her mind, injected herself with Dr. Hempel's drug, and was already...

No. I wouldn't let my mind go there.

"Will she listen to you?" Shiloh asked. "Do you think you can get her to come back to New Caelum with us?"

I leaned my arms across the steering wheel. "I have to convince her that it's the only way."

"Does she really hate New Caelum that much?"

"Wouldn't you?"

"If I blamed them for my parents' deaths and for exposing me to Bad Sam?" Shiloh tilted her head side to side while biting her lower lip. "Yeah. I guess I would. You'll have to convince her that you're going to change New Caelum."

"How do I do that?"

Shiloh paused a few beats, having no answer. "Are you going to tell her about Annalise? About your mother's insistence that you be matched soon?"

"You think it would help?"

"It might."

Shiloh and I would have to agree to disagree on that point. I wanted Cricket to help me convince the people of New Caelum that it was safe on the outside, that the only way to become a strong nation again would be to spread out within a defined area, live off the land, and grow and prosper again. I didn't want her distracted by a girl who meant nothing to me.

It was late in the day, and the gray sky looked as if it could dump snow on the land any time. Staring at the house, I tried to imagine Cricket living there. This was a family home—one to raise kids in and grow old. I could hardly believe my nineteen-year-old mind was drifting to thoughts like this.

But it didn't matter. I was here to convince Cricket that she had to return to New Caelum, not spend the rest of her life with me. Not yet, anyway.

Static erupted from my PulsePoint, followed by a voice. "West! West! Can you hear me? You have to turn around. He's got a gun."

"Is that Cricket?" Shiloh asked. "What did she say?"

A blur of movement caught my attention on the right side of the house. "There." I pointed. "Someone just ducked behind that shed over there."

"Did she say someone had a gun? Who could be here with her?"

"I have no idea. But we're not going to stop them with a Taser."

I lifted my PulsePoint. "Who was that? He's behind a shed on the right side of the house. Are you okay?"

"I'm fine. It's a kid from a nearby settlement. He *will* shoot you. You need to leave."

"Got any weapons in there? Because we're not leaving."

The kid appeared from behind the shed and pointed the gun at the truck.

"Duck!" I yelled. The window beside Shiloh shattered.

I put the truck in reverse, backed up a few feet, then turned the truck and floored it toward the boy. He fired the gun again. Sparks flew as the bullet ricocheted off the hood and zipped past, busting the driver side mirror.

Just before we reached him, he darted into the forest. I slammed on the brakes.

"Cade!" Cricket yelled. She jumped off the front porch and headed in our direction. She had what looked like a crossbow aimed into the woods. "Come out now. No one's going to hurt you."

"Cricket," I said into the PulsePoint. "Do you even know how to use that thing?"

"Yes," she yelled, not even bothering with the PulsePoint this time.

Cade appeared from behind a tree. "You're one of them," he said. He raised the gun. "You have one of those electronic things. Like the others."

"No," Cricket answered. "I *was* one of them. Many years ago. And only for a brief time. But I contracted Bad Sam and left the city forever in order to recover."

"You're lying. No one survives Bad Sam." This kid was making me worried the way he was waving the gun around with shaky hands, and Cricket didn't even look nervous as she inched closer.

"I hope you know what you're doing," I said under my breath.

"I survived," Cricket said to the boy. "And I know how to cure others. I'd like the chance to tell your settlements that we can beat the virus. Maybe even prevent it in the future."

Was she serious? Did she think the leaders of these settlements would listen to her? Then again, they'd surely listen to her before they'd ever listen to *me*, a leader of the enemy city. Another reason we needed her on our team.

"Then who is that?" the kid said, jerking his head in my direction.

"That's no one." Cricket didn't even glance our way.

"Ouch," Shiloh said. "She didn't mean that."

I threw her a sideways glare.

The kid aimed the gun back and forth between Cricket and the truck. "If he's no one, then you won't mind if I get rid of him." He pointed the gun straight at us again.

I punched the gas and sped toward the boy. He started backing up while still aiming his gun. I slammed the brakes just short of running the kid over. Losing his balance, he fell backwards to his butt. The gun flew from his hand as he thudded to the ground. Cricket ran over to him and pointed the crossbow at his chest as he struggled to his feet.

I couldn't hear what Cricket said next, but the boy stared at her for a minute, then turned and ran off into the forest.

Shiloh and I climbed out of the truck and joined Cricket. "Who the hell was that?" I asked. "He couldn't have been more than thirteen."

"Twelve." Cricket bent over and grabbed the gun. "What are you doing here, West? I thought we made it clear that I wanted to be alone."

"You call that alone? Who was he?"

Cricket didn't answer. She walked to what had once been steps to the front porch, and I followed. Blood stained the splintered wood in the middle of the steps, where it was clear someone had fallen through. My eyes followed a trail of what looked like smeared, reddish-black paint up onto the porch.

"What happened here?" I asked. "That's not your blood, is it?" I grabbed Cricket's shoulder and forced her to turn, letting my eyes travel the length of her body. I wanted to open her coat and examine her body to make sure she was okay, but thought better of it when she rolled her eyes.

"I'm fine. No, not my blood."

Shiloh cleared her throat behind me.

"Hi, Shiloh," Cricket said. Shiloh must have nodded, but she didn't speak. Cricket leaned the crossbow against the house then locked eyes with me. Any second now she would order me to get back in my truck and drive the hell away. I braced for it. My fingers curled into themselves at my sides. I badly wanted to pull her into my arms and tell her how much I missed her.

"Why are you here?" Cricket asked.

I approached her slowly and lifted both hands to stroke her hair and cup the sides of her cheeks. "I came to make sure you didn't inject yourself with the protein compound from Dr. Hempel."

She cocked her head, then leaned away from my touch. "What? No. I almost did, but... No, I didn't."

There was a strange tone I didn't recognize in her voice. A huge weight left my shoulders though.

Cricket looked to Shiloh and back to me. "You both came all this way just to make sure I hadn't injected myself with that medicine?"

"And to make sure you weren't sick," Shiloh said.

"You haven't turned on your PulsePoint. I was worried. And then..." I stopped myself from explaining more about the protein compound or about the murders in the city. "Can we go inside? Or are you going to send us away?" It would be nice to not have to stand out here on the front porch while I detailed the latest news.

After several heartbeats, she nodded. She grabbed the crossbow, pulled the revolver from her waistband, and led us into the house. Closing and locking the front door behind us, she told us to make ourselves at home, then disappeared into the back of the house.

"Nice house," Shiloh commented when Cricket was gone. "The kind of house dreams were once built on. It's seen better days though."

I could only nod. Anyone inside New Caelum who had memories of the outside had to remember the kind of living that involved land, views, and few neighbors. And though most of the houses and buildings on the outside were run-down, the Blacks' house appeared to be in decent shape, apart from the need for a few minor repairs... like the front porch.

I pointed at the steps through the small window beside the front door. "What do you think happened out there?"

"Animal of some sort," Shiloh said. "There's fur stuck to the wood. It was recent. Some of the blood is still fresh."

I moved further into the house and walked directly into a cobweb. All the furniture was covered with sheets, and those sheets had a layer of dust so thick you'd practically need a shovel to remove it.

"Please don't judge me, but I miss the dust-free climate of New Caelum already." Shiloh picked up a pillow that was so dingy it needed to be trashed.

"But would you trade it for the freedom of never having someone know your exact whereabouts at all times?" I asked. "Never having to turn over your temperature to some computer that's just waiting for the next flu outbreak or worse?"

"Good point."

I lifted a sheet off of a table, revealing a few picture frames face down. I lifted one. It was a picture of a young Christina when she had dark hair. Little curls hung around her face. Her bright blue eyes practically glowed; they were electric. Her mom and dad were on either side of her. She had her arms draped over their shoulders, and she was smiling so big you could almost hear a giggle. Her mom had platinum blond hair, which made me wonder if that was why Cricket bleached her own hair when she decided to disguise herself.

"Please put that down." Cricket stood in the doorway.

"I'm sorry." I replaced the picture and let the sheet fall back in place. Despite the brief moment of closeness in front of the house, Cricket and I were strangers again. In the hours since I'd seen her, she'd managed to put a steel barrier between us. But I was not going to let her shut herself off from me. Not completely. She needed me, and dammit, I was going to make her admit it. "Cricket, we need—"

She raised a hand. "Don't."

I raised a brow. "Don't what?"

"I know what you're going to say."

"Oh yeah? And what are you so sure I'm going to say?"

"That we need to talk. You're going to try to convince me that New Caelum is a safer place for me."

I glanced at Shiloh. She widened her eyes and urged me to continue. "Actually, I'm pretty sure that New Caelum is the least safe place for you at the moment." No matter how much I wanted her there, I couldn't ignore the fact that someone had tried to murder Key, and had successfully murdered Dr. Hempel.

And then there was the case of the missing Bad Sam virus.

Cricket crossed her arms and jutted out a hip. Something about the way this beautiful girl in front of me was always ready for a fight made my lips twitch. I loved her, and yet she was always ready to argue and challenge me.

"So why are you here?"

"I'm here to persuade you to return to New Caelum." I smiled.

"Of course you are. You just admitted that New Caelum was unsafe for me, yet you... Never mind. It doesn't matter. You're wasting your breath." She waved a hand and turned on her heel, walking away from me. "I've got things to do," she yelled over her shoulder as she disappeared. "You and Shiloh are welcome to stay, but I want you gone by morning."

I looked at Shiloh and muttered, "Well, we knew this wouldn't be easy."

Cricket returned with a pile of what looked like...

"Why do you have hazmat suits?" I asked.

"I stocked the house years ago just in case."

"Just in case what?" Shiloh asked.

"Just in case I would ever need them. Follow me."

chapter thirteen

Cricket

I wasn't sure how West and Shiloh were planning to talk me into returning to New Caelum with them, or if I would let them, but since they were here, they could at least help me get rid of the bodies in the back.

They followed me to the shed at the edge of the woods without saying a word. I didn't have to look at West to know he was watching every move I made.

I scanned the woods for any sign that Cade was still out there, but he was probably long gone. He had to have been afraid that more city people meant more Bad Sam. He could have gone to get help. In that case, I was probably in danger. As were West and Shiloh.

I'd have to tell West that the settlements west of here were looking to come after New Caelum, and about the scouts already on their way to spy on the security on the outer wall. But first things first. After unlocking the padlock on the door, I entered the shed and spotted the tools I needed.

"Cricket, you're starting to freak Shiloh out. What's with the protective gear?"

Freak Shiloh out, right. I returned to the shed entrance with two shovels and a large canvas tarp. I gave one of the shovels to West and the tarp to Shiloh. "Well, I'm sorry to freak *Shiloh* out, but we have bodies to bury.".

Ignoring their gaping mouths, I headed in the direction of the German shepherd and Steve. West and Shiloh were close on my heels. Just as I was about to round the corner, I stopped and pulled the protective hood and mask over my head. West and Shiloh followed suit, saying nothing.

I faced them and spoke through the mask, my voice slightly muffled. "I had a little run-in with a German shepherd when I arrived last night. That's what the blood on the front porch was from. Then a couple of guys showed up this afternoon. Before I could decide if they meant me harm or not, the dog attacked."

"Was one of them the kid who shot at us earlier?"

"Yes, and his friend is dead."

"Why the hazmat suits?"

"The dog appeared to be sick. It's probably nothing, but..." I shrugged. It would be the worst possible luck to find out the virus had mutated and spread to animals. "I don't want to attract more animals, so we need to bury the bodies."

I felt the heat of West's gaze on me as I turned and continued to the back of the house. When we reached the scene, Shiloh sucked in a breath. "It ripped his throat out."

I tried not to look at Steve's mangled body as Shiloh and I spread the tarp. Shiloh gagged, fighting to keep her last meal down.

I stood and was about to position myself at Steve's feet, intending to roll his body onto the tarp, when West stepped in front of me. He placed a hand on my arm, forcing me to look up at him. "I'm going to help you," he said. "Then we're going to talk."

I blinked several times while studying the intent behind his gaze. He and I both knew I was defeated. My choices were diminishing.

~~~~~

Four hours later, the sun was setting. I set a couple of metal buckets beside the opening to the property's well. For the first time since I'd arrived, I was getting a look at the solar panels. They were going to need some work, and I'd need them in order to get running water from the well to the house consistently.

Realizing that I was not going to have working electricity anytime soon, I set the first bucket under the spigot and began manually pumping.

"What are you doing?" West asked. I got a whiff of bleach. After drenching both porches and ourselves with a disinfectant of bleach and water, we had disposed of our protective gear, but the stench of the strong chemical lingered.

"This pump will send enough water directly into the house for use in the toilets and the sinks. We'll also use the buckets to warm extra water by the fire in order to take bucket baths."

"Seriously? And here I wasn't sure if you'd actually considered how you would live out here on your own."

I smiled. "Did you think I'd run off to live like a hermit with no access to water or resources?"

"I should never underestimate you. I've seen your ability to survive firsthand."

There were many meanings hidden in West's words.

"The well has plenty of water thanks to a rainy fall," I said.

"Nina said you don't come here often."

"Nina is my best friend, but she and Dax could also tell you stories about how I'm known to disappear from time to time."

"Which explains why this place doesn't scream of six years of neglect." West covered my hand, stopping my motion. "Let me." He took over the pumping of water.

I looked off into the woods. Darkness was growing. I couldn't see much beyond the first row of trees. "This house and land is full of squashed hope. Empty promises," I said.

West stopped pumping for a moment. Beads of sweat formed across his forehead despite the cold temperatures. "I don't understand."

"Look at this place." I gestured around the property. "Solar panels, manual water pump attached to a well. My parents were planning to survive out here. You don't equip a house with the things this house has if you're planning to join the ranks of New Caelum." Or run off to Africa. They'd had every intention of returning here.

West went back to pumping water. "Maybe they were just preparing for all possibilities."

"Maybe."

"Except—" West stopped abruptly.

"Except what?"

"They had to have known the risk of leaving the country. And even though this house is well equipped, they sent you to live inside New Caelum. Why?"

"It doesn't make much sense. Neither does the fact that your mother allowed me to leave the city with Caine and knew where I was all these years."

"She couldn't have known you were going to survive."

"Hmm." I thought about the bloodstones. Did President Layne know about them? I'd pretty much drawn the conclusion that my parents had returned to Africa with the hope of obtaining more bloodstones in order to bring back enough to study the medicinal value of the gem. I had never considered whether anyone else knew what my parents were doing, or if anyone besides my parents knew that I had been injected with them. "There is one thing I still don't understand..."

"Only one?" West joked.

I smiled weakly. "My parents had to have had some proof about the bloodstones. They wouldn't have injected me if they hadn't believed it would protect me." I paused, then remembered West's worry when he first arrived at the house. "Why were you so freaked about Dr. Hempel's drug? Is there something I don't know?" If I was going to figure out a treatment, I needed to know everything.

"Dr. Hempel admitted to me that the protein compound wasn't safe for someone who already had the virus running through their blood. Everyone who has received his compound *after* developing the virus..."

"... is dead," I finished for him. My heart ached for the many New Caelum citizens the city had experimented on.

"However, it appears that everyone who received the compound *prior* to contracting the Samael Strain has recovered... with the help of whatever concoction you gave them."

"But not without pain. They still suffer every excruciating symptom of the disease." But it was still interesting. "So, Key, Ryder, and Willow—"

"And Dr. Hempel. All received the protein compound before contracting Bad Sam. And all have survived. The virus, anyway."

"What does that mean?"

West's brows tilted inward. "Dr. Hempel is dead."

"What? How?"

"Murdered."

My heart sped up slightly. Dr. Hempel knew so much about Bad Sam and the possible ways to fight another outbreak. Without him...

"Someone poisoned him." West shifted his stance and stared over my shoulder. "There's more."

"Tell me." I began filling a couple of large buckets with water from the spigot.

"Someone also tried to kill Key."

I paused, but then handed him one of the filled buckets. I picked up the other and began walking toward the house. "But she's okay?"

"She was all right when I left. I put as many guards as I could on her."

I held the door open for him. "I guess you're going to tell me what this has to do with me?"

We carried the buckets through the kitchen. He spoke over his shoulder as we walked. "I think someone's trying to remove anyone inside the city who knows anything about curing or getting rid of the Samael Strain."

"And that's your pitch for getting me to return to New Caelum with you? Telling me that I might be next on the list if I were to reenter the city?"

I set my steel bucket on a platform near the fire. West followed suit.

"No, I'm just trying to be honest with you. I'll give you the pitch after we've both cleaned the dirt and sweat from burying two dead bodies in the back yard."

Shiloh entered the room, a PulsePoint in her hand. "We have a problem."

West gestured impatiently, urging her to continue.

"Your mother has moved the gala to tomorrow night."

~~~~~

While the water warmed, I showed West and Shiloh their choices for dinner. It wasn't New Caelum gourmet, but my parents had planned well for a zombie apocalypse. Rows and rows of canned vegetables and non-perishable food sat on floor-to-ceiling basement shelves.

I could eat for many months without ever leaving the house. Thankfully, I'd never had to rely on my parents' stash. Yet. People in the settlements and other survivors had learned to grow and hunt for food. And many of the larger grocery stores still had canned goods stocked. There simply hadn't been enough survivors to deplete the supplies.

While Shiloh and West ate SpaghettiOs warmed on the hearth, I filled a container with enough warm water to wash the grime from my body after burying Steve and took it to an upstairs bathroom. Though it was refreshing to rid my body of the dirt and sweat, the air in the house—every room except the living room—was so cold that I had to rush through the process.

When I was clean, I changed into a fresh pair of pants and a fitted turtleneck sweater. I was combing fingers through my hair and staring at the dark circles under my eyes in the bathroom mirror when someone knocked lightly. I tensed, thinking it was probably West, and I'd only just then gotten dressed.

"Come in."

I turned to find Shiloh pushing the door open. Her hair was damp, and she wore a clean gray uniform, a New Caelum standard for government guards.

"You shouldn't come very close," I said. When she flinched, I quickly added, "I don't have a fever or any symptoms. I'm just trying to keep your exposure to a minimum." The more time that passed, the more anxious I became.

She nodded, relaxing a bit. "West won't tell you this, but..." She walked further into the bathroom and closed the door. "He's getting pressure from the council and his mother. They want him matched."

"Matched? As in married?" What did this mean? Was that why he was here? Just weeks ago, his mother had announced to the entire city that West would marry me. The people inside New Caelum had seemed pleased at the announcement, though they had no idea at the time who I was, and I had thought it was just an act on West's and my part. West knew how I felt about living inside New Caelum. And we had only just found each other.

"Yes. And not to you," Shiloh added, answering my unspoken question.

I gnawed on my lower lip, trying to hide the disappointment I had no right to feel. Then I turned and began to clean up the mess I had made in the bathroom. "That's good. He should find happiness inside the city. Our engagement was an act." I poured what was left of my dirty bathwater down the drain.

"This is all part of the original plan for New Caelum," Shiloh explained. "When citizens reach their eighteenth birthday, they are required to be matched. By their nineteenth birthday, they are to be married. And West is the future leader of New Caelum."

And nineteen, I thought to myself.

"He's under pressure to live by the principles that the founding members laid out in order to keep his status as vice president. And he's managed to evade this rule until now."

"Of course it was part of the plan." I nodded and tried to convince myself that it was better to agree with New Caelum's founding principles. "And he *should* comply, as leader of the last great city of survivors." Even I heard the weak crackling of my voice as I rambled. "He should lead by example."

"He's also under pressure to reproduce. Quickly."

"To help the human population rebuild, and all that." That was New Caelum's plan from the very beginning: save the human race by repopulating. I swallowed hard. None of this should matter to me. "Why are you telling me this?"

"I just thought you should know... as you decide what to do." Shiloh turned, but she paused at the door and looked over her shoulder at me. "President Layne and Councilman Gatewood plan to match West with his future bride at a ceremony tomorrow night. If he isn't there, they will know that West isn't capable of a position in leadership and they'll name another vice president." Shiloh slipped out, closing the door quietly behind her.

My hands shook as I gathered up my dirty laundry. I would need to wash everything tomorrow. After West and Shiloh returned to New Caelum.

It was time I learned how to live on my own. And what better place to do it than the house my parents had stocked with everything I could possibly need? I would just need to figure out how to get the solar panels working again. And fix the broken window somehow.

I would also need to make sure I had plenty of water inside in case I did come down with Bad Sam. I already knew I had plenty of bandages in a large plastic container somewhere. I remembered sitting with my mother at the kitchen table, when I was eleven, and we were shredding white sheets into strips. I didn't know it at the time, but we were making bandages. My parents knew what the Samael Strain did to people. They'd seen it firsthand on their travels to Africa. And they had done everything to prepare me.

If I got sick, I had the supplies to take care of myself—and hopefully, with a treatment already in my bloodstream, my symptoms would be manageable. And if I didn't get sick, I'd continue to study Caine's notes and the treatment that now seemed to be working for Willow and the others. As long as I stayed well, I'd rejoin Caine, and together we'd develop a vaccine for the outside world.

West had his agenda and responsibilities, and I had mine.

I dropped the armful of muddy clothes, leaned against the door, and slid to the floor. My forehead touched my knees as I wrapped my arms around my legs. And I cried. My entire body shook as stored up emotions consumed me.

I wasn't sure if I was crying because I had been exposed to that horrible virus again, or because my exposure to Bad Sam was dictating what my next choices in life would be.

Or was I crying because West had come back into my life after all these years?

And I was about to lose him all over again. This time, it would be forever.

....

chapter fourteen

West

Bathed and dressed in the only change of clothes I'd brought with me, I prepared for an argument with Cricket—someone who refused to see reason at times. My reason anyway.

I handed Shiloh a stack of down comforters. "If it gets too cold, come back in here by the fire."

"I'll be fine," she replied. "Do what you need to do. She needs you as much as you need her." Her lips formed a thin line. I despised the look of pity she gave me as she left in search of some much-needed sleep.

The sun had set and the house had grown darker. I placed another log on the fire. Staring into the flames and at the flying sparks, I breathed in the piney smell of burning wood. While waiting for Cricket to finish up her bathing, I had examined every part of the house. It was a solid structure. It needed some love and attention, but as far as neglected houses go, this one looked better than most in the outside world. Maybe because it was off the beaten path, it had been safe from passersby looking for a place to crash. The large biohazard symbol painted on the outside probably helped too.

"Hi," Cricket said in a small voice behind me. I hadn't even heard her enter the room.

When I took in her appearance—her damp hair in a side braid, long bangs covering her scarred cheek, and a turtleneck that did nothing to hide her very feminine curves—I wanted nothing more than to scoop her up in my arms and forget everything we were up against. If only for a few minutes.

I wanted to approach her, but I hesitated. I needed her to come closer to me. I needed her to believe she was in control of her own life. As much as any of us could feel that way. And I needed her to trust me.

"Feeling better?" I asked.

"I feel cleaner." She wrung her hands in front of her.

"Look," I started. "I see that you have your life all figured out. And I'll go as far as to agree that this house is close to perfect. It has most of what you need..."

"But..." Cricket challenged.

"It doesn't have everything. I know you. I saw the miniature medical lab you've started in the kitchen."

"And you don't think the house is enough," she said. It was more statement than question.

I glanced toward the fire, looking for inspiration for how to keep her from getting so defensive that she'd do anything just to win the argument. This wasn't about winning. One wrong decision, and we would all lose. "You don't have everything you need to develop a treatment for Bad Sam," I said. "And you know it."

She didn't argue with that. Pulling a long stick from a cylinder tube, she struck a match, then proceeded to light a small oil lamp and several candles placed around the room. The flickering light bounced off the walls and cast a warm glow upon her cheeks.

She blew out the match. I didn't move when her shoulder brushed against my chest and she tossed the burnt match into the fireplace. I breathed in her clean smell—the fragrance of soap on her skin and her freshly washed hair—and I contemplated running my fingers along her damp braid.

Unable to stop myself, I grabbed her upper arms and turned her gently to face me. "I need you to come back with me to New Caelum. I'll keep you safe there."

She blinked up at me through dark eyelashes. "I don't need your protection."

My lips twitched. I wasn't even about to try to convince her that she would not successfully fend off every wild animal and group of outsiders that came along. "I know you don't. This is not about what you need."

"Then what's it about?"

"I know you can survive here. And by the looks of it, you'll manage quite well. But I have an entire city of citizens to think about. I've been preparing to run that city for a long time. And those people are changing—starting to want different things." Hell, I wanted different things than I once had.

"What does that have to do with me? I told you I was never going to live inside New Caelum."

"Yes, you've made that perfectly clear." Anger seeped into my voice, and I reminded myself that I only had one chance to get this right. One wrong statement, and she could be forcing me to sleep in my truck tonight. "I respect your wishes. But I'd like to make a deal with you." I massaged her arms. I wanted to touch more of her, to pull her closer. God, what I would do for her to admit she wanted me just as badly.

"What kind of deal?"

"If you'll come back with me to New Caelum and finish helping our doctors come up with a cure, I'll provide whatever you need to make this house exactly what you need it to be. I'll get the solar panels working. I'll get someone to fix your front porch. And anything else you need."

"Why would you do that?"

"It's what you want."

"How do you know I don't want to go back to Boone Blackston?"

"I've been watching the way you've moved about this house. Nina said you haven't been back here in years, but I know different."

"And what makes you think that?"

"You know where everything is, and how the house operates. You move throughout the inside and around the outside of this house like you've studied every nook and cranny."

She crossed her arms. I was practically holding my breath while I waited for her to agree. Who wouldn't take me up on this proposition? New Caelum had the best builders and engineers. I would make this house perfect for her.

As I studied her crossed arms, the thin line of her pressed lips, and the way two vertical lines formed between her narrowed eyes, I knew it wasn't the time to invite myself further into her life. She'd grown skeptical of me since we spent those two nights on the roof of the Biltmore. I suspected it was because of Dax, because of his accusation that I had brought Bad Sam back into the world—and his insistence that Cricket was the reason Dylan hadn't fought the disease successfully. And now she was putting up walls faster than I could tear them down.

"I'm sorry, West," she said with absolutely no emotion. "I can't go back to New Caelum."

chapter fifteen

Cricket

"**W**hat? Why not?" West practically screamed. I walked to a large decorative wood trunk beneath one of the front windows and pulled out two folded quilts. "These should be good if we sleep in front of the fireplace. We should be warm enough as long as we don't let the fire go out."

His jaw hardened as he glared at me. "That's it? We're not even going to discuss this?"

"There's nothing to discuss." I thrust a blanket at him, forcing him to take it. "Where's Shiloh? She'll freeze if she doesn't sleep near the fire." I needed to construct a barrier between us. I would never be able to watch him go tomorrow if I let him get too close tonight.

"She's fine. I gave her enough comforters to keep her warm. We're not done here."

It didn't matter how much I wanted him to hold me or how much I craved his body heat. Nor did it matter that I'd slept most peacefully when he was near. He made me feel safe, like the world around us wasn't this frightening place filled with rabid dogs, deadly diseases, and people who were ready to wage war on each other.

But with Shiloh near, I could push back against my needs—and the desire that West so obviously emanated. What confused me though was: Why had he made sure we had this alone time when he was preparing to return to New Caelum to be matched with someone else?

West tossed his blanket on the floor, then stalked toward me, his eyes clear with intention. He rested a hand at my waist where the hem of my sweater just barely met my pants.

"West, don't." I started to pull back, but stopped when I felt the warmth of his touch on my skin.

His hand traveled to the small of my back. "What's changed?" His fingers stretched wider, splaying across my back. "You act like I'm trying to force you to live inside New Caelum against your will forever. I'm only asking you to help me save our friends and family."

"*Your* family." I blinked up at him. "I have none, remember?" It was a low blow, even for me.

His cheeks drooped, and he released me. I immediately felt the drop in temperature when his hand left me.

"Caine, Nina, Dax—they're your family," West said. "What are you planning to do? Live out here in this house by yourself forever? What happens when the next group of outsiders from the western settlements stumbles upon your house?"

My back stiffened, and my face must have reflected my thoughts.

"What is it?" he asked.

"The two boys. They said the six settlements west of here were discussing ways to attack the city. They believe New Caelum sent the virus to them on purpose. To them it was an act of war."

West nodded and turned away, toward the fire. "I've suspected this could happen. But so far, we've received no word from the other missing scouts."

"According to Steve and Cade, all four of them were infected with Bad Sam, and the leaders of the settlements killed them."

"Did the virus spread?" West asked.

I nodded. "Cade said it did."

He rubbed the back of his neck, the weight of New Caelum's increasing problems resting on his shoulders. I couldn't help myself from sliding my arms through his, reaching my hands up to grip his shoulders, and pressing my chest into his back. "Are you sure you want to take on a leadership role inside New Caelum? How much are you willing to give up to do so?"

He turned, but when I started to pull back again, he wrapped his arms around me. He stared into my eyes. "I've been trained for this. Most of the people inside New Caelum just want to live out their lives with a chance at happiness, and to make a difference in how our country survives beyond Bad Sam. They didn't want to inflict the disease on anyone ever again. That was just Justin, Dr. Pooley, and whoever helped them. I have to see my city through this. And somehow..."

"What?" I asked when his voice trailed off.

"Somehow my city... no, not my city. I, as the next leader of New Caelum, have to make things right with the outside world."

"How are *you* going to do that?"

"I have no idea. Dr. Pooley obviously can't be trusted, and my best infectious disease doctor is dead."

I hugged him tighter and leaned my face into his chest, breathing in that rugged scent I'd come to know.

"I understand why you don't want to return with me to the city," he said, "but I need your help. You know more than anyone else about the treatment that actually worked against Bad Sam."

I closed my eyes. My forehead rested against his shirt, and he stroked my long braid. What would my parents want me to do? How would our society ever thrive again? "I'm so exhausted," I said. "I just don't know what to do."

"We need sleep." He held me at arm's length. "Things will look clearer in the morning."

I nodded, but I had never really understood that statement. No amount of sleep would make my decision—whether or not to return with West—any easier. And West would still be returning to New Caelum to be matched, a fact he had yet to mention.

"You're right. Let's get some sleep." I turned before he witnessed the moisture pooling in my eyes at the thought of him marrying someone else, and at the thought of him leaving me in the morning, maybe for the last time.

I grabbed cushions of the couch and laid them on the floor in front of the fire. "You can use these." When I finally lifted my head to look at him again, his throat bobbed like he was attempting to hide his emotions. "They'll be more comfortable than the hard floor."

"I don't care about the stupid hard floor."

I looked away. "I can't do this, West."

"You can't do what?" He stepped closer and tried to reach a hand to my cheek again, but I pulled back.

"I can't be close to you."

Something close to fear flashed in his eyes. "Why are you pulling away?"

"Don't you get it?"

"Apparently not."

He and I were in two very different places, going in two very different directions. I was losing him, and he was refusing to be honest even with himself about his future matching. "I'd like to sit in the chair for a while. I have a lot of thinking to do, and I need to sleep. I need you to let me process this my own way."

He finally nodded, then lay on top of the cushions and covered himself with one of the blankets. I knew he was exhausted, and it wasn't long before his breathing evened out.

Wrapped in a hand-stitched quilt, I was curled up in a wingback chair thinking about my very few good options. Mostly, I listened to West breathe, memorizing the way his face looked in the light of the candles and the fire. Every once in a while, lines formed across his forehead and the muscles around his eyes tightened like he was in pain.

When I couldn't take it any longer, I crawled out of my chair, blew out the remaining candles, and joined him on the floor. As if a sixth sense had taken over, he felt my presence. He opened up his blanket and folded me into his body, adjusting our blankets until we were so snug that sleep found us both.

~~~~~

I woke with a start in the middle of the night, and I could have sworn it was from a loud banging noise. The embers in the fireplace glowed a magnificent orange. Wrapped in the warmth of two of my grandmother's quilts, West's and my limbs were intertwined so tightly that I couldn't move, and I was burning up.

How we'd ended up that way, I barely remembered. I had sworn to myself last night that I wouldn't let it happen. We were just putting off the inevitable heartbreak. He belonged with the people of New Caelum. I belonged in a place where I could be free.

A faint knock from the front door caused my entire body to tense up. Was that what had woken me up? I looked down at West, who continued to sleep. Should I wake him? Sensing movement from the back of the house, I lifted my head. Shiloh, who had obviously been awakened by the disturbance as well, was crouched low and armed with her Taser. She lifted her finger to her lips, telling me to be quiet, as if I'd planned to be anything but.

I shook West gently. His eyes popped open. He was disoriented at first while trying to focus on my face, but then the sound of the knock registered.

"What the...?" he whispered.

I pressed my hand over his mouth. "I'm going for the gun."

I rolled out of his hold and padded in sock feet to retrieve the gun from Dad's office. All three of us then moved to look out the two front windows onto the porch. A dark shadow was moving away from the door to the window opposite the one I was peering through.

Then I saw the figure's face, and I let out a huge breath. I went to the door and unlocked the two deadbolts. West's eyes widened, but he didn't stop me. I pulled the door open wide. "What the hell, Zara?"

My voice echoed into the silence of the early morning. It was near pitch black, and the rush of freezing air forced me to wrap my arms tightly around my own body. West and Shiloh both breathed heavy sighs.

Zara removed what appeared to be a set of night goggles, something she liked to use when guarding Boone Blackston at night. She didn't say anything.

"Zara? What are you doing here?" I stepped back and allowed her to enter the house, quickly shutting the door behind her in order to keep more cold from entering.

"And why in the middle of the night?" West added in an aggravated tone.

Zara pulled her gloves off, one by one. When she lifted her face, tears filled her eyes—something I'd never seen from her. "It's Dax."

"What's Dax?" I asked, a slow panic forming in the pit of my stomach. When she didn't answer right away, I grabbed her arms and gave her a little shake. "What happened to Dax? Did he run away?" I studied her expression, looking for any hint of why she would come all this way from Boone Blackston by herself in the middle of the night. "He does that. You know this. Things got tough, so he left. He'll be back."

"He didn't run away," she said softly.

My heart was racing. I suddenly couldn't breathe. "Tell me!" I managed to scream at her. I backed up a step, letting my hands fall to my sides.

HEATHER SUNSERI

"He's sick. It's Bad Sam. He's been infected."

West grabbed me just as my knees gave out. I stared straight ahead. My face must have started turning colors, because West pushed hair out of my face and began screaming at me. "Cricket, you have to breathe. Look at me! Breathe!"

And I did. I gulped in a huge gasp.

"That's it." He pressed my head to his chest, and I realized I was sitting in his lap. "In. Out."

When I'd caught my breath again, I stared up at Zara. Her face was wet with tears. She knelt in front of me, but her hard stare shifted from me to West. "If he dies, I will never forgive you or your city. Caine got word that the settlements to the west are plotting revenge. If Dax dies, I will do more than just join them, I will personally set out to make sure every other settlement in existence joins us to take down New Caelum."

She then looked at me and continued. "I know you're already suffering. And you'll suffer even more if Dax doesn't survive this. I hope it's the worst pain you'll ever feel, even more than the pain of Bad Sam itself. But I also know that you can fix this."

I climbed out of West's lap. Zara and I stood before each other. I looked deeply into her eyes. I didn't find the hate for me she usually had, but more of a desperate need.

But what if I was sick, too? How long did I have before I succumbed to a fever? How long did I have to figure out a way to save Dax?

It didn't matter. I had to try. I would do whatever it took to save my best friend from Bad Sam. I owed him that.

Then I remembered the supplies I'd brought with me. They were still strewn about the kitchen table. They suddenly felt so... insufficient. I knew I couldn't come up with a treatment on my own—or even with the limited equipment Caine had. Not in time to save Dax. I needed fully equipped laboratories. I needed access to water, decontamination chambers, and refrigeration. And there was only one place that had all that.

I turned to West. "I'll go with you to New Caelum. I'll go, and I'll find a way to save Dax."

"Then you should know," Zara said. "You don't have the Samael Strain."

West and I both faced Zara. I stared, barely able to comprehend her words.

"How do you know this?" West asked.

"Caine begged me to come and tell you about Dax, and to let you know that you were in the clear. It was my choice not to tell you about your own blood test until you agreed to help Dax."

I narrowed my eyes. How had Caine tested my blood? That didn't make sense. But neither did Zara withholding the results. "You hate me that much? You thought I wouldn't do whatever I could for Dax? Do you and Dax and Nina honestly believe I didn't do everything I could to help Dylan?"

West slipped his fingers into my hand. "Nina knows you did the best you could. I saw her before I came here, and she's very sorry for how she let you go. She's just devastated over losing Dylan."

"Did you see Dax?" I searched West's expression. I knew that Dax was still overcome with anger at everybody, but especially at me.

"You and Dax will talk again, and you'll forgive each other." He pulled me closer and smoothed my hair behind me. "Why didn't you tell me you'd had Caine test your blood?"

"He was supposed to give *you* the blood," I said. "I knew you would come looking for me. I didn't think Caine had the capability of testing my blood prior to having symptoms." But none of that mattered. He had found a way, and I wasn't dying. But Dax...

"How much time do you need to get ready?" West asked.

"Twenty minutes. But..." I eyed Zara again. "I need Caine to bring Dax to New Caelum. With Dr. Hempel gone and Dr. Pooley untrustworthy, I'll need Caine's expertise. And Dax will get better care inside the city."

"I'll put my most trustworthy guards and medical staff on Dax," West agreed.

"There is no way Dax will agree to return to that place," Zara said.

I grabbed Zara's hands in an unusual display of friendship. "I don't care about your or Dax's hatred toward New Caelum or toward me. If you want him to survive, you'll get him there."

She jerked her hands away. "How can I trust you?"

I flinched.

"I'm sorry," she quickly said. "I didn't mean that."

"Zara, you have my word that we will do everything we can to save Dax." West held my hand again. It was as if he wanted Zara to know he and I were a united front. Or maybe he was trying to convince me. "You are welcome inside New Caelum as well. As my guest."

I glanced up at West. *Were* we a united front—he and I? He had only asked me to return to New Caelum to work on treatments for Bad Sam, never to live there with him. At least not since I'd made my intentions clear. Was it because he knew he was to be matched with someone else?

Not that his matching mattered. Dax's survival had to be my primary concern.

"I cannot return to that place," Zara said. "Besides, if Caine agrees to bring Dax, Nina will be left alone."

"You're right," I said. "Nina is my best friend. Caine and I will be able to work faster and with less distractions if we know Nina is being taken care of."

Zara nodded. "Consider it done."

....

chapter sixteen

West

I had never experienced weather this cold. I figured it had to be unusual this far south, but I wasn't sure. I was only a little boy the last time I spent any time outside in the winter.

Cricket insisted upon setting up homemade booby traps outside the house to discourage anyone from entering. Though she hadn't said much, I think it freaked her out a bit that two guys from the west had stumbled upon her house. Frankly, I was surprised no one had occupied the home sooner. It was perfectly equipped for anyone who wanted to live on their own off the grid. However, the large painted biohazard symbol on the front really was a nice deterrent. People probably wouldn't risk the possibility that the virus might have withstood the passage of time.

Cricket locked the padlock on the shed, then faced me. When our eyes met, she hesitated, standing very still. Her eyes darted left, and then she did a one-eighty to stare into the forest behind her. She pulled her father's gun from her waistband. My hand tightened around my Taser as I joined her at the forest's edge. "What is it?"

"I thought I heard something, and... I don't know. It's just a feeling."

I had felt it too. Like we were being watched. Maybe it was the young boy. Was he stupid enough to come back, knowing he was outnumbered and we were armed?

I placed my arm around Cricket's shoulders and led her away from the shed. "Let's get going."

Zara and Shiloh climbed into the truck. I stood at the passenger door and held my hand out to Cricket. After a long look at her house, she slid her fingers into mine. Her hand was cold and slightly calloused, whereas mine was smooth—the hand of a boy who'd spent his entire life inside the city.

I pulled her closer and urged her to look at me. "We're going to do everything we can for Dax."

She breathed deeply, then nodded while letting out a long sigh. "I don't trust your city, but I know it's Dax's only hope."

"I hope you'll give me the chance to prove to you that New Caelum can change."

~~~~~

At the hospital near Boone Blackston, Caine explained to us that Nina had discovered Dax beside his brother's grave outside the settlement's walls, collapsed with fever and uncontrollable shakes. They didn't think he'd been near anyone since developing symptoms—other than Nina, and she was immune to Bad Sam.

Fortunately, Caine didn't put up much of a fight before agreeing to accompany us to New Caelum, but he did appear nervous, and he made it clear that he was uncomfortable leaving the settlement without knowing if the virus had spread further. He was put somewhat at ease when Zara and Nina announced that they would stay behind to aid the people of Boone Blackston, who had quarantined themselves inside their homes until the Bad Sam scare passed.

Shiloh rode up front with me in the New Caelum truck, while Caine and Cricket rode with Dax in the bed, all three of them suited up with protective gear. The plan was to keep Dax from infecting others by bringing him into the city the same way anyone who'd been outside would enter—through the hospital's decontamination wing, the same way Cricket and I had reentered after I found her the first time.

We rode toward New Caelum in silence for a long time before Shiloh finally spoke. "West," she said quietly. "What's going to happen?"

"Can you be more specific?" I asked without taking my eyes off of the dirt road that led us home. It was a bumpy ride, and I was watching for obstacles or potholes that would make the trip more difficult for the passengers in the back.

"Do you think the guards around the perimeter of New Caelum are going to let us bring in someone contaminated with Bad Sam?"

"It's already been arranged." I eyed her sideways. "The emergency medics are standing by."

"How did you manage that?" Shiloh asked, but then held up a hand. "No, you don't have to explain. I already know. It's what I've been trying to tell you for months: the people of New Caelum are ready to do whatever you tell them to do."

"Not everyone," I reminded her.

"Enough people are."

"Do you really think so? Because when people find out that I've brought the disease into our city—"

"West, our city started this war."

"It *is* going to be a war," I said, my voice full of regret. "The outside settlements aren't going to let us get away with what we did to them without seeking revenge. But that's not what I'm most afraid of right now." I swerved to miss a hole in the road. "I'm most afraid of the people out to ensure that we never open up the gates of New Caelum—the people who sympathize with Justin. And I have no idea who, or how many, fall into that camp."

"Any idea why someone stole the vials of virus?"

"Not yet. I have theories. But the people working against those of us who want to throw open New Caelum's doors permanently are motivated by fear, and eventually they'll lose." Fear always loses. At least that was my hope.

"Where does Cricket fit into all of this?"

I glanced in the rearview mirror at Cricket. She was holding Dax's gloved hand, facing forward. Through her mask, I could just make out the blue of her eyes and the pale skin around them. "I'm not sure." I knew how I *hoped* she would fit into my life, but that was going to take some work.

I glanced at Shiloh out of the corner of my eye. "But I have a plan."

....

chapter seventeen

Cricket

I couldn't shake the feeling that we were being watched as West drove the truck carefully along the bumpy road, attempting not to jostle Dax too much. I loved him for trying.

We arrived at New Caelum, and the solid wrought iron gates immediately began to open inward. Two people appeared in bright red hazmat suits—guards from the emergency sectors. The muscles in my neck tensed, and my grip on Dax's hand tightened.

Dax groaned. Through the mask, I could see that he was licking his lips, anything to moisten the dry, cracked skin around his mouth. His flushed cheeks were a stark contrast to his otherwise pale skin.

Behind us, trees rustled in the frigid winter temperatures, but the forest was otherwise quiet as the truck came to a complete stop. Yet I still had the distinct feeling that someone was watching us from somewhere deep in the woods. It was a sixth sense I knew well, since I myself had spied on others many times in the past.

The city guards approached the driver's side of the truck. After a few words, West ground the truck into gear, and the guards backed away to allow us to pass through the entrance.

Just as the truck lurched forward, a shot rang out from the forest behind us.

One of the guards shouted from inside the gate, followed by a shrill scream from Shiloh. At the front of the truck, the guard fell backward, his mask shattered, his forehead marked with a dark, round dot.

West sped up and steered the truck inside the gate, but more shots rang out, and the other guard collapsed to the ground. Caine pulled me down, and I immediately scrambled to cover Dax's body with my own. He grunted from my weight.

With both guards down, no one was left to shut the gate. I scrambled to the back of the truck and practically hurled my body over the edge and climbed to the ground. Caine yelled for me to take cover. Shiloh and West were close behind me. We reached the gates, and were pushing them closed—me on one side, West and Shiloh on the other—when at least ten people emerged from the forest with rifles, shotguns, handguns, and crossbows raised and aimed at Caine and Dax.

We froze. We'd never close the gates quickly enough to prevent a clean shot to the back of the truck.

I looked nervously at West, who held his hands out to the side. He motioned for Shiloh to get behind him, but she refused. Instead, she stood protectively in front of her vice president. His eyes darted from me to the armed men in front of us.

Finally, he held his arms higher and stepped out to the side. "What do you want?"

A man with a burly beard smiled. Standing over six feet tall—only slightly taller than West—and built like a bear, he wore layers of plaid flannel, a camouflage hunting jacket, and combat boots. He tipped his shotgun barrel up and dropped it to his side, then walked toward West. "We only need one thing, boy, and then we'll be on our way." He nodded behind him and to the right.

That's when I saw Cade. A woman pushed him forward. "Cade here tells us that the pretty young lady there..."—he nodded my way— "... is close to developing a cure for Bad Sam."

I stared at Cade.

"I'll ask again. What do you want?" West asked. "And I would answer fast. Soon this place will be crawling with armed guards. And they won't be asking questions." I was positive West hoped his guards would be pouring out of the city's inner buildings any second.

The bearded man laughed, the sound low and deep. A sound that made the little hairs on the back of my neck rise and my pulse pick up speed. "We'll be taking her with us, son."

West straightened. "The hell you will." He pinned me with a hard stare. "Cricket, get inside the truck."

Several people redirected their weapons from me to West. Shiloh shifted, and her hand drifted slowly in the direction of her weapon. I had no idea what she planned to do with a Taser against this small army.

"The way I see it," the bearded man said, "you don't have much of a choice. She comes with us."

With eight or so deadly firearms pointed at West, I walked forward and stood in front of West to face this brawny man.

"What do you want with me?" I asked in the calmest voice I could manage. It came out muffled through my protective mask. "And just to be clear, I *always* have a choice."

The man laughed at that. "You're one brave little girl, aren't you?"

"Or crazy," West said under his breath behind me so that only I could hear him. "Don't be a hero, Cricket."

"Maybe," Cricket answered the man. "But the way I see it, you have no idea who I am. Why would you take the word of that little boy that I can actually heal Bad Sam?"

"Because he tells a story of a girl who saved his life after a feral dog killed my son."

"You're Governor Jackson?" I curled my fingers into my palm to hide the fact that my hands were now shaking uncontrollably.

"That's right. And since you act like the name means something to you, I can only assume you know that I get what I want."

I concentrated hard on not letting any emotion—especially fear—show on my face.

"Cade says you invited him into your house, and inside, he spotted a table of medical equipment. Just before he left, he said you told him that you had survived Bad Sam and could cure others."

"And here I thought people would be nice to me when they thought I could help them." I nodded at the men and women poised to shoot me and my friends.

"You'll have to forgive us for not trusting a bunch of city folk. You people are the reason we need this cure."

This might have been the right time to tell Jackson I had heard nothing but evil things about him, and that I was not a citizen of New Caelum. But I couldn't think of a good reason to give him that information. "How many people in your settlements are sick?" I asked.

"You'll find out soon enough. Tell your friends goodbye."

"No."

"I don't think you understand, sister. Like I said before, you don't have a choice."

"And like I've already said: I always have a choice."

The governor smiled.

"Mr. Jackson," I said, "I mean no disrespect, but the reason I'm entering the Land of Oz behind me—"

"Cute," he interrupted.

"Thank you." I smiled with as much sincerity as the German shepherd I'd faced days earlier. "As I was saying... I cannot develop a cure without the supplies that are only available inside New Caelum. It's that simple. I also need help from the wizard, also only available inside New Caelum." I was lying, because the wizard was in the back of the truck behind me.

"I don't know if you're bluffing, but I thought you might say something like that."

I risked a look over my shoulder toward West. Tension radiated off of him and warmed my backside. When my eyes met the governor's again, a shiver started at my neck and moved down my spine.

"In that case, we'll take your passenger in the back of the truck with us."

I turned toward the truck, panicked as I followed the governor's line of sight—not to Caine, but to Dax. "Are you crazy?" I asked. "You know he has Bad Sam, right?"

Cade's hands shook as he stuffed them into his front pockets. The governor picked up his rifle and slung it over his shoulder. "I know exactly who he is and what he has," he said. Then he shouted over his shoulder, "Bring the lady out!"

From the forest, a girl was shoved forward. *Zara*. Behind a veil of chocolate brown hair, the fiery anger in her eyes burned into mine. "I'm sorry," she said. "Nina is fine—"

The woman behind her jabbed the butt of a rifle into Zara's back. She grunted and stumbled. "I will kill you when I get the chance," Zara growled.

"I believe you know this feisty one?" Governor Jackson asked. "She all but offered up you and your patient here as being the key to finding a cure to Bad Sam."

"Not on purpose," Zara barked. This time the woman hit her in the head. Zara fell to her hands and knees. I made a move forward to help her, but stopped when a crossbow was aimed directly at me. "They were eavesdropping," Zara continued. The woman hit her again, and Zara immediately began puking. She apparently didn't know how to stop talking.

I fidgeted with my hands while trying to figure out what these people could possibly want with Dax. They'd already killed the city boys that had arrived on their doorsteps with Bad Sam.

"Why do you want a man sick with Bad Sam?" I finally asked.

"According to your friends, you're the only one who can cure this kid—a man you apparently love—of the Samael Strain."

"So?" I asked, seeing no reason to deny what he was suggesting.

"Well, when you have the cure, you'll bring it to us."

"Why would I do that?"

"Because if you want to see your boyfriend again, you'll cure our people first."

"And if I say no?"

"Then he dies, and we continue with our plan to take down this city."

I looked immediately back at West, begging him with my eyes not to react to this statement. We both knew it would take a small army to take down New Caelum. But I had no way of knowing how many of Governor Jackson's people had already trained for such a battle.

The governor pulled a handgun from his waist, and after two quick strides, he pointed it at Zara's head. "What's it going to be?"

Zara looked up at me, still on her hands and knees, her face pale. Though she usually came across as quite intimidating, she now appeared vulnerable and helpless. I wasn't sure if it was the nausea from the concussion she was probably suffering, or if she thought this man was about to execute her.

"How do I know you can keep Dax alive while I find a treatment? And not infect your entire settlement in the process?"

"You'll just have to trust us—the way I'm going to trust you." It was then that I noticed a man and a woman suiting up in their own set of protective gear and gas masks.

I stared at Zara's pure determination to stay strong with a gun aimed at her head. "Fine. But if Dax is dead before I make it to Morgan Creek, I will personally see to it that you *never* see a cure or a vaccination to Bad Sam." I refused to fear Governor Jackson any more than I would fear the big city behind me.

"I'll make sure they take care of him." These words came from Shiloh, who had remained silent until now.

We all turned to look at Shiloh—me, West, Governor Jackson, and even Zara.

"I'll go with Dax wherever they're taking him," she said.

"Shiloh," West said. "You're not immune to Bad Sam."

"Well then, it's a good thing I don't plan on becoming infected with the virus, now isn't it?" She smiled uncomfortably. When West grabbed her hands and pinned her with an are-you-sure stare, she continued. "I'll check in daily. You and Cricket have your jobs; I have mine. My job is to protect."

"We'll allow that," Governor Jackson announced.

Large metal garage doors opened at the base of the city, and out poured West's armed guards. "On my command!" West shouted at them. They moved into position and aimed their weapons at the people standing outside their gate.

West turned to Governor Jackson. "Mr. Jackson, I am vice president of this city that you obviously know nothing about. The men and women behind me are willing to die to protect what New Caelum has worked the last six years to preserve. If Shiloh does not report to us each day, I will send my own army out to your settlement."

West and I had no choice but to take Governor Jackson's next words as an agreement to our terms. "We'll be taking the truck, too," he said. When I raised a brow, he explained: "How else do you suggest we transport your sick boyfriend?"

"I'll just get my things," I said. I turned, and before anyone could stop me, I climbed up into the bed of the truck. Caine had mostly kept his back to the entire conversation that had just transpired.

Caine uncurled his fingers to reveal a syringe and needle lying across his palm. "I know him. I don't trust him."

"You know him?"

Caine ignored the question, but I supposed I shouldn't have been surprised, since the governor's settlements weren't all that far away from our own. "I think we should inject Dax with a dose of the treatment you used on the others," Caine said.

I met his gaze with widened eyes. My heart had practically stopped. "What if it kills him, like it did Dylan?"

"A boost of your antibodies is Dax's best chance. It will help him fight the virus until we can come up with something we know will work. I think this is our only choice."

Dax's eyes flickered open. "I'm sorry." He coughed.

I didn't know what he was sorry for, but it didn't matter. I had to make sure he recovered so that we could both be sorry later. "Shh. It's going to be okay." I nodded to Caine, then dug through my backpack in a crazy hurry until I found what I was looking for.

"Duct tape?" Caine questioned.

"It can fix anything." I flattened the layers of clothing and protective gear against Dax's arm. He was shaking from a fever that had climbed to who knew how high. "Be quick," I instructed Caine.

Caine jabbed the needle through Dax's hazmat suit and into his arm, and plunged the syringe. As soon as he pulled the needle out, I slapped a strip of duct tape over the tiny hole in the protective gear, and Caine dropped the used syringe into a biohazard bag.

"Cricket? Everything okay?" West walked up beside the truck. "The city guards are getting restless."

A line of guards stood in front of the truck. I grabbed the biohazard bag and stuffed it into a side pocket of my backpack. "Yes. We're ready." I touched Dax's mask and forced him to look at me, though he could barely keep his eyes open. "I will come for you." I touched my fingers to his mask, over his lips.

I climbed down out of the truck. Caine followed and managed to keep his back to the governor as he stood off to the side. I faced Shiloh. "Thank you."

The members of the governor's entourage with protective suits climbed into the back of the truck. Shiloh followed. The governor and a couple of others climbed into the main cab. And the truck drove off down the road, leaving the other members of the governor's contingent to disappear unceremoniously into the woods outside the walls of New Caelum.

Just outside the gate, Zara had fallen unconscious, face down in the dirt, probably due to repeated hits to the head. Without words, West knelt down beside her. He turned her over, lifted her in his arms, and carried her inside the city.

....

chapter eighteen

West

"What the hell were you thinking?" Mom said when I entered the Presidential Suite. A server approached her with a pot of what I assumed was her favorite hot tea. Mother waved her off. "Not now."

The server set the tea on the service cart beside the coffee and fresh pastries, then scurried out of sight.

"Relax, Mother. You act as if—"

"Relax? You promised me you were ready to lead this city."

"I am," I said, my voice deceivingly calm as I approached the service cart.

"West, you watched one of our country's most brilliant doctors die, and then you fled like you'd actually shot him up with poison yourself. Not even that, you fled *outside*."

I faced Mother. "I didn't kill—"

She held a hand up to silence me. "The nurse who injected the poison has already been locked away. She confessed the minute the guards found her."

"That seems strange, doesn't it? Did she say why she killed him?" I turned over two delicate coffee cups and set them on their matching saucers. I filled one with coffee and the other with hot water and an herbal tea bag.

"No. After confessing, she killed herself."

"What? Why?"

"No idea. She injected herself with the same poison she used on Dr. Hempel before the guards could even take her into custody."

I stirred a couple of sugar cubes into the tea while attempting to process why this nurse would murder Dr. Hempel and then kill herself.

"Are we expecting someone?" Mother asked, gesturing at the two cups.

I picked up the coffee and faced her. "Cricket is here."

"You *have* lost your mind. She was exposed to the Samael Strain, West." She tapped her perfectly manicured nails against her elbow.

"Yes, she was." I took a drink of coffee while attempting to keep my pulse, and my temper, placid. "Do I need to remind you that *we* are responsible for exposing Cricket?"

"*We* are not responsible. Justin is, and he's being dealt with."

"Is he?" As far as I was concerned, being locked up, fed regularly, and allowed to shower and breathe was not punishment enough. I waved her off, giving her permission to ignore my question. "Not to worry. Cricket and I have both been cleared of any outside diseases, including Bad Sam."

Mother's personal assistant entered the suite carrying two black garment bags. He laid one across a dining chair and opened the other. Mother eyed the long, black sequined dress. "That looks fine, Dale. And the other?"

Dale opened the other bag and turned it toward me. "A tuxedo?" For the Founders' Day Gala tonight. "Perfect," I said, not even bothering to hide my sarcasm.

"You *will* attend the gala this evening," Mother said. "You are to be matched to Annalise Gatewood in a short ceremony at ten p.m. sharp."

"Please leave us, Dale," I ordered.

"Very well, sir." Dale bowed and exited quickly.

As soon as he was gone, I turned to Mother. "I will not be matched to Annalise Gatewood. Not tonight or any other."

"If you wish to keep your newly appointed position as vice president, you will accept the matching."

My chest rose and fell in heaving breaths. I could not allow the council to name another leader of New Caelum. Not yet. "That sounds like a threat, Mother."

"No, here's the threat: You will agree, or Cricket will be sent back outside the city without the supplies she brought in."

"An empty threat. Cricket's the only one who knows how Willow, Ryder, and Key were cured. Besides, you owe Cricket way more than you can ever repay after she unselfishly entered our city and saved Willow's life. You won't be sending her anywhere." I took another drink of coffee, hoping the caffeine would give my muscles the pick-me-up they needed, while camouflaging my anxiety.

"Westlin Layne, I will remind you that I am president of New Caelum, not you."

"Yes, and I am vice president. And since you taught me so well, I'll remind you that I have almost as much authority inside this city as you have. I also have the ear of half the council, plus my own guards."

Mother stepped closer to me and picked a piece of lint off my shoulder. "Well, look who's developed a backbone."

"I've always had a backbone, Mother. I've just always chosen to give you the respect you deserved. Until you started threatening me, that is."

A smirk touched the corner of her lips. "And by respect, are you speaking of the cast of cronies you've quietly built behind my back?"

"That has nothing to do with my relationship with you, and everything to do with protecting myself in case I ever needed to step into a higher role. Leadership 101 taught me that I couldn't always count on you as a safety net."

"Ah. Well, I'm glad you've been paying attention. But your training in chess should have taught you to anticipate the unexpected moves."

"Meaning?"

"Annalise Gatewood has been trained to lead this city as well. Not as your wife. But as one of the council's choices in case you weren't up to the job."

"What?" I was stunned. How had I missed this? That lipstick-wearing, cleavage-flaunting girl has been prepping to take my job? "When did this happen?" I asked.

"Apparently, while you were organizing your own guards for a quiet intifada."

"An intifada, Mother? That's a little melodramatic, even for you."

"That doesn't change the fact that Mr. Gatewood and I have arranged for you and Annalise to join forces and keep peace and order inside our city. In case you haven't noticed, our city is a bit... restless."

Restless? Just wait until those who wish to leave the city discover that the virus is in the settlements, and that the leaders of the settlements are not happy. "I will entertain Annalise this evening," I said, "but I'd like more time before our engagement is announced. You can make that happen, right?"

Mother gave me a considering look. "What shall I tell the Gatewoods?"

"Tell them that the city will hardly take me seriously if I suddenly hop from one fiancée to another." Not to mention if people discover that Cricket is still inside this city. Anyone who witnessed me around her would see straight through me. "I'd like time to... what's a word you would use? Court? No, woo. Tell them I'd like time to *woo* Annalise. Do whatever you have to do to postpone the ceremony."

Mother sighed heavily, then pulled me into an uncharacteristic hug. "What we're doing for the people of New Caelum matters. You believe that, right?"

"More than anything else." If I didn't, I wouldn't have returned. I would have stayed with Cricket in her house and worked on a very different future.

"Good. You have until the eve of the Renaissance Ball. That's the best I can do. You *will* be matched."

Which meant I had less than a week to convince Cricket to stay inside New Caelum—to join me in leading our country into the next era. And to come up with a plan for what the next era would look like. That wasn't much time.

The door to the suite opened behind us. I turned as Cricket and Caine entered. Caine wore a white lab coat and white scrubs, the uniform of a New Caelum doctor. But to my surprise, Cricket was dressed head to toe in beige. She wore khaki pants and a soft beige sweater. Her blond hair hung loose around her face. Her jaw was set in rigid determination instead of the distraught devastation her face had held when Governor Eli Jackson drove off with her best friend.

An audible gasp escaped Mother's lips behind me, and I was pretty sure it wasn't at the sight of Cricket. "Dr. Caine Quinton," she said. "West, you didn't tell me Dr. Quinton had returned with Cricket."

"I was getting to it." I handed Cricket the cup and saucer of hot tea. "Interesting color choice," I whispered so that only she could hear.

She only shrugged, taking a sip of tea.

I had instructed my assistants to get her white clothing, the same as Caine. I didn't think anyone on the council would argue that the woman who had saved four of our citizens from dying of Bad Sam deserved anything but the color of our highest physicians and medical researchers. And I didn't think Cricket would accept the royal blue I desired for her.

Obviously, Cricket had gone out of her way to request something different—clothing the color of New Caelum's lowest sector.

"Hello, Ginger. It's been a long time," Caine said, holding out his hand to Mother.

Mother seemed cemented to the floor. And as she slid her fingers into his palm, I could have sworn beads of sweat formed along her forehead.

Cricket and I traded questioning looks. Obviously neither of us knew exactly what history existed between Mother and Caine.

"Mother, Caine and Cricket will be staying in the guest suite down the hall," I said. "As you can imagine, they'd like to continue the work of Dr. Hempel and Dr. Pooley. By combining their findings with Caine's own research, they hope to destroy the Samael Strain once and for all."

By now, Mother had regained her poise. "Caine, I'm surprised. Why have you returned to our fine city? I was sure that when you told me you'd find enough resources on the outside—or you would die trying—you meant it. Have you failed?"

I cringed. "That's quite a welcome, Mother, to the people who may be our only hope to rid the world of Bad Sam."

"It's okay." Caine shook his head, smiling. "I deserve your Mother's cold reception. I disappointed her, and your mother doesn't take well to disappointment."

It was a direct right hook, delivered with finesse and a calm tone.

"I hate to cut this reunion short," Cricket said beside me. "But Caine and I need to get back to work. We've already begun a round of lab tests. We want to thank you both for the staff of nurses and the young doctors. They've been very helpful." She took another drink of tea, then set the cup and saucer on the service cart.

"Well, it's the least my city can do for the young lady who saved my daughter's life." Mother looked nervously at me, and I wasn't sure what was causing her the most distress—the fact that Caine was here, or the fact that our city was being forced to rely on outside help in finding a cure to Bad Sam. "Christina." Mother walked closer and grabbed both of Cricket's hands. "I am terribly sorry about what Justin did to you. On behalf of New Caelum, please accept my apologies."

145

Cricket angled her head, studying Mother. "I accept your apology. But please don't misunderstand my acceptance as a declaration of trust in you—or in anyone inside this city." She pulled her hands free, and after a brief glance in my direction, she faced Caine. "I'll meet you back in the labs." Then she turned and headed straight for the door, where Derek waited.

At least she hadn't balked when I'd told her earlier that Derek would be going everywhere she went. Like it or not, I would protect her inside my city this time around. Especially with multiple murderers running amok.

I turned and faced my mother one last time. "Mother, you will handle that little issue we discussed?"

Her lips squeezed into a thin line, but she nodded nonetheless. At least that would give me some time. I would need to find a way to secure my position as vice president without Annalise in the picture. I refused to live any part of my life married to that opportunist.

~~~~~

I jogged to catch up to Derek and Cricket. "Cricket."

She stopped but didn't turn. Derek backed up, giving Cricket and me some space.

"Are your quarters all right?" I asked.

She turned and smiled. "Yes, Caine and I will be perfectly comfortable in a plush, three-bedroom flat with a fully stocked refrigerator and servants who will get us anything we desire."

I rubbed my mouth with my fingers. "It's too much. I'm sorry. I just wanted you both to be comfortable."

"We are. Thank you. Is that all?"

"We're going to get Dax back. I promise." My heart ached at the obvious pain she was in. "Do you and Caine need anything that will speed up the process of finding a cure?"

She seemed to relax slightly. "No, but thank you." She glanced over my shoulder. "Someone's coming."

Before I'd even turned fully, I breathed in the scent of Annalise's intoxicating perfume.

"Hi, West. You've been hiding. I was afraid I was going to have to send out a search party to find you before tonight's gala."

I cringed inwardly, as I had hoped to avoid introducing Annalise to Cricket this soon. If ever. And I had hoped to keep the gala a secret for now, knowing I was not going to subject Cricket to the city's lavish display of food, drink, and clothing typically worn on such an occasion. And that didn't even begin to explain how I was going to tell Cricket that the council was attempting to match me to Annalise.

"As you can see, there's no need for the dramatics," I said. "I'm present and accounted for."

Annalise was dressed in black pants and a red strapless top—colors of the emergency and government sectors she represented. Sapphires dangled from her ears in a show of the color of our pending matching. I risked a peek at Cricket. Her arms were crossed and her brows stretched high toward the ceiling.

"Who are you?" Annalise angled her pointy chin down toward Cricket for the first time, scanning the length of her beige clothing. "And what are you doing in the government sector?"

"Annalise, this is—"

"I was lost," Cricket said, cutting me off. "Mr. Layne was just pointing me in the right direction. I apologize. It won't happen again."

"See that it doesn't." Annalise linked an arm with mine. "Mr. Layne doesn't have time to play GPS to lower sector citizens."

Cricket tilted her face to the ground, letting soft strands of blond hair fall forward against her cheek. "I'm sorry, ma'am." She turned and walked off toward the medical sector, her hands clenched into fists.

Derek started to follow. "I'll just see that she finds her way, sir, and give the two of you some privacy."

Though I was sure Annalise didn't hear the sarcasm behind Derek's statement, I knew he was mocking me. He knew more than he should about my feelings toward Annalise. And toward Cricket.

"You didn't need to make her feel like that," I said to Annalise when Cricket was gone.

Annalise placed her hands on my elbows, attempting to pull me closer. "She's nobody. Why do you even care?"

The tension building in each vertebra of my spine was enough to make me want to shove Annalise into the nearest wall, but besides the fact that I would never hit her, I knew I had to act agreeable for now. At least until I figured out what was happening inside my city.

....

chapter nineteen

Cricket

Seated on a metal stool, I stared in disbelief through the glass door into an empty lab refrigerator. The vials of my antibodies were gone. As were many vials of active Samael Strain virus, according to West.

"Who would take those? And why?" I muttered. Luckily, Caine had more of my early antibodies, which were still capable of fighting the virus.

"I think you're asking the wrong questions."

I practically fell off my stool. I stood and turned toward the voice. I hadn't even heard the woman enter. We stared at each other through our hazmat masks. "Who are you?" I asked, while putting a lab table between the stranger and me.

"I am Rinala Canary. Ryder is my son."

I let my eyes wander to the large windows that looked out into the area just outside the lab, and I remembered Justin pounding on those windows, trying to get inside the lab to stop me from developing the very same treatment that was currently working its way through Ryder. "And how is Ryder?" I asked, meeting her warm brown eyes.

"He's doing much better, thanks to you."

I fidgeted with my gloved hands. "And Key? Is she okay? West said there was a situation."

"Key is getting stronger every day. Maybe even faster than Ryder and Willow."

"You said I was asking the wrong questions," I prompted.

Rinala wore dark gray protective gear, the color of leadership. She ran her fingers along the stainless steel tables as she strolled around the lab. "West wants the citizens of the city to have the freedom to leave New Caelum any time they wish. What do you think about that?"

"I think that as long as people can be peaceful, they should be allowed to wander anywhere in the world they wish."

"Do you think citizens of New Caelum can live peacefully with those already on the outside? And vice versa?"

"Why are you asking *me* that?"

"Because you see all sides," Rinala said, as if she knew me and the things I'd witnessed.

"The outsiders have been threatened. New Caelum infected them with Bad Sam."

"Yes. Justin and people who helped him were scared their city would no longer exist, or even need a leader, if West's plan to liberate the citizens of New Caelum worked. People sometimes resort to horrible actions when they feel threatened."

"You make it sound like your citizens are imprisoned."

"Aren't they? Isn't that why you left?"

"I left because I wanted to save Ryder and Key... and my friend." And I wanted to breathe the outside air and see the stars at night.

"I meant when you fled as a child six years ago."

Rinala Canary obviously knew who I was. And she was right. I did think New Caelum was a prison.

"Take a walk with me," she said. "As a council member, I'd like to show you around."

"I'm not here to tour your city." But to be honest, I *was* curious about New Caelum. And I could see kindness in this woman's eyes.

She smiled. "I know you're not. But watching those machines isn't going to make them run your experiments any faster."

She had a point. And Caine had disappeared again, leaving me nothing to do here but sit and wait. "Okay," I said.

~~~~~

After decontamination, I exited the dressing room. Rinala was already waiting for me outside, wearing black dress pants and a yellow and green silk blouse. The bright colors of the blouse accentuated the dark color of her skin, and a matching yellow and green scarf tied her hair away from her face.

"West says that council members often wear the colors of their sector or sectors in addition to the black or charcoal gray of government," I said.

"That's correct," Rinala replied. "And I see you've chosen the color of the people."

I was still dressed in beige. "That's an interesting way to put it. I met someone earlier today who didn't see my clothing choice in such a positive light."

"Mmm." She held out her hand and gestured toward the exit. "Shall we?"

Rinala led me through corridor after corridor, down stairs, and down an elevator. West had never taken me very far into the city, and never this far down. By the time we exited a second elevator, I was lost.

"Do the citizens ever tire of the bright colors everywhere?" I asked. Everywhere I looked, I saw vivid, cheerful colors.

"New Caelum was intentionally designed with festive colors to promote happiness."

"But it's manufactured happiness," I said before I could filter my words. "Don't get me wrong. I like the sleek modern and clean feel of New Caelum," I lied a little, "but after a while, it seems the people would see through the facade." I knew I did.

Rinala only smiled. She smiled a lot. Another facade?

She held open a door, and I entered what looked like an indoor playground. Children from a wide range of ages climbed on large structures and slid down slides. One wall was a rock climbing station, complete with a rainbow of fake rocks that seemed to reach four stories high. All the children—from toddlers on up—were dressed in shades of beige. No other colors.

I noticed two girls, age five or six, sitting in wheelchairs at a table by one of the windows. One was a fair-skinned blond with rosy cheeks and bright blue eyes; she was coloring with short, broken crayons. The other was a black girl with what looked like a hundred adorable braids all over her head. She sat and stared through the window at gardeners tending one of the city's gardens.

"What happened to them?" I asked.

"One was born that way."

"And the other?"

"She fell from the rock wall." Rinala nodded toward the wall where some of the kids were hooked to harnesses, and some weren't.

"There was nothing the doctors could do?" I had thought that was the appeal of living inside this fortress with the best of the best.

"They're part of the lowest sector. The resources inside New Caelum are limited."

"Limited to what?" My voice came out louder than I had intended. Several kids looked my way, and I played with the loose strands of hair that covered my scarred cheek. "Or should I say, limited to whom?"

"Limited to only those who can pay for the highest of medical care."

"I thought anyone inside New Caelum was part of the elite. That anyone allowed inside was entitled to everything the city had to offer. Wasn't that the point?"

Rinala only shook her head.

I redirected my attention to the little girls in wheelchairs, and I wondered if their lives would have turned out better if they'd lived on the outside. "What is she staring at?" I pointed to the girl with braids, dressed in a beige skirt and off-white sweater. She wore small brown boots on her feet. I walked closer and turned so that I could see out the window. It wasn't a window to the outside, but to an area of the city that tried to mimic the outside with greenhouse technology. "It's so much like our gardens in Boone Blackston in the summer."

"Those are the vegetable gardens," Rinala said. "Her father works the irrigation system. She only sees him once or twice a day if she's lucky, so she watches for him through that window."

My breath caught in my chest, and I swallowed hard. My eyes darted from the little girl to the gardens and back. Something in her eyes squeezed at my heart: hope. She watched the gardens intently, just for the off chance that she would see her father pass before her, even if only for a brief glimpse.

"Cricket, has anyone told you about your parents? Their positions inside New Caelum?"

I turned to Rinala, surprised by the subject change. "Their positions? No. I think they intended to stay outside New Caelum." Why else would they have prepared their house for living off the grid? "I was only sent inside because they needed to return to Africa." That's what I was told anyway.

"No, your parents were supposed to lead the medical sector inside New Caelum. And your father was slated to be president."

"President? What are you talking about? That's not true. They never would have turned their backs on the millions of people left outside the walls."

"Not forever, maybe."

"Not *ever*," I insisted. My parents had devoted their entire lives to people who had less. To people with fewer opportunities and fewer resources. They never would have imprisoned their passions for medicine and helping others by enclosing those passions inside these evil towers. "If they considered living inside this city for even a minute, it had to be for a good reason."

My PulsePoint pinged at my waist. I lifted it to read a message from West: *Why did you ditch Derek? He's for your protection.*

Not smart. Please tell me you're okay. And why are you in the lower sectors? Derek is headed your way.

I sighed.

"West?" Rinala asked.

I nodded. I wanted to ask Rinala about West. Had he ever wanted to be anything other than vice president of New Caelum? Would he be happy if he married Annalise? Did she think he would successfully lead the citizens of New Caelum to the outside? What would that look like?

"Are you attending our Founders' Day gala tonight?" she asked.

"I didn't return to New Caelum to celebrate your city's made-up holidays," I said. I couldn't hide the anger from my voice. The idea that this city actually celebrated the sealing-off of so many people from the outside world made my neck tense. "My friend is dying because of the people inside this city." Then it dawned on me, and I blurted it out before I had a chance to think. "He contracted Bad Sam because your son and his girlfriend brought the disease into my settlement."

Rinala's lips thinned into a straight line. "That's right."

I tilted my head. "Why did you bring me here? To this playground?" I gestured to the room of children around me.

She turned and walked back to the door. She turned just as she reached the doorway and pointed to a plaque on the wall. I stepped closer. The plaque read: *In Memory of Drs. Catherine and Henry Black.*

I brushed my fingers along my parents' names.

"I think you're in this city for a reason, Christina."

At the sound of my birth name, I faced Rinala.

"And the reason goes beyond developing a vaccine for Bad Sam—although I do think you and Dr. Quinton will succeed with that."

What other reason could I possibly have to be inside New Caelum?

My PulsePoint pinged again: *Can you at least respond that you're okay?*

This time I typed: *I'm fine. Have fun at your gala tonight.* If he could read the tone of the text, I would sound like a jealous girlfriend. As far as West knew, I only knew about the gala because of the interaction with Annalise in the hallway. He had no idea that Shiloh had warned me of the council's intentions to match him with Annalise Gatewood.

I lifted my head and met Rinala's maternal gaze. "I better get back to the labs. Caine will be wondering where I am."

We were a few steps outside the playground's doors when Rinala turned to me again. "I'm struggling with something." Two lines formed between her eyes as she grasped my elbow to hold me where I stood. "You chose to leave New Caelum when you got sick, and before the doors were to close on New Caelum for the foreseeable future. Why didn't—"

She cut herself off in mid-sentence. Her hand slapped against her neck.

"Rinala?"

After a few seconds, a small trickle of blood streamed down her neck into her yellow and green blouse. Her eyes widened, and searched mine. Her free hand squeezed my forearm tightly. I placed my hand over hers. My pulse sped up, and I looked around frantically. "Help!" I screamed.

"Christina." She backed up against the wall and slid down it to a sitting position.

I knelt in front of her. "Somebody help!" I screamed again.

She let her bloody hand slide down until it rested on the ground beside her thigh. I now saw that a small dart stuck out from her neck. "Christina, listen to me."

I leaned in closer to hear her whispered voice.

"Your parents helped create this city. There is power inside New Caelum that belongs to you. Don't let them take from you the power that is rightfully yours. The citizens, like the ones in this sector, deserve a chance to live the way your parents intended. They deserve to know you. And Christina?"

I moved slightly so that I could look into her eyes.

"Be careful. They will kill anyone who gets in the way of their plan to keep New Caelum closed up forever." She grabbed on to my sweater and pulled me even closer. "Be careful. Question everything."

A hiss escaped her mouth, and she went limp.

chapter twenty

West

I didn't even knock before entering Caine's and Cricket's apartment. Across the living room, a small lamp dimly lit the space. The entire room was reflected against the large window.

Neither Cricket nor Caine were anywhere to be seen.

Derek stood at attention just inside. He wouldn't make eye contact with me until I stood directly in front of him. When his eyes finally focused on mine, he let out a huge sigh of frustration. "I'm sorry. She said she would stay in the lab. Caine wanted to visit the three patients recovering from Bad Sam. Said he had questions for them and wanted to see records of their vitals."

"How long were you gone?"

"I swear, West, I was only gone ten minutes. I don't even know how she had time to decontaminate, dress, and disappear."

"Was she the target? Or was Councilwoman Canary the target?" How was I going to tell Ryder that his mother was dead?

"She was killed with a dart from a blowgun. This tells me that the killer knew exactly who he or she was targeting."

I rubbed the back of my neck, relieved that Cricket wasn't the target. Not this time, anyway. Until a short while ago, crime had been nonexistent in the city. Now there were murders, the theft of a dangerous virus, and even the arrests of council members.

"Why did Mrs. Canary take Cricket to the lower sector?" I asked.

"And why the children's hospital wing playground?" Derek added to my growing list of questions.

"That's where they were?" I asked. "Do we have video or audio of their visit together?"

"Nope. None. They stood mostly out of range of the video cameras. If I were a betting man, I'd bet my life that Mrs. Canary deliberately kept them out of video and audio range."

"Strange."

"Very. There are very few places in New Caelum that aren't monitored by video. Few people know that."

"Why don't you ask *me* what we talked about?" Cricket spoke from behind me.

I whipped around. In three quick strides, I stood before her. Her eyes were slightly bloodshot, and her hair was wet; she'd obviously just showered. "Are you all right?" I asked.

She crossed her arms, hugging a thick, white terrycloth robe tighter, and pulled in a labored breath. "No, West, I'm not. How *could* I be?" She turned her head and looked off toward the apartment's big windows. On the other side of those windows, in the distance, were the western settlements where Dax had most likely been taken. "Someone was murdered right in front of me today. And that was just hours after I watched one of my best friends be stolen away. Dax is sick and alone, and I might be the only one who can help him."

I reached out and tried to touch her arm, but she flinched, taking two steps away from me. I let my hand fall to my side. The pain of seeing Cricket pull even further away from me seized the muscles around my heart. "Dax is not alone," I said. "Shiloh is with him. They're in a hospital southwest of here."

Cricket lifted her head. "You heard from Shiloh?"

"Yes. Dax is hanging in there. Despite the look of the men and women who took him away, Shiloh says they're pumping him full of fluids and antibiotics. She said the hospital is run-down, but the infectious unit where they've placed Dax is sterile, and he has round-the-clock care. They even set up a cot near his room where Shiloh can sleep."

"Is she being careful? We don't know if she's immune."

"She's being very careful." I tried to offer her a smile. She would never stop caring about those around her—even people she barely knew. "I'm more concerned about you." I had promised she would be safe inside New Caelum. And if I was ever going to show her that there was a place for her here, I'd have to show her she could trust me again.

"I'll be fine. But Mrs. Canary said something..."

"What?"

"She knew things about my parents."

"What kinds of things?"

"She said my parents were a part of the initial development of New Caelum. My father..." Her voice trailed off.

"Your father what?"

She gave her head a little shake. "Oh, nothing." Her entire demeanor changed. She offered a small smile, but it was far from genuine. "Don't you have a celebration to get to?"

I glanced down at my PulsePoint. It was getting late. I had promised Mother I would be on time to the gala. Even after the murder of one of the council members, Mother and the council had refused to cancel the gala.

I narrowed my gaze at Cricket. "What else did Mrs. Canary say?"

"It doesn't matter. You should go."

"What's happened to us?" I couldn't leave Cricket this way. She was further away from me right now than when I didn't even know she was alive. "Is this about Annalise?"

"You mean the girl who shooed me away earlier like I was a fly on her delicate finger sandwich?"

"Yes, her. Who told you?" I looked back at Derek. He pretended to not be listening.

"Who told me what, West? That you would be matched to Annalise?"

"Yes."

"You just did."

I inhaled sharply, then let it out slowly. Both of our lives were complicated, and I hated that this farce of a matching was complicating it further. "It's an act. All of it. I won't marry her. In order to keep my title of vice president, and in order to help the people of New Caelum, I have to jump through the hoops set forth by the council. And the council, at the moment, is mostly Mr. Gatewood. And his daughter is..."

"Annalise Gatewood."

I moved closer, but I didn't touch her this time. I didn't think I could stomach the sight of her flinching away from me again. "It's just an act," I repeated.

"Just like *we* were, when your mother announced to the city that you would marry me?"

The city had hardly even gotten a good look at Cricket that day. The announcement was made solely to appease my mother. And Justin. "I wasn't acting then. You know that. I want you by my side. But right now..."

"I know. The timing isn't right."

"That's not what I was going to say. Right now, we both have other people counting on us. I'm here for you. I'm by your side any time you want me. Just say the word." I stepped closer and, against my better judgment, slid my hand to the small of her back. The muscles along her spine tightened at my touch, but she didn't pull away. I brought her closer to me, and leaning in, I kissed her on the forehead, breathing in her freshly showered scent of lavender. "Get some sleep tonight. Caine says you and he are close to a treatment. You'll need your strength for when we leave to get medicine to Dax." And for when we retrieve my most loyal guard. I had a strong feeling that Governor Jackson wouldn't release either of them without conditions, or some sort of fight.

She nodded, and though our conversation was far from over, I turned and left.

chapter twenty-one

Cricket

When West left, probably to find his tuxedo for the big party, I touched my fingers to the spot on my forehead he had kissed. What an endearing act—to kiss someone's forehead. It felt more like an act of protection than an act of passion or love. Maybe West was starting to see the unreasonableness of the idea that he and I would ever be anything more than political allies in this broken world.

My PulsePoint pinged at my waist. When I looked at it, I discovered a message from an unknown source: *Your presence is desired at New Caelum's Founders' Day gala.*

I risked a glance at Derek, who was still angry with me for leaving the lab earlier and getting him into trouble with West. My PulsePoint pinged again: *You have everything you need in your closet.*

"My closet?" I whispered. After another glance at Derek, who narrowed his eyes at me this time, obviously curious as to who was sending me messages, I headed in the direction of the bedroom.

The bedroom was elaborately decorated in gray and white. A crystal chandelier hung above a four-poster ebony bed. I opened the closet doors to reveal the same set of clothing that had hung in the guest room of the Presidential Suite the first time West brought me back inside the city, including the sapphire-colored dress decorated with sequins and jewels. It was strange before, and it was strange again now, to see, hanging in my closet, the color worn by people who'd been matched to their forever mates.

I read the PulsePoint messages again. There was no way I was wearing a royal blue dress to some gala like someone's betrothed. West hadn't even bothered to invite me. And there was no way I was going to watch him be matched to another woman while dressed in that color. I was no one's fool.

But if I was being honest with myself, it wasn't the dress I was upset about. It was the matching. Yes, I was doing everything I could to distance myself from West, but the truth was, I still couldn't stomach the thought of him spending his life with someone else.

And now someone was trying to get me to come watch it happen?

I typed a message: *Who are you?*

A friend. The dress you're looking for is in the black bag.

I glanced around the room and looked up at each corner, wondering if I was being watched. Turning back to the closet, I found the black garment bag. I lifted it off the rack and carried it to the bed. Scared to open it, I just stood there, staring. My feet were cemented in place.

Was I actually considering going to this gala? And wearing whatever was inside this bag?

"This is stupid." I grabbed the bag and jerked the zipper down, revealing layers and layers of soft golden fabric. "The color of the people," I whispered. And the color was not the ugliness that the upper echelon of New Caelum tried to make it out to be. No, this dress was layers and layers of gold shimmers, decorated with soft lace and delicate pearls and golden beads. I ran my hands along the fabric; it felt soft like fresh rose petals.

I looked down again at the messages on my PulsePoint. *A friend.* I had no friends inside New Caelum—except Caine, and sometimes West. I typed: *Why would I wear this?* And why would I go to some ridiculous gala? I kept the second question to myself.

The people who know about you are dying, one by one. Only you can stop it. Go to the gala tonight.

~~~~~

An hour later, I sat on a stool in front of the bathroom mirror and stared at my scraggly strands of hair, the results of letting it air dry.

But I wasn't really looking at the mirror. I couldn't get the vision of Mrs. Canary out of my head. I kept seeing her collapsing against the wall, her eyes glassy. And I kept thinking about the things she'd said about my parents.

The part that continued to stand out—the part that bothered me the most—was Rinala's claim that the citizens of New Caelum deserved to live the life that my parents had planned for them.

What did that mean? What *had* my parents planned?

I didn't have time to traipse all over this city looking for people who knew about my parents and who were willing to talk to me. And I didn't want to, either; I couldn't shake the feeling that Rinala was killed *because* she was talking to me.

I buried my face in my hands and let my fingers massage my forehead. This new information was causing me to lose sight of my real objective for being inside New Caelum: helping Dax. My heart ached just thinking about him suffering from Bad Sam. Had the shot we'd given him helped? Were the people who kidnapped him truly being kind to him? Was he in pain?

Of course he was. I was running out of time.

And I wanted to know what Rinala was talking about, and what the person messaging me on the PulsePoint was leading me toward. And where better to get a good look at the people of this city than at the annual celebration gala? I'd just have to get myself ready.

The sound of people entering the apartment interrupted the debate I was having with myself. I exited the bedroom to find Caine and Zara in the living area. I braced for Zara's anger. West and I had brought her inside the city—this city she loathed almost as much as I did.

She was talking to Caine, but she stopped when she saw me. "Hi, Cricket. I..." She fidgeted with her hands. She wore light beige, like me. "I'm sorry."

I blinked a few times. "You're... sorry?"

"Those people wouldn't have found you guys if I hadn't been so stupid in talking too much and..." She walked further into the suite. "I'm just sorry."

"How are you feeling?" I asked.

She tilted her head in Caine's direction.

"She has a concussion. As long as she avoids future knocks to the head, she should be okay."

"I still have a killer headache," Zara said, "but New Caelum has come a long way in the area of pain medication. So. What's the plan?"

"The plan?" I asked. I was still taken aback by the fact that she wasn't pissed off that West and I had brought her inside New Caelum.

"We have to get Dax back," Zara said, as if it was obvious. "And Caine says he thinks he's close to perfecting a cure."

I looked at Caine, who hadn't spoken yet. "Caine?"

He nodded. "Based on the treatment you gave the others, and the many tests we've run over the years, I think we're almost there. I really do. We just need to run it through the simulation."

My face dropped. "The simulation? Are you serious? We're going to trust a simulation?" Did that mean that the first time we'd know if the treatment truly worked would be after we injected it into patients in the western settlements and into Dax?

"Do you have a better idea? I haven't come across any rats inside New Caelum to test on."

"Of course you haven't," Zara said. "The medical sector inside New Caelum was created with the promise they would never harm animals in their scientific research."

"But they would harm *humans*?" I couldn't keep the rise in volume out of my voice, but then I closed my eyes tightly. "I'm sorry. It's just difficult to separate the evil inside these walls from the good."

"There *is* no good inside these walls," Zara said. "Only varying degrees of evil." She just might be even more tainted by her memories of New Caelum than I was.

She was wrong, though. Wasn't she? *West* was good. I was sure of it. Shiloh was good. No one, especially not a person from New Caelum, would have volunteered to go with Dax, to an area infected with Bad Sam, unless that person was the opposite of evil.

"So, how long before we know if we have a treatment to take to Dax?" I asked Caine.

"I'm shooting for the day after tomorrow. I think we'll know by then."

And hopefully no one else will have died of Bad Sam before then.

Caine sank into a leather armchair and rubbed his temples. Only then did I notice the dark circles under his eyes. He probably hadn't slept much since West, Ryder, and Key had arrived at Boone Blackston. I wondered if he'd slept at all.

"Caine? You okay?" I asked.

His hand slid around to the back his neck and massaged the muscles there. His tired eyes met mine. "I know Nina must be going crazy out there. She has no contact with the inside. Zara was supposed to be my contact with her."

"She'll be fine. She's resourceful and mature enough to know we can take care of ourselves. She's probably got Boone Blackston running like a well-oiled machine."

Caine chuckled.

A knock at the door interrupted us. Derek opened the door to a cart of covered plates. A server rolled the cart in, and as he and another server began setting a table, I motioned for Zara. "I need your help."

She eyed me. "With what?" She followed me down the hall toward the bedroom. Caine watched us go, his eye twitching with curiosity.

When we entered the bedroom, I stopped in front of the bed. Zara looked down at the sheets and sheets of glamorous fabric and the bodice of delicate pearls and golden beads.

"What. Is. That?" Zara asked.

I looked from the dress to Zara. Her cheeks had a little bit of color. Her short hair, which was in a major need of a wash, was tousled about. She walked closer and leaned over the dress, but appeared too frightened to touch it.

"It's not going to burn you."

Her lips twitched. "Are you sure?" She turned back to the dress. "What is it?" she asked again.

"It's a dress. A ball gown."

She squinted at me. "I can see that. What's it doing in here? And who in all of New Caelum would make a dress the color of drab beige?"

I glanced at Zara's clothing. "*You're* wearing beige."

"Yes, and I love it. But no one who thinks highly of themselves inside New Caelum would be caught dead wearing that color."

I studied the dress again. It really couldn't be described as khaki or beige, and definitely not drab—more of a gold shimmer. It was beautiful. "I need you to help me look good in this dress," I said.

This time when she faced me, her eyes had doubled in size. I could see a complete layer of white around her espresso irises. "You." She looked down her nose at me and raised a single brow. "*You're* planning to wear *that*?"

I looked down the length of my body. What was so wrong with thinking I could wear that dress?

Zara began to laugh. And not just a small giggle. It started with a slow chuckle, then erupted into a full, deep-from-the-belly laugh. She pressed her palm to her stomach. "You had me going there for a second."

I grabbed her arm and forced her to turn toward the door, then pushed her out of it. "I should have known this was a mistake. Get out."

"Why? What did I say? You weren't serious, were you?" Her eyes went wide again. "You *were*. You—"

I slammed the door in her face, then turned abruptly and faced the dress again. I was going to have to do this by myself.

The bathroom was filled with makeup and styling products. Of course, I had no idea how to use any of them. Approaching the bathroom mirror, I looked at my face. It was just as pale as it always was. I sat down on the black velvet stool in front of the vanity, then picked up a foundation that appeared light enough in color. I dabbed the liquid foundation around my face and tried to rub it into my skin. If only Nina were here. She'd know what to do. She'd probably even know how to cover up the scars on my face.

"I'm sorry."

I lifted my head to look at Zara's reflection in the mirror behind me.

"I don't know what this is about," she said, "but I'd like to help. I could fix your hair and makeup."

"I'd like that." I turned and faced her. She finished spreading and massaging makeup into my skin. When she was done with foundation and powder, she moved on to blush, eye shadow, and mascara. Then she braided portions of my hair and tucked the rest into a bun.

After thirty minutes of primping, I slipped into the dress and faced the mirror. Zara zipped up the dress, and we both admired the finished product. I had never worn something so beautiful in my whole life. I almost didn't recognize my own face or hair.

"Now, are you going to tell me what this is all about?" Zara backed up and sat on the edge of the bed. "Where did you get this dress?"

"It was waiting here for me after I returned from seeing a woman who was murdered right in front of me."

"Mrs. Canary? I heard about that. The guards were talking about it. They're pretty freaked out about it. But what does that have to do with this dress and the Founders' Day gala?"

"She said there are people inside this city who know about my parents and about me. That my parents left a legacy or something for me here. My parents were part of the original organizers of New Caelum."

Zara showed no emotion or surprise. "Have you asked West about it?"

I shook my head. "No."

"Why not?" I stared at her, attempting to keep all emotion from my face, until she answered her own question. "You think he might already know? And he's not telling you?"

"Possibly."

Immediately Zara began shaking her head. "No way. I might not like West—or any other asshole inside this city—but I'm good at reading people, and there's no way that the prince of New Caelum has been hiding something that big from you."

"You think so? I honestly didn't want to think badly of West, but I wasn't sure if I was letting my feelings cloud my judgment."

"You really like him?"

I hadn't had a conversation this long or this open with Zara in a long time. Maybe not ever. "It doesn't matter," I said. "West needs to lead this city, and I need to save Dax. I belong on the outside. West belongs on the inside."

"Have you not been listening to him? His number one goal as leader of New Caelum is to give people the freedom to pass in and out of the city walls."

"How do you know that?" I knew it was true. I think his mother even knew it was true, but I didn't think it was public knowledge.

"The guards. They talk a lot. And they say a huge announcement is going down tonight."

"I guess I better get going, then. The party has already started."

When I exited the bedroom, I slid my hand through the drawstrings of a small bag that matched my dress. It held lipstick and my PulsePoint.

Caine's head popped up from his dinner. "What do you think you're doing?"

"I'll let Zara fill you in. I'm running late."

I turned to Derek, who was now dressed in a formal guardsman uniform. My mouth fell open slightly. "How did you..."

"I received a message that said you might need me." He held out an arm as if to escort me. "Shall we?"

I slipped my hand through his arm and instantly felt a touch safer. Yet I still had no idea what I was about to get myself into.

chapter twenty-two

West

M other thrust a glass of red wine into my hand. "You look uptight. Relax." She walked off to greet a couple of government aides.

I didn't even like red wine, but I sipped it anyway as I scanned the perimeter of the room. The gala was in full swing.

"Hi, West." Annalise slinked into the spot beside me. She wore a black dress with a plunging neckline that would make any man's eyes wander directly to the curves of her breasts peeking out from beneath the fabric. She clinked her glass of sparkling champagne against my dark, burgundy wine. "Here's to our eventual matching." She batted her fake eyelashes while tipping back her tall, thin glass.

I wanted to tell her that I would never marry her—that if the future of this city was dependent upon us marrying and producing offspring, then we might as well kiss humanity goodbye. But she would have heard the doubt in my statement. I was dedicated to helping our country recover. In the end, I would do what I had to do. Still, I was holding out hope that there was another way besides the pairing of two people who obviously didn't love each other. "It was only right to postpone a matching ceremony until our people had grieved the loss of Councilwoman Canary," I said. I gulped down the rest of my wine. Talking to Annalise was driving me to drink more than I normally did.

"I suppose." Annalise shrugged, then rolled her shoulders back and faced me. With five-inch heels, her eyes were almost level with mine. "However, I hope this isn't some lame attempt to stall for that waif your mother and Justin almost matched you with at the last town meeting." She ran a red, manicured fingernail down my lapel.

I squeezed my wine glass a little tighter. I was certain now that Annalise had no idea that the girl she'd run into in the hall earlier today was the same person my mother had practically introduced as my matched. "I need another glass of wine." I craned my neck, looking for a server.

Annalise rested a hand on my forearm, urging me to look at her. "I didn't say anything to upset you, did I? Surely you understand the importance of our city growing stronger. Not to mention, our city needs to see that its leaders are serious about growing our population." She laughed. "Though we can wait a few months before we seriously start trying to make babies, I suppose."

The urge to loosen my necktie was immense. I scanned the room in an attempt to find someone else—anyone else—to talk with.

Annalise and I were surrounded by government officials dressed in black formal attire, guards in light gray, and a few men and women dressed in the jeweled color of royal blue. The royal blue was what got my attention tonight—the color symbolizing future weddings. Key had been matched to Ryder in a quiet, private ceremony. Even I, as their best friend, wasn't asked to be present. However, when I was formally matched, there would be a public ceremony during a social event or party. A shiver moved through me at the thought that our matching had almost happened tonight.

But there was one thing I still didn't understand. If Mr. Gatewood and the rest of the council had been so certain that I should marry his daughter, why had Justin insisted I marry Cricket? This was a piece of the puzzle that didn't fit. Cricket was even provided with a full closet of royal blue when she arrived inside New Caelum—a wardrobe I had moved to her new bedroom in hopes that she would continue to wear them. I wanted to believe that there was somehow still a chance for us.

But I wanted her to *choose* it, not acquiesce to it because of some rule dictated by the council of New Caelum.

Above us on the various levels of the atrium were people dressed in a rainbow of colors: green, yellow, red, orange, and even a few beige, though not many of the lower sector of New Caelum were present at the gala tonight. It was interesting that Cricket had insisted on beige clothing when she returned. That was probably to spite New Caelum snobs like Annalise and my mother. But it didn't matter what she wore; she was beautiful in anything.

The sounds of whispers rustled through the crowd, and the cool draft of the expansive room was replaced by an unidentifiable warmth. I lifted my head and looked around.

"West?" Annalise prompted, snapping her fingers in front of my face. "Did you hear me? My father insists that we dance."

But I couldn't even look at the mad snapping woman in front of me. The sea of guests in front of me parted slowly, and I just glimpsed the golden glow of someone's dress on the other side of the room. I knew the instant her electric blue eyes broke through the crowd that it was her.

"Who the hell is that?" I heard a voice say beside me. "And what the hell is she wearing? How dare she—" It took several seconds for the voice and her words to sink in before I realized the voice had come from Annalise, and she was now headed straight for Cricket.

A waiter stepped in front of me. "Another drink, Mr. Layne?"

"No, thank you." I thrust my empty glass at the server and darted around him. Annalise was almost to Cricket, and Cricket appeared to be surveying the crowd. Was she looking for me? Well, it wouldn't matter in a second, because Annalise was on a mission to put her in her place before I could stop it.

chapter twenty-three

Cricket

Annalise, the pretentious snob who was with West in the hallway earlier, was headed straight for me. Her face was perfectly made up. Her bright red lips were pursed into a thin line, and her emerald eyes narrowed, forming several unattractive trenches between her brows. I saw no way to avoid the imminent confrontation. What had I been thinking when I decided to attend this gala?

"What are you doing here on this floor? You don't belong here!" Annalise's voice boomed over the soft music.

People all around us stared. I glanced down at my feet for courage before looking at her again. "I'm sorry? This floor?" I knew what she meant, but I wanted to hear her explain.

"No one from the lower sector is allowed on the main ball-room floor." She scanned the length of my dress, much like she had once-overed me earlier that day. "Where did you get that dress?" She practically spit the words.

It was difficult to take this person seriously. She was dressed in a long ball gown, black and charcoal gray, her deep red hair hung in loose curls well past her shoulders, and she was putting way more energy than necessary into tapping a sparkly, silver peep toe shoe against the floor.

West was hurrying toward us. I attempted to read the look on his face, but it was cryptic.

"Do you speak English?" Annalise snapped.

I redirected my gaze from West back to the porcelain doll in front of me. "Yes, I speak English. And French. A little bit of Spanish. And I'm pretty good at pig Latin." Nina and I had made it our mission to learn multiple languages, mostly out of boredom, between the ages of thirteen and sixteen. We'd tried to pull Dax and Dylan into our multiple-language phase, but they had refused.

"Are you mocking me?"

I held up two fingers half an inch apart in front of my face. "Maybe a little," I said with no emotion whatsoever.

Her face reddened, nearly matching her hair.

"What's going on here?" West asked in a very calm, matter-of-fact tone when he finally sidled up to Annalise.

"This tramp is making fun of me. And she's not even allowed in here." Annalise crossed her arms across her bodice, pushing her breasts even further up on her chest.

"She's not making fun of you." West flashed a stern look at me as I struggled not to laugh. "Annalise, this is Christina Black."

If I hadn't been ultra-sensitive tonight, looking for anything out of the ordinary after the incident with Mrs. Canary, I might have missed the way Annalise stood a little taller and hardened her stare at me. "Christina Black? The girl who survived the Samael Strain?"

"That's right," West answered, though Annalise's question had been directed at me. "And she is my guest inside New Caelum. You will treat her as such."

A waiter was passing by with a tray of drinks.

"Well, in that case, you should have a drink." She grabbed two glasses of champagne and thrust one at me, sloshing it onto my hand when I took it. "It even matches your dress. Interesting color, by the way. Where did you get it?"

"This old thing?" I asked, looking down at my gorgeous dress while flinging droplets of spilled champagne off of my hand.

"You're new to New Caelum," Annalise sneered, "but you should know that that is not the color someone of importance should choose."

"Funny. I met two beautiful little girls today that convinced me that this was exactly the color I should wear this evening." I took a sip from the glass while looking around the room for any sign of President Layne. Would she be disappointed to see me here tonight? "Nice party, by the way."

Annalise's eyes widened at my words. She was close to exploding.

"Annalise, will you excuse Miss Black and me?" There was a playfulness in West's expression.

"What? But West, you were supposed to dance with me. This was supposed to be our night." She squared her shoulders, looking down on me. "West and I are to be matched, you know."

West stiffened at her declaration, but he kept his eyes focused on mine. Actually, he hadn't taken his eyes off of me since he'd first stalked me from the across the room. "The matching isn't happening tonight, though," West reminded Annalise, but I knew he was just making sure that I knew that piece of good news. Finally, he tore his eyes away from mine and grabbed Annalise's hand. He lifted it to his mouth and planted a small kiss on her fingers. "And like I said, Christina is my guest. You and I will visit soon."

Annalise huffed, like a petulant four-year old, and then turned on her heel and stormed off.

No matter how much I wanted to, I had no right to question how West could possibly allow himself to be attached to that brat for the rest of his life. Of course, maybe matchings weren't a life commitment the way I always dreamt marriage would be—the way my parents had been committed to each other.

West took my glass from me and set it on a nearby table. He grabbed a cloth napkin, dipped it in an abandoned glass of ice water, and returned to wipe my hand clean. When he was finished, his head lifted. The corners of his lips twitched, but he remained serious. "I wanted to ask you to come here with me tonight."

I pulled my hand away from his lingering touch and rubbed the spot where his skin had heated mine. Angling my head, I studied the intensity of his gaze. The gold specks glittered against the green of his irises. "You don't have to say that. You have a job you feel you must do." And now I had a job I needed to do. West opened his mouth like he was going to argue my point, but I cut him off. "Where is your mother?"

He didn't even look. "She's behind me somewhere. Speaking to council members, I'm sure. Everyone is fairly stressed about Mrs. Canary's death." Something in West's eyes dimmed with sadness.

"She was your best friend's mother. I'm sorry for your loss."

"Thank you."

"I'd like to speak to your mother."

"Why?"

"Assuming she's the official hostess of this celebration, I'd like to thank her."

Massaging his five o'clock shadow, he analyzed me a moment longer. "Why do I feel like you're hiding something from me?"

I took his question as rhetorical and remained silent.

"It doesn't matter. I've had too much to drink to really care tonight." He grabbed my hand and pulled me through the crowd, weaving in and around partygoers who'd also had too much to drink. As we walked, he leaned into my ear. "After you speak to my mother, I'd like to dance with you."

My breath caught at his words, but I didn't have time to react further because we were approaching a group of people dressed in nothing but black, including President Layne.

"Mother." West interrupted a conversation between President Layne, two men, and two other ladies.

President Layne turned, and when she saw me, her mouth gaped slightly. "Christina." Her voice faltered, which I found rather interesting. "Don't you look... lovely? And that dress..."

Her hesitation had me lifting a brow. "Thank you, ma'am. I found the dress in my closet, and I hated to see such a beautiful gown go to waste." My knees shook as I spoke. Something about the intimidating look in her eyes frightened me. She was a completely different woman than she'd been on the day I saved her daughter's life—the same day she escorted Dax and me out of the city.

"Inside your closet, huh?" President Layne looked at West.

"Don't look at me. Where would I have gotten such a dress? And in such a gorgeous golden color?" West slid a hand to the small of my back, the warmth of his skin soaking through the fabric and giving me a burst of strength.

"Ms. Layne," I said, "I just wanted to tell you how sorry I am for your loss. I know that Mrs. Canary was a dear friend to you."

"And how do you know such a thing?" the president asked.

"She told me just before she was murdered. We had a lovely talk this afternoon. I just don't understand why anyone would kill such a kind woman. And an amazing historian. She knew so much about your city." I gave my head a little shake and smiled. "Anyway, I just wanted to say that I'm sorry."

President Layne appeared speechless. A man at her side held out a hand to me. "I don't believe we've met. You must be the infamous Christina Black. I'm Councilman Gatewood. I believe you've already met my daughter, Annalise."

I shook Mr. Gatewood's hand. His hand was smooth and cool to the touch, and when I lifted my eyes, I found the same frigid temperature in his facial expression. Though he had thick, black hair and pale skin, the result of many years spent away from the sun, I immediately recognized the resemblance between him and his daughter. "It's nice to meet you," I managed.

"My guards tell me that you and Dr. Quinton won't be staying long inside our city, but that you're once again working on a cure to Bad Sam. Why? Was the first one not good enough?"

President Layne's face had lost most of its color. She stared straight ahead with a blank expression.

I smiled at Mr. Gatewood so that anyone looking on would think I was having a pleasant conversation with this man. "Well, apparently your city kept secrets from me when I was here last time. Your city doctors are responsible for killing my best friend. So now I'm here to ensure we have a more reliable cure for future outbreaks."

Mr. Gatewood tensed. "How dare you. You are—"

"Dancing," West announced.

"Now, now, Howard." President Layne, apparently recovered, placed her hand on Mr. Gatewood's arm. "This is a celebration. Christina is just emotional after losing a dear friend. As are we," she reminded him.

West grabbed my hand and tugged me in his direction before leaning in and whispering in my ear: "Let's dance before you stoke any more fires."

....

chapter twenty-four

West

All eyes were on Cricket as I twirled her to face me and brought her body flush with mine.

She stared into my chest. Her small hand fit perfectly inside my palm as I held it between us. My other hand rested snugly at the small of her back, and her fingers grasped a handful of my tuxedo jacket at my waist.

We moved to the music, a slow, orchestrated waltz.

"Want to tell me what that was all about?" I asked.

"Not really. Not here anyway." She laid her cheek against my chest. Her grasp on my jacket loosened slightly. "To be honest, I'm not sure what came over me just now. I've never spoken to anyone like that before."

I scanned the area around us. Derek and five other guards stood at the edge of the dance floor. I hated that so many eyes were on us. I wanted Cricket to myself.

Glancing up, I noticed the balconies above us had become more crowded. I'd always loved the kickoff to the annual week of celebration. People attended the gala in their finest outfits, and many women even had new dresses made for the occasion. After the gala, citizens saw to decorating the common areas of the city with twinkle lights and ribbons. It was a happy time inside New Caelum.

But this year, the atmosphere inside the city was different. A dark cloud hung over the gala tonight. What with Justin's and Dr. Pooley's arrests—and now, the murders of two of our leaders—the city's citizens were on edge, and the air inside this grand atrium seemed thick with tension.

As I looked up at the citizens above us in their colorful attire, I was struck by something. There were more citizens dressed in beige dresses than I'd ever seen at a celebration gala. And many people on the higher balconies were now staring down—not just at the main floor or toward the city's government officials, but at Cricket and me.

Actually, I was fairly certain they were staring at Cricket. I looked down at her. She was looking straight ahead at a spot on my shirt, her eyes unmoving.

"Hey." I crooked a finger under her chin and lifted. "What are you thinking about?"

Her bright blue eyes met my gaze. "Someone went to a lot of trouble to get me here tonight. I know it has to do with what Rinala told me today, but..." She squeezed her eyes tight. "I watched Councilwoman Canary die right in front of me, and when she looked at me as she took her final breath, it was as if..."

"As if what?" I prompted.

"As if she knew she would die, and she was willing to do so." Tears welled at the edges of her bottom eyelids. "She was willing to die for *me*, West. Why would anyone do that?" A tear escaped her eye and streamed down her face, leaving a streak in her makeup.

"We need to get you out of here," I said. I didn't know what Mrs. Canary could possibly have told her, but I agreed with one thing: someone had gone to a lot of trouble to plant this dress she wore inside her closet. Besides, something was definitely off tonight. The council members had been whispering in corners all night.

"I think I will go, but you should stay." Cricket stepped closer to me. She leaned in and placed her lips on my cheek. When she pulled back, she wiped her thumb across my cheek, I assumed to remove the lipstick there. "I'm glad you weren't matched to Annalise tonight," she whispered.

Then she turned and walked away.

....

chapter twenty-five

Cricket

Derek rode with me in the glass elevator. When the doors opened several floors above the main ballroom, I was greeted with a crowd of festive partygoers. Unlike the main floor, the citizens at this level were dressed in a rainbow of colors: red, orange, green, yellow, purple, pale blue, and even a little black and royal blue sprinkled in.

I was getting ready to turn away from the people celebrating and head toward the wing where Caine and Zara would be waiting for me when some children caught my eye. It was the two girls in wheelchairs from earlier that day.

"Cricket," Derek said. "I was ordered to escort you back to the suite."

I eyed Derek. The guard beside him didn't even look at me. "And you will. I'm just going to say hello to these children."

I walked closer. I felt the stares of men and women all around me. When I reached the dark-skinned girl—the one who had been waiting patiently for a glimpse of her father working the irrigation system—I knelt before her. "Hi."

Her brown eyes darted around nervously before they settled on me. "Hi." She wore a simple beige dress and the same boots she'd worn earlier that day. "I like your dress."

"Thank you. I like yours, too." My face warmed when a smile spread across her face. "What's your name?"

"Gloria." She looked away bashfully.

A tall black man stood behind the wheelchair. "Who are you? Why are you speaking to my daughter?"

I stood and backed away immediately, keeping my head slightly bowed and instinctively allowing the loose strands of hair on one side to cover my scars. "I'm sorry, sir. I didn't mean any harm."

"He didn't mean that you weren't allowed to," Derek said beside me. "He just doesn't understand why you are."

"Oh. Well." I made eye contact with Gloria's father. "I think your daughter is beautiful, and I'm sorry that she fell."

Gloria tugged on my dress. "Are you the princess that is going to save our city from falling?"

I looked down into the most hopeful chocolate brown eyes. But her words confused me. "Your city is not going to fall."

"My aunt told me that you would help us."

I angled my head to Gloria. "Who is your aunt?"

"Aunt Rinala. She was my mommy's sister."

I glanced up at the man who gripped the handles of the wheelchair. "Where is Gloria's mom now?" I asked.

"She died years ago."

"And she was Rinala's sister?"

"That's right." He opened and closed his fingers around the wheelchair handles nervously.

I knelt in front of Gloria again. "Would you mind if I came to see you at the playground again?"

"I would like that." She smiled, revealing a couple of crooked front teeth that added to her major cuteness.

A voice came over the speakers. "Welcome, citizens of New Caelum, to the seventh annual Founders' Day gala. Six years ago, our city was preparing to be sealed away from the outside world. It is the day you and I were saved from the worst fate this generation would ever know."

I stood slowly as every citizen around me either looked to the large screen hanging in the middle of the atrium or peered over the balcony to the main ballroom below.

On the screen was Councilman Gatewood. His daughter stood to his right. To his left were President Ginger Layne and Vice President Westlin Layne.

"We know you were expecting a matching ceremony tonight," Councilman Gatewood continued, "but in light of today's tragic news that Rinala Canary has moved on to be with our Creator, the council and I felt that the timing wasn't right. However, we would like to assure the citizens of this fine city that the council, your president, vice president, and future leaders"—he looked at Annalise—"are dedicated to seeing to it that we are safe for years to come.

"There have been whispers and grumblings that our city is in danger from the Samael Strain. That is not true. In fact, we have specialists inside the city who are working diligently to provide every citizen with a vaccine so that no one in New Caelum will ever need worry about the Samael Strain again."

I glimpsed movement out of the corner of my left eye. I had just started to turn when several things happened very quickly:

something knocked against the handbag hanging from my wrist, Derek tackled a man to the ground, Gloria screamed the horror movie of all screams, and three guards forced me away from the balcony's edge and down a hallway.

The guards didn't stop rushing me through the hallways until I was back inside our assigned suite.

"What was that?" I asked when the door to the suite was closed and Derek was backing away from me, breathing hard.

Derek spoke into his wrist. "She's safe. The hallways and suite are being swept."

I could hear the faint sound of words coming from his earpiece. He winced when they grew louder.

"Very good, sir. I will, sir."

When Derek had obviously finished his conversation, I asked: "Who was that?"

"Mr. Layne, ma'am." It was Mr. Layne and ma'am, now. He gestured toward my bag. "May I?"

I looked down. A tiny metal object was sticking out of my bag—a dart. The same kind of dart that had been used to murder Rinala. "Did someone try to kill me?" I searched Derek's face, then the blank expressions of the other guards. All were unreadable.

My PulsePoint pinged. Before I could reach for it inside my bag, Derek took the bag and laid it on the glass dining table. "There are probably remnants of the poison in the fabric," he said. He pulled the few items out of it, including my PulsePoint, which he handed to me.

The screen was lit up with a text message: *Hope you enjoyed dressing up for the gala. My suspicions were correct. The powers that be were not happy to see you there, especially in that dress.*

uprising

What the hell? I typed: *You set me up? Are you trying to kill me?*
Like my killer would confess his intentions.

Of course not. But we need your help to take down President Layne.

....

chapter twenty-six

West

I loosened my bow tie with unsteady fingers and paced in front of Key and Ryder. According to Derek, someone had just tried to poison Cricket. My heart had practically stopped when I saw him and the other guards hustling her away from the celebration.

Key sat up in bed, her hands folded gently in her lap. Ryder slept in his own bed beside her.

I took a cleansing breath to regain focus. "Does Ryder know about his mom?" I asked with my back turned to Key.

"Yes," she said. "He's refusing to talk about it, though."

I nodded. My heart ached for my best friend. Finally, I faced Key. "Where did you get the dress?"

"How do you know it was me?"

I angled my head. "*Key.*"

"*West.*" She mirrored my tone.

"Willow has been bedridden since she got sick. Only you two and my mother could have found that particular dress. And based on Mother's reaction, I know she didn't give it to Cricket."

After several beats, she sighed. "I haven't told you every-thing." She glanced nervously at Ryder. "I need you to sit, and I need you to have an open mind."

I glared at her for several beats, then scooted a chair closer to her bedside and sat. "Fine. I'm sitting. And my mind is open."

Key smoothed the blanket along her thighs before folding her hands in her lap again. Ryder, Key, and Willow weren't contagious any longer, but Ryder and Key weren't strong enough to be out of bed for more than a few minutes at a time, and Willow was still too weak to even hold her head up.

"Ryder's mom found the dress," Key said finally. "I told her where to look."

"Why? Why would Rinala want it? And why give it to Cricket? It will only hurt her to find out that the dress be-longed to her mother."

"Why does she need to know where the dress came from?"

I angled my head at Key. "You and Rinala manipulated Cricket into attending the gala in Catherine Black's dress. I want to know why."

"Rinala wanted to rattle your mother and Councilman Gatewood."

I sighed heavily, losing patience. "Again, why?"

"I only know that Rinala came to Ryder and me after you left the other day and began saying all sorts of crazy things."

"Like?"

"Like Cricket was always supposed to return to New Cae-lum. Like it was her job to continue the legacy of her parents. And she was certain that Cricket *would* do these things."

"I don't understand. Ryder's mom felt strongly that Cricket belonged inside New Caelum? What does that have to do with her digging up a dress that Cricket's own mother wore more than seven years ago? A dress that, though beautiful, is also the same color worn by the lower sector of this city?"

"I know it sounds crazy."

"Do you?" I stood and paced. "It doesn't even make sense."

"Cricket's parents helped fund the building of New Caelum."

"What? How do you know this?"

"From Rinala. Apparently, everything we thought we knew about Bad Sam and the formation of this city is only a tiny portion of the truth. According to Rinala, the Blacks were supposed to be the original leaders of the city, not your mother. She claimed that your mother and others manipulated the Blacks into relinquishing their titles inside the city. This was how the council got so much power. The founding members backed your mother and shared the power by becoming New Caelum's first council members."

When I said nothing, Key continued. "Look at this city, West. It took years to build this many buildings and connect them with the tunnels and the airtight technology that would keep our air clean of a deadly virus. Not to mention secure us from those left on the outside."

"Yes, the people who built New Caelum clearly had a unique vision."

"Not just unique. Prophetic," Key corrected.

My eyes narrowed. "What do you mean by that?"

"Why build this monstrosity of a city, why go to all this trouble... unless those who built it *knew* we would need it?" Key looked down and played with a loose thread in her blanket. When her eyes met mine again, moisture had pooled in them. "West, someone, or a group of people, *knew* that Bad Sam would be the deadly force of mass destruction it turned out to be." A tear streamed down her face.

"Knew about it? And let it happen?" The words stung the tip of my tongue.

"I don't know. But look around you. Look where we are. In this beautiful, well-planned, and airtight city. Kind of a big coincidence that it was built right before Bad Sam came along, don't you think?"

"That's a heavy accusation, Key."

She shrugged. "I'm just telling you what I learned from Rinala."

I sat again and buried my face in my hands. What Key was saying couldn't be true. But at the same time, I knew everything she said made sense. I felt the burning in my eyes as I thought of the destruction of our nation. And what was now left of our population.

When I lifted my head, Key was smiling reassuringly. It was obvious she'd already had some time to process all of this.

"Why didn't Rinala tell me any of this?" I asked.

"She wanted to. She's been watching you. She says your following—the people who are clearly loyal to you—within the sectors reaches many tens of thousands, probably more. But then—well, after you were asked to marry Annalise, you just stood by your mother and agreed to everything Mr. Gatewood was asking. To her, that was... concerning. Though she's done nothing to discourage the people of the city who think you're the next in line to run New Caelum."

"I will never marry Annalise Gatewood," I practically spat.

"I know that. But Rinala..."

I sighed. "What does any of this have to do with Cricket? Why did Rinala insist that Cricket attend the gala? And how did Rinala know that Cricket's presence would rattle my mother and Mr. Gatewood?"

"Rinala said that your mother, Councilman Gatewood, and the rest of the founding members of New Caelum were hiding something huge—a secret that could destroy our city. And this secret goes well beyond the fact that they'd somehow manipulated the Blacks all those years ago."

"Rinala isn't a founding member."

"No, but she somehow discovered their secret. And she claimed Cricket was the key to exposing your mother and Councilman Gatewood."

....

chapter twenty-seven

Cricket

I padded out to the panoramic windows lining the living room. This was obviously a celebrated feature of the suite because a sofa was positioned to face the night sky. And with most of the lights turned off inside the suite, I could clearly see the stars I longed to sleep under.

I sat down on the carpet in front of the windows and leaned against the base of the couch. Bringing my knees to my chest and letting my thin white gown cover them, I looked up at the sky and thought of my parents. Were they out there somewhere, or was that just something I *wanted* to believe— something I told myself in order to get through the hard times?

There had been a lady in Boone Blackston who used to read to Nina and me from the Bible at night. She taught us of a heaven and a hell, of good and evil, of lessons from parables. I once compared New Caelum to Noah's Ark, but this lady warned me that for New Caelum to be Noah's Ark, God would have had to have wiped out the rest of life on earth—that only the people and animals inside New Caelum would have survived.

But that's not what happened. Which was why this lady always spoke of a God who hadn't turned His back on us.

I never definitively decided if she was right, but I did know that I'd witnessed enough evil in my lifetime to know that *it*, at least, existed. I'd also experienced the good in people—my parents before they were taken from me, Caine who delivered me from this city and from Bad Sam, my friends inside Boone Blackston, and now West.

The door to the suite opened behind me. I peeked over the back of the couch. I was hidden in the dark shadows. West entered, followed by Derek, who stayed by the door. West continued toward the hallway, not even glancing in my direction, and slowly entered the room where I was supposed to be sleeping.

Seconds later, he flew out of the room. "She's not in there."

I stood slowly, knowing that my white gown would glow with what little light shone in the room. When West saw me, he stopped and just stared. I crossed my arms in front of my chest.

He moved toward me. "I couldn't go to sleep without first seeing that you were okay." He was still wearing his tuxedo, but the tie was gone and the top two buttons of his shirt were unbuttoned.

I turned back to the windows. "With the lights off, I can see the entire sky." In the reflection of the glass, I saw West turn toward Derek.

Derek lowered the lights even further and exited the suite, most likely no further than just outside the door. I was almost positive Derek never slept.

It was now nearly pitch black in the apartment, and the stars winked at us from their places in the sky. "As soon as Caine has a treatment for Dax, I'm leaving," I said.

West didn't say anything. Not at first. I heard him slide out of his jacket and toss it on a chair. He sat on the couch behind me and took off his shoes. The air around us seemed to thicken.

He walked up behind me. Slowly, he brushed his fingers along my arms. After sliding my hair to one side of my neck, he leaned in and kissed my shoulder. A chill started at the base of my neck and moved down my spine and arms, leaving goose bumps in its wake. He formed a trail of kisses along my shoulder and up my neck until his lips reached my ear. "Let's not talk tonight," he whispered. His breath warmed my cheek. "I just want to hold you." He started another line of kisses down my arm. When he reached my fingers, I nearly got the strength to stop him.

I slowly turned toward him. "West, I—"

He closed in on me and covered my lips with his, silencing my attempt to stop him. It obviously wasn't a very convincing attempt.

Because I did want this. There was not a single doubt in my mind that I wanted the man in front of me with every ounce of my heart, soul, and mind.

He kissed me harder, sucking lightly on my lower lip. A fire erupted within every nerve in my body. I would not be able to turn back in three, two—

West pulled away, first with his lips, then with his hands. He let go of my arms and stretched his fingers wide as they still hovered close. "I'm sorry. I shouldn't have done that. It's just..." He backed away and sat on the couch, looking up at me.

"What is it?" I asked. My voice sounded small, weak.

"Tell me what I have to say," he said in a heavy sigh.

I stood staring at him. My thin white gown hung to my mid thighs, and my feet were bare. After that kiss, my entire body felt like it would break out into a sweat any second. "What do you mean?" Did he want the right words to be able to kiss me again? To sleep with me? My pulse sped up, but I managed to walk closer and stand between his legs. I reached my hand to his and linked our fingers together.

My breath caught in my chest as we touched. I knew I couldn't stay inside New Caelum, but I also knew it was getting harder and harder to imagine saying goodbye to Westlin Layne, the boy with whom I had shared my first kiss before I'd even reached four and a half feet. He had left his city to find me when his sister became sick and when he thought his city was in trouble.

Anyone could have come to find me. Ryder and Key would have found me. They *did* find me. But West came because he and I had a connection. He came because he wanted to protect me. Not everyone inside New Caelum had good intentions, and West knew—as evidenced by what was happening inside his city now—that if anyone else had found me, he might not have ever seen me again.

So what was he asking me now? He was looking up at me with a hunger I didn't recognize. It was late, and he and I had had little sleep in the last forty-eight hours.

"Tell me what I have to say to get you to stay with me forever," he said. "Fight with me, Christina. Do it for your parents.

Do it for me. Do it for yourself and for all the children who don't have a voice in this city. Do it for future children."

I dropped his hand. Turning, I faced the windows and thought of the two little girls in wheelchairs. I drilled the heel of my palm into my chest while trying to will myself to breathe. My skin, hot only seconds earlier, now shivered from the distinct change in temperature. I tried to rub warmth back into my arms.

West stood, grabbed my arms, and steered me back to sit on the sofa.

I turned in my seat to face him. "Someone tried to kill me tonight."

"I know." His fingers lightly grazed my knee. "I can keep you safe."

"West. You can't be with me every single second of the day. And I have no desire to live like a prisoner inside a city that doesn't want me here."

"Are you saying you would stay if the threat to your life was removed?"

I sighed. "No, I'm not saying that. Why are you asking me this again? You know the many reasons I won't stay here."

"Because I want you to help me," West said. "Help me make the world a better place for the citizens of New Caelum. Help me give people on the outside more opportunities. The outside settlements and New Caelum would be better if we worked together, rather than fighting each other. I know this, and you know this, and you and I, together, can convince others of this." He grabbed my hands and held them both. "You and I would make a great team. I know we can find a way to make it work."

"West, earlier this evening you were close to being matched with someone else. The leaders of New Caelum want you to produce children with... that woman." I stood and walked away from him. I couldn't let him touch me while thinking about that redhead spending her life with him.

I didn't hear him come up behind me, and when he spoke, I flinched at his nearness. "I was never going to commit to Annalise. I told my mother this. I just don't know how to play their game and get what I want at the same time. But I'm close to figuring it out."

I couldn't help the laugh that escaped my lips. I turned and lifted my eyes to his. "Do you hear yourself? 'Play their game'?" I lifted my hands and then let them fall in frustration. "This is not a game. I'm inside your city so that Caine and I can heal a virus that people inside *your* city revived. Many of the leading members of your government have recently been locked up for corruption. Just today, someone killed one of your council members and tried to kill me, and you have no idea who or why. And you're calling it a game?"

"No. That's not what I meant. It's not a game." He ran his hands through his hair, leaving it sticking out in all directions. When I lifted a brow at his irritation, he said, "I know!" He moved closer. Took in a cleansing breath. "I need you here, Cricket. I need your help in fixing my city." There was desperation in his voice.

I glanced toward the hallway, to the rooms where Caine and Zara were sleeping. I thought of the text I had received earlier: *But we need your help to take down President Layne.* Why would anyone think I would get involved in New Caelum's corrupt politics? "Listen. You need sleep. We both need sleep. I'm not leaving yet." I crossed my arms. "Hell, I've left once already, and look where I'm standing."

That made him smile, seemed to relax him a little. He stalked closer, pulled my arms loose, and proceeded to guide them around his back. When he placed his arms around me and held me closer, I finally let the muscles in my back ease up. The current fight was over.

He leaned his chin into the top of my head. "Can I stay here?" he said. When I hesitated, he continued. "I'll sleep on the sofa. I just won't be able to sleep, knowing someone inside my city might try to kill you again."

I pulled back. "I thought you came here 'just to hold me.'" I put air quotes around "just to hold me."

"And apparently to beg you to stay inside New Caelum. Which," he added, "I'm not above doing again in the morning. So, can I stay?"

"Yes, but I can't let you sleep on the sofa. The stars are very distracting."

I smiled, then slid my hand into his and led him to my room. And I knew with every step we took toward my bed, I was simply making it even harder to eventually say goodbye.

....

chapter twenty-eight

West

An alarm sounded in the predawn hours. Cricket and I sat straight up in bed. The front of my body was radiating heat from holding her so close while we slept.

"What is that?" Cricket scrambled from bed and slipped some khaki pants on under her nightgown.

"That's the alarm."

She angled her head and raised a single brow.

"Sorry. I'm still asleep. That means our border has been compromised."

There was a knock at Cricket's bedroom door. "Come in," I called.

Derek entered the room and flipped on the light switch. I flinched at the bright light and quickly glanced toward Cricket, who had turned away from Derek. Though nothing had *really* happened between Cricket and me, and she was completely clothed, I didn't want her to be embarrassed.

I moved to block Derek's view of Cricket. "This better be incredibly important."

"Sir, you need to come with me."

"What's happened?" I asked.

"There are people all along our border walls."

"What do you mean?" I stood and put my black slacks back on. I needed a change of clothes.

"I mean, people—thousands of them—are lined up with torches and weapons along our entire perimeter."

Never in the past six years had anyone attempted to threaten our outer walls. Leadership had begun to assume there simply weren't enough on the outside to try.

I crossed to Cricket and placed my hands on her shoulders. "Do not leave the suite. I'll be back."

She shook her head. "No. Caine and I need to go to the labs. The need for a cure to Bad Sam could be the very reason your perimeter is being attacked."

I brushed her hair back and held her cheeks. Though we'd stopped ourselves before going too far last night, I felt we were on more even ground this morning. I had broken through some of those barriers she'd constructed. And now this. "We are *not* being attacked. They're simply testing us. This could be a good thing."

Cricket and I both knew I didn't believe that. But communication had to start somewhere. The outside settlements would be sorry if they attempted to breach our walls. The guards and emergency sector inside New Caelum were trained to defend our perimeter, though they'd never been tested.

I leaned in and pressed my lips to hers. "I'll find you later."

She nodded, and I left.

~~~~~

The situation room, located at the highest point in the city, one floor above the government sector's offices, was buzzing when I arrived. Mr. Gatewood, dressed mostly in red, was already speaking to his three top leaders in the emergency sector.

Mom was talking into her PulsePoint. She motioned for me the minute she saw me.

As my most trusted guard currently inside the city, Derek remained on my heel, assuring me that he'd left competent guards with Cricket.

"Where were you?" Mother flipped through some images on her PulsePoint.

"Sleeping."

"I've been calling you for two hours." She stood and faced me. "If you're going to lead this city, you need to be aware of situations prior to an alarm sounding."

"Are you saying you knew there were people threatening our borders before the alarm sounded?"

"I did."

"How long before?"

"That's not the point. I came to wake you to tell you before I sounded the alarms. Your bed hadn't been touched."

"Is this really what you'd like to discuss right now, Mother? Where I slept last night?"

By now, Councilman Gatewood's ears had perked up, and he was glancing toward us while giving orders to his guards.

The door to the situation room opened, and Annalise entered wearing a mixture of red and black.

I turned to Mother. "Why is *she* here?"

"I told you she's been studying and gaining experience in government. She's now a split-sector and the newest member of the council."

"Taking whose place? Not Dr. Pooley's. She's certainly no doctor. And she's not representing the gardening or the food production sectors that Mrs. Canary covered."

Mother's lips thinned as she took in a deep breath.

I grabbed her elbow, then turned my back to the rest of the room as I pinned her with my glare. "Are you telling me that Annalise Gatewood is filling *Justin's* spot?"

"No. As vice president, technically you hold Justin's spot. And I've also put you in charge of the medical sector to fill Dr. Pooley's responsibilities until a more suitable person is available." She pulled her arm from my grasp. "Annalise will oversee the gardening and food sector in place of Rinala for now." When I narrowed my eyes further, she added through gritted teeth, "I've been telling you for days that your position in this government is fluid. Now we have a situation. You can either rise to the occasion, or you can cry over the fact that you have some competition. That's assuming you still have no intention of marrying her."

She stepped around me to face everyone in the room, leaving me speechless and staring at the wall before I also turned. "Can everyone take a seat." She nodded to one of her assistants by the door, who dimmed the lights.

After everyone sat, Mother and I took our seats as well. A screen lowered from the ceiling, and high-resolution images of our outer walls popped up. Mother clicked through the various angles of video and camera surveillance. "As you can see in these pictures, there are people—thousands, I am told—camped out on our perimeter." She stopped on a photograph of people sitting around a campfire beside our wall. "There are hundreds of other photographs just like these."

"What are they doing?" one of the emergency sector guards asked. "It looks like they're just sitting there singing camp songs and roasting marshmallows." Several in the room laughed.

"Councilman Gatewood, you will control your guards."

With a stern look from Mr. Gatewood, the emergency guards fell in line. Annalise cupped a hand over her mouth in an attempt to hide her smile. Her wide eyes gave her away though.

Mother continued. "If you'll look closely at this image..." With a remote, she zoomed in on the picture. "You'll notice the weapons leaning against rocks, strapped to people's legs, or slung on their backs. Like the crossbow on this man." She zoomed even closer.

"They don't appear to be gearing up to attack," I said. "These pictures are obviously a couple of hours old. What are they doing now that the sun is up?"

"The same." Annalise paced. "They're just hanging out. But there are groups of them around the entire perimeter. Thousands of men, women, and even children."

I eyed Annalise curiously. I wasn't used to her being in the situation room or in council meetings, and I didn't like it. "Are they testing us? What could placing people around our perimeter possibly prove? What do they hope to gain?" The question was mostly rhetorical.

"Isn't it obvious?" Annalise asked. "They want what we have. We knew they'd come for what we have eventually."

Attempting to be subtle, I cast a sideways glance toward Mother, letting her know I thought Annalise was full of crap.

She answered by placing a gentle hand over mine for a brief moment—her way of telling me to stay calm.

"Howard, are our outer walls secure?" Mother asked Councilman Gatewood.

"Yes, ma'am. More secure than ever. The electric current running through the wiring embedded in the walls has been activated. Anyone who attempts to climb the walls will get quite the shock. And guards have been posted on our roofs and at every interior entrance with weapons aimed at the gates. No one is going in or out of our city."

"Good. Keep me informed of any movement."

"Yes, ma'am. I'm headed to security headquarters as soon as we're done here."

"And West, you will also report to the security headquarters. I want you to see to it that we have plenty of guards and security personnel in place, and with enough weapons, in case these people attack."

"Do you really think *those people* have the resources to attack?" Annalise asked dubiously. The disappointed look on Mr. Gatewood's face spoke volumes.

I narrowed my gaze at her. "Yes, Annalise. Just because *those people* weren't invited into your elite world doesn't make them stupid."

She crossed her arms, and I could tell she was swallowing the urge to throw a fit as she shot daggers through those green eyes—the eyes of an angry snake.

"On to other matters," Mother said quickly. "Last night was a horrible failure. Derek, how is our guest?"

I angled my head toward my guard. I found it funny that she was asking Derek and not me. But I guessed with Mr.

Gatewood and his daughter present, it was probably not a good idea to advertise my apparently rebellious relationship.

"She's fine, ma'am. I delivered Christina, Dr. Quinton, and our other guest, Zara, to the labs this morning."

"Are they close to having what they came here to develop?"

"I wouldn't know, ma'am." Derek's eyes stayed glued to my mother's.

"Fine. I will visit them later. Howard, what have we learned from the man who tried to shoot a dart into Christina?"

"You know who it was?" I looked to Derek. He shrugged, letting me know this was news to him too.

Mr. Gatewood cleared his throat. "Yes, we found the assassin. I'm afraid we don't know much, Ms. President. But my people are working on it. I'll let you know as soon as I have something."

"West," she said, "have you spoken to Ryder? I hope you gave him condolences from the entire council."

I nodded. "I did," I lied. "He was extremely appreciative." I lied again. Ryder had stopped me before I could say anything that resembled regret or pity.

Mother continued down her list of business items to discuss with the council, then she made plans to reconvene before lunch, or sooner if there was movement on the wall.

As everyone stood and began to exit the room, I accessed a few classified files on my PulsePoint—one on the woman who poisoned Ryder's mother, one on the man who had tried to kill Cricket, a third on the nurse who had injected poison in Dr. Pooley's IV drip, and a fourth on the person who had tried to smother Key. It was easy to identify commonalities in their methods: three of them had used poison and two had used blowguns. But there appeared to be no commonality among the alleged perpetrators. They came from different sectors and different backgrounds. None of them had a record of any wrongdoing inside New Caelum. And I could see nothing that would motivate any of them to commit the crimes for which they stood accused.

I wanted to discuss my thoughts with Mother, but when I looked up I noticed that Annalise had hung back while everyone else was filing out. As Annalise drew closer to me, Mother continued to scroll through something on her PulsePoint, refusing to take the hint. I loved her for not leaving me alone with this pain in my ass.

"Is there something you need, Annalise?" Mother asked, peering over her reading glasses.

Annalise appeared wounded. "I was hoping to speak with West, but I don't mind if you hear what I have to say."

Mother's gaze shifted to me, and in her twitching lips I could see that she was enjoying this. She knew I hadn't slept in my own bed last night—not that it was anyone's business. I was old enough to make my own decisions, as was the woman I held through the night. But Mother also knew that Annalise would figure things out eventually.

"West," Annalise started. "You and I are to be matched at the Renaissance Ball. And the city needs strong leadership after the whole Justin fiasco."

Mother raised her brows further.

Annalise continued. "I was hoping you and I could reassure the city by making appearances together. Dad says you asked for more time so that you and I could get to know each other.

I'd like to start by eating together, maybe get coffee. And you know..." She wrung her hands. "... go on dates."

"Go on dates," I deadpanned.

"Yes." Her demeanor was the complete opposite of the display of power she'd shown in front of Cricket the night before at the gala. "We know nothing about each other. We've had so few classes together, since my father has always insisted teaching me himself."

"Yes, your father did keep you and your government aspirations quiet, didn't he?" My mother asked, but I didn't think she was looking for a response.

"So, what do you say?" Annalise asked.

"I agree. If you and I are to be matched, I think we should get to know each other better. I'll call you and set something up."

"*When* we are matched," she stated.

"What?"

"You said 'if' we are to be matched. I just wanted to clarify that it's 'when.'"

"Yes, well—"

"West, we *will* be matched." She smiled, leaned into the table where Mother and I still sat, and clicked her manicured nails against the wood. "Our matching has been properly arranged. You can postpone it, and you can have your little side fling with the outsider, but this *will* happen."

I tensed when she described Cricket as a fling. I didn't have to look at Mother to know she was sending me a warning vibe. I opened my mouth to tell her that we would never marry, but Mother spoke first.

"Annalise. West is well aware of the needs of our city, and he has told you that he will call you. Now, if you'll excuse us, I have city business to discuss with West. In case your mind wasn't fully present in the meeting just now, I'll remind you that there are people threatening our city perimeter at the moment."

Annalise looked sufficiently put in her place. "Yes, ma'am." She looked pointedly at me. "I'll await your call."

When Annalise was gone, Mother faced me. "Now that that's been taken care of, we have something more important to discuss."

"Okay." I gestured for her to continue.

"What has happened to your best guard?"

"What do you mean?" I glanced nervously at Derek, who was waiting for me by the door.

"Don't patronize me. When you stood up to Justin and took his place at the top of this government, Shiloh didn't leave your side. You insisted that she was the one guard you would not do without. You even promoted her. And now she's nowhere to be seen. Where is she?"

"She's on the outside."

Mother's eyes widened. "You left her outside our walls?"

"She volunteered."

"Why would she do such a thing?

"Cricket's best friend, Dax, has Bad Sam. People from a western settlement captured him outside our gates when we were bringing him to New Caelum for treatment. They're holding him hostage and will only release him to Caine and Cricket once we've healed the members of their settlement infected with the virus. They allowed Shiloh to stay with Dax. She reports in to me regularly." Though I hadn't heard from her in over twenty-four hours, which was disconcerting.

"Do you know why people are gathered around our city walls?"

"I can guess as well as anyone. They're pissed off that we sent Bad Sam back out into the world."

"Maybe. Or could it be that they've witnessed one of the leaders of our city outside the walls, and they're sending us a message?"

"What message would that be?" I asked.

"That they've heard that our citizens wish to venture outside, and that they wish us to know: We are not welcome beyond the walls."

....

chapter twenty-nine

Cricket

We were dressed in the usual protective gear. Caine mixed vials, while Zara organized and labeled them. I crushed one of the precious remaining bloodstones into a fine powder using a mortar and pestle. We had limited raw materials, especially the bloodstones. If it turned out that the bloodstones were a key ingredient in the vaccine to prevent Bad Sam, we couldn't afford to waste what little we had, knowing I had left the majority of the bloodstones hidden inside my parents' house for safekeeping.

Caine lifted his head from the microscope. He'd been peering through the lens for what seemed like hours, but it had really only been about thirty minutes. A smile slowly crept across his face.

I set the mortar and pestle aside. Wordlessly, I sidled up to him, and he gestured for me to look at the microscope. I waved him off, knowing that I wouldn't know what I was looking at. "Just tell me." My fingers shook, and I wrung them, waiting for Caine to speak.

Zara stopped what she was doing too, and circled the laboratory tables to join us.

"That, my friends," Caine said, "is what the Samael Strain looks like after it has been zapped with my cure."

"Really?" I practically squealed. I threw my arms around him. "You're sure it will work?"

His happy face faltered slightly. "As sure as I can possibly be."

"Of course you're sure. You were already so close before."

"And with Dr. Hempel's notes and the information you learned and used to help Ryder and Key…"

I bit my lower lip. I had helped Willow, Ryder, and Key, but not Dylan. I gave my head a little shake. "So, what's in this?"

"Well, it has your antibodies…" I knew he meant antibodies from before they had weakened. "… combined with elements of the protein compound developed by Dr. Hempel, certain ingredients from my original treatment, and a small amount from the bloodstone in order to help the body fight the breakdown of the major organs."

"I thought injecting the protein compound into someone already affected was a problem."

"It was, but I've altered the compound such that that should no longer be a concern."

"But this still won't prevent healthy individuals from contracting the virus, right?" I asked. "It's not a vaccine."

"No," Caine said, "that's a little trickier. But I think I'm pretty close."

"How much of this treatment do we have?" Zara spoke for the first time since we'd arrived at the lab.

"Enough to send out to Governor Jackson and to cure Dax. I'll make a couple of additional doses to have on hand."

"And when will we have the vaccine you're talking about?" she asked.

"I'm not sure. I need a few more days, I'm afraid." Caine appeared slightly defeated. He'd slept very little since we arrived, and I knew he wanted to get back to Boone Blackston.

"Are you thinking about Nina?" I asked. "I know in my heart that she's fine. Better than fine. She's probably got Boone Blackston completely prepared for the long winter."

He nodded, and seemed to shake off the dark mood. "So, how are we going to get this treatment to Dax?"

"I'll go. Governor Jackson is expecting me, and I owe Dax."

"I figured you would say that. West tried to get me to promise I wouldn't let you go."

I laughed under my breath. "And did he suggest a way for you to stop me?"

"No, but he made me promise that I would at least tell him when we were close to a treatment."

"He wants to go with me. But that's not possible. If Governor Jackson were to discover who West is, he'd likely take him hostage to give himself an edge against New Caelum."

"And that would be a bad thing?" Zara spat. Her hatred for New Caelum ran deep.

Ignoring her, Caine said, "West could at least send guards out with you."

"Any New Caelum guards sent out with me will be killed. I saw the look in Governor Jackson's eyes. He wants the city to pay for the lives he lost. Besides, I can do this."

"West is committed to protecting you."

"I know. I'm not running. I just need to get to Dax. West can't help me with this particular errand."

Caine walked to a nearby fridge and pulled out a half-filled syringe.

"What's that?"

"While I don't have a general vaccine, I do believe Dr. Hempel had already inadvertently discovered a way to vaccinate *you* against Bad Sam."

I angled my head, studying the syringe, then understood. I thought back to the slides Dr. Hempel had shown me with the broken antibodies, and then the slides after being treated with the protein compound. "Of course. His protein compound can strengthen my broken antibodies. Do you think it will work?"

"Yes. I've tested it and retested it. I think this will revive your immunity. I'll give it to you on the other side of the disinfectant chamber."

Caine turned to Zara. "I'll continue to work on the vaccine for you and everyone else. For now, you're at least protected by the protein compound. It seemed to help Ryder and Key."

Zara nodded. "I'll just have to take my chances, then."

I angled my head. "What do you mean by that?"

"I want to come with you. I can help you reach Dax, and then I can return to Boone Blackston."

Caine and I traded glances, and I knew immediately that Caine thought it was a good idea.

"Fine," I said. "But Dax is my first priority. If you cause any trouble because you can't manage your attitude, I *will* leave you."

"Understood."

chapter thirty

West

My PulsePoint pinged with a message from Cricket: *Meet me on the roof. We need to talk.*

I looked up from my spot inside the security control room where I had been scanning the images of outsiders around our walls for any clues as to what the small army was planning. Councilman Gatewood was speaking with several guards in red, along with Annalise, whose eyes lifted to meet mine every minute or so.

I read the message again. I hadn't had many girlfriends over the last few years, but I knew enough to know that when a girl said "We need to talk," it was never good. But I also knew Cricket wasn't the type to summon me unless it was important.

I stopped by the Presidential Suite and grabbed a coat before climbing the stairs to the rooftop—the same rooftop I had shown Cricket the last time she was inside New Caelum.

She stood with her back to me, hugging a cream-colored down coat close to her body, obviously a new addition to her New Caelum wardrobe, which was interesting since most people inside New Caelum had no need for winter coats. Light snow flurries fell from the sky and disappeared into her blond hair.

When my feet crunched on broken concrete, she turned. "Hi." She looked down at her feet, then up again. Though she'd spent the previous night in my arms, her shy nature had returned. It was just one of the many things I loved about her.

Of course, I couldn't tell her this. It seemed any time I mentioned a reason we were destined to be together, she pulled further away. For now, I would respect her need for distance.

"I'm leaving," she said, her voice barely above a whisper. "I have the treatment Dax needs."

I nodded, lifting my head to peer over the rooftop wall and toward the forest behind her. There was no use arguing with her about the need to reach Dax. "The wall is surrounded." She knew this already, but it deserved repeating.

"Have they done anything that would suggest an attack?"

"Not yet. At this point, we aren't even sure what they want."

"I can find out."

I met her calm gaze. "How do you propose to do that? I can't even reach Shiloh." It had only been two days, and already Shiloh had stopped checking in.

"I'll be unarmed. I'll dress in the beige clothes of the lower sector, and I'll demand to see Governor Jackson. He's expecting me. They need what I have, so I don't think they'll harm me."

"What if he shoots you once you show up with the cure? You think he'll let Dax survive once he has what he wants and you're dead?"

Cricket nodded toward her backpack. "I have several vials of the treatment ready. I also have vials filled with an identical-looking substance, but with no active medicinal ingredients. He won't know the difference."

My lips twitched upward. "Clever. Your idea?"

She answered with a grin, a rare show of confidence from her.

"What's the status of a vaccine?"

"Caine is staying to work on it. He thinks he's close." She took a step toward me, reached out, and laced her fingers with mine. "Caine tested Dr. Hempel's protein compound and confirmed that it strengthens my antibodies. He gave me an injection. I'm once again immune."

I released her hand and wrapped my arms around her, bringing her body flush with mine. "That's good. Really good." I placed my chin on top of her head. "I'm sending Derek out with you."

She pulled back. "No, West. I don't want the responsibility of anyone else's life. Zara will leave with me. She's strong enough. She wants to leave the city and knows the risks."

I placed my hands on her cheeks, leaned in, and kissed her gently. "It's taking everything in me to let you go back out there. I know you have to do this, but you've got to let me protect you the best way I can. I realize I can't go with you. Governor Jackson has surely discovered who I am by now. But Derek is trained in Muay Thai and hand-to-hand combat."

A brow arched high up on her forehead, and a smirk reached her eyes. "Muay Thai? Seriously? Just how are Derek's martial arts skills going to help me fight thousands of outsiders?"

"None of this is funny. Our walls are surrounded." She continued to smile until I finally mirrored her light mood. "Why are you insisting on minimizing the threat?"

"I'm not. Not really." She closed her eyes briefly. When she opened them again, all traces of sarcasm were gone. "Do you trust me?"

"What do you mean? Of course I trust you."

"You and I want many different things, but we also want many of the same things. You have to trust me if we are ever going to find a way to meet in the middle."

I inhaled sharply. It was the first time she'd ever hinted that we might have common ground in our future. "I want to trust you. I want to trust that you have feelings for me even though you're not ready to admit what those feelings are." When she looked away, I touched gentle fingers to her cheek and brought her eyes back to mine. "I want to trust that you won't take unnecessary risks with your life while you're trying to save others. Let me send Derek with you, and I will trust that you will come back to me."

"West... I..."

"What? You're asking me to trust you, but you don't want to commit to coming back inside New Caelum? Is that it?"

Her chest rose and fell quickly. She was nervous about something. "I can't promise I'll come back inside New Caelum. You know that. And your loyalty lies with New Caelum. The people inside need you." Her throat moved as she swallowed hard against my fingers. "I need to find Dax. I need to give him a fighting chance. Only then can I decide what's next for me."

"A fighting chance." Something she hadn't given Dylan. That's what she left unsaid. "Dylan wasn't your fault," I said.

"Maybe not, but if I don't do everything I can to save Dax, I will never forgive myself."

"Fine. Do what you need to do. I trust you." I had no choice. She felt an obligation to people on the outside. I felt one to the people on the inside. I had enough faith for both of us that we'd always find our way back to each other.

I moved my hand around to the back of her neck, leaned in, and kissed her again.

She slid both her arms inside my coat and around to my back, allowing me to deepen the kiss. I knew she was kissing me like it was our last. I could feel it in the way she hugged me closer. When we broke away, a tear slid down her face. I wiped it away, then kissed the dampness left behind.

"I need to show you command central, where our guards and emergency team members are monitoring the situation along the outer wall. I have an idea of how to send you, Zara, and Derek out. But you're not leaving until I have confirmation from Shiloh that she and Dax are still—"

"Alive. I get it. But I still haven't agreed to let Derek come."

"I'm sending Derek out. You don't really have a say in it. He works for me."

She sighed. "Fine, but while we're waiting for word from Shiloh, I'd like you to take me to the person who tried to kill me."

~~~~~

"He killed himself?" I asked, stunned.

We had reached the overpopulated holding cells, and Derek was giving me a full report on the man who tried to poison Cricket. "He had an extra dart, apparently hidden well, and

233

when no one was looking, he stuck it in his own neck. Poisoned."

While Derek and I spoke, Cricket walked down a hallway, passing doorways with windows constructed of both glass and steel bars. Standing on the tips of her toes, she peered into one window then another. When she got to a third, she stopped and lingered.

"That's Justin's cell," Derek said to me.

Keeping one eye on her, I continued with Derek. "What was his name?"

"John."

"What was John's demeanor when the guards took him into custody?"

"That's the strange thing. The guards said he was out of it, in a trance, like he was on some sort of drug, but the toxicology came back completely clear."

"They said the same thing about the man who tried to smother Key."

"I want to talk to him," Cricket said, pointing toward Justin's cell.

Derek and I traded uneasy glances.

"Why would you want to talk to *him?*" I asked, walking closer to her. "He tells nothing but lies."

"That may be, but I'd like to ask him a few questions. This John person is dead. I obviously can't speak with him now. Justin tried to kill me too. Indirectly, anyway."

In a show of trust on my part, I ordered Derek: "Restrain Justin, and let her in."

"Are you sure?"

"Yes. The lady says she has questions."

Derek approached the door and knocked on it. "You know the drill, Mr. Rhodes."

We heard the sound of a metal chair scraping across the industrial tile floor. Derek unlocked the door. He entered with confidence and quickly had Justin handcuffed to his chair with his hands behind his back.

Derek reappeared at the doorway. "He's all yours," he said to Cricket.

She entered, and wasted no time firing her first question at Justin. "The first time I entered the city, why was it so important to you that I agreed to stay inside New Caelum?"

He cocked his head. "To cure Willow of Bad Sam, of course."

That was expected. To Cricket, too, by the way she didn't miss a beat but continued with her questioning. "Did you—do you—know about the bloodstones?"

A grin spread across his face, lighting up his eyes.

"My parents—or someone else—told you about the bloodstones, didn't they?"

Justin remained quiet. I walked farther into the room. Derek remained by the door with a hand on his Taser.

"What do you know about my parents' last trip to Africa?" Cricket continued.

"I will tell you, but not him," Justin said, nodding toward me.

Before Cricket even turned toward me, I figured she was going to ask me to leave. I braced for it. She'd lived in the dark most of her life regarding her parents.

But she didn't turn, and she didn't ask me to leave. She walked closer to the table that separated her from Justin and placed her palms flat against the metal surface. "No. West stays. Tell me or don't. It doesn't really matter."

"Oh yeah? You don't want to know who else besides President Layne took your mom and dad away from you? You still think Ginger made the decisions alone?"

I moved closer, my hand now resting firmly on my Taser.

"I never assumed she made the decision alone." Doubt crept into Cricket's voice. Even I noticed it.

"Did you know that the man you've loved like a father was partly responsible for what happened back then?"

Cricket straightened and stumbled backward, falling against me. I grabbed her arms from behind to steady her.

"Caine?"

I wanted to reassure her that Justin was lying, but I couldn't. Caine *had* been inside the city when Cricket contracted Bad Sam. And now that I'd heard that Cricket's parents were instrumental in the initial construction of New Caelum, I was sure about one thing: there was a lot about the original leaders I didn't know.

Cricket shrugged out of my hold. "Who else?"

"He leaves," Justin said.

Several beats ticked by before Cricket turned. "We're done here." She gestured toward the door.

Shock forced my eyes wider—shock that Cricket would just leave. I wanted to hear the rest even if she didn't. I turned and walked through the door first.

In hindsight, I should have seen the signs—the red-hot anger on her face, the way her hands closed into fists. Derek held the door open for Cricket, but she was lightning fast. By the time her intentions registered in my mind, it was too late. In one fluid motion, she had grabbed Derek's keys and his Taser and shoved him through the door and into me.

"Cricket!" I recovered and made two quick steps, but I was too late. She slammed the door in both our faces.

....

chapter thirty-one

Cricket

"**M**ake it quick. I'm sure more guards are on their way to knock that door down." My heart was pounding. I tried to block out West's voice behind me.

Justin's grin grew. "Impressive." He leaned forward, pushing his chest against the table while his arms remained restrained behind his back. "You think I'm the only leader of New Caelum who wants to keep this city sealed from the outside world? You think Dr. Pooley and I are the only ones to make risky, possibly immoral, decisions to keep our citizens safe? Even back then, that was the issue, and every leader on the initial team wrestled with how far to take the plan to shut off the city from outsiders."

I slammed my fist down on the table. "You killed people."

"We've also saved people. Kept them safe, fed, and clean. And let's not forget healthy."

"Healthy. Right. And now I guess you and Dr. Pooley were thinking of the greater good when you used your own citizens to test Bad Sam treatments."

"Yes. Times are desperate. Citizens want to leave the city. We needed to prepare for another possible outbreak. In case you haven't noticed, our population can't take another big hit. We need to repopulate, not die off."

"So why send Bad Sam out into the settlements?"

A smirk tipped the corners of Justin's mouth upward. "We were trying to stall the re-entry of our citizens into the outside world."

"You're nothing but a bully." But this was all old news. We already knew that Justin had sent Bad Sam out into the settlements to keep the citizens locked inside by their own fear. "What does all this have to do with President Layne and Caine stopping air travel and keeping my parents from returning to the United States? Who else was responsible for closing down our nation's borders?"

"Don't you get it? We *all* were—all of the founders. And we all had secrets that needed to stay hidden."

The door jiggled behind me. I turned and held the Taser in front of me as I peered through the tiny window at West. "I will Taser whoever comes through this door. Give me two more minutes."

West's panicked eyes softened. "Two minutes." His voice was muffled through the glass.

Justin's brows lifted further. "You handle him well. You'll make a fine leader someday."

"It's called kindness and trust."

"Trust? You really think West doesn't know the many ways his mother manipulated her way into the top position of this city? How she took over the position your father should have held? Do you trust that West's not just like her?"

240

That's when I smiled. "Bark up another tree. West isn't like either of you. He doesn't know my parents' history with the city. If his mother purposefully forced my parents out of their rightful position inside New Caelum, West doesn't know."

"Are you sure about that?"

"Quite."

"He might not have known since the beginning, but he knows quite a bit now, and he hasn't shared it with you."

My thoughts stalled for a moment. I wanted to say Justin was lying. But something stopped me—a heavy pressure over my chest. I thought about the dress and the messages inviting me to the gala. Did West send me the dress? Had it been his plan all along to have me come to the gala and stir up trouble with the leaders? And why? Just to stop West's and Annalise's matching? Did he already know that my parents were supposed to be leaders of New Caelum when his mother took over all those years ago? Why would he keep that information from me?

"Why do you think someone requested your presence at the gala?" he finally asked me.

"Why do *you* think someone wanted me there?" I knew Justin was playing with me, and I was getting tired of his games.

He angled his head. "Someone wants you to know the founders' biggest secret. Your presence and your attire were very subtly orchestrated."

"What does that even mean?" I narrowed my eyes, but Justin only shrugged, infuriating me. I took in a deep, calming breath and tried to refocus on what else I could possibly learn from Justin. "So, you sent Bad Sam out into the settlements so that the citizens of New Caelum would know that it was still unsafe to merge with the outside world." We already knew this—that Justin was the worst kind of evil. "In doing so, the need for a sealed city and continued leadership would be necessary. But you were falling out of favor with the people."

Justin tilted his head side to side. "Arguably."

"Someone on the council, besides President Layne, knew about me. Knew that I held not only antibodies against Bad Sam but the bloodstones as well." This gave me some power inside the city. Would the bloodstones lead me to this big secret the founders were keeping? How could they? It wasn't like I had enough to keep everyone safe from Bad Sam. That was why my parents had to return to Africa.

"True. But only Ginger knew where you were—where Caine had taken you."

"And she protected me until Willow contracted Bad Sam."

"Also true."

"Why did you try to reinfect me? And why is someone trying to kill me now? You still don't have the bloodstones. Only I know where they are."

Justin smiled, and I cringed inwardly. I had just confessed that I knew where my parents' bloodstones were.

"Amazing the lengths people will go to keep secrets hidden."

"Secrets," I said softly to myself. *Too many secrets.*

"Tell me something, Christina. Where did your parents hide their secrets?"

I thought about my father working in his home office, the papers and medical journals scattered across his desk and on the floor. But his secrets—our family's top secrets? They were in the basement in a vault behind heavy metal shelving stocked with food. The bloodstones had been locked away there, along with important papers—papers, and stones from Africa I'd never bothered to care about. Until now.

"Open the door!" President Layne's voice came through the door, and I jumped.

"Why tell me these things?" I asked, my voice rushed. "What's in it for you?"

"You're going to need me eventually. Councilman Gatewood is threatening to move me."

"Move you? Where?"

"The city dungeon."

"Dungeon? That sounds so medieval."

"Nonetheless, I'm kind of hoping they do. And after this little talk, I'd say my move is imminent. You'll find me there when you've figured this all out."

"Why not just tell me this big secret?" The sound of a key entering the lock forced me to my feet.

"I'm waiting." Justin smirked.

"For what?"

"To see who ends up on top. I have no intention of staying locked up in New Caelum's jails. Whether it's you, West, or the current president, the secret I'm holding will eventually set me free."

Derek, West, and President Layne flooded into Justin's cell.

"Why would you leave her alone with him?" President Layne boomed at her son.

I backed away slowly while absorbing Justin's words. "West had no choice, Ms. President. Don't blame him or Derek."

Caine turned the corner. He must have come with President Layne. Instinctively, I curled my fingers into fists until my nails cut into my palms. Did I want to confront Caine right now? West shot me a look of warning. I swallowed hard.

President Layne's face morphed from angry authority to something much softer, motherly. I was starting to see through her many personalities, though, and learning that most of them were insincere. "Christina, sweetie," she said, "Justin is a liar and a master manipulator. I hope you haven't believed a word he said."

"I think Christina Black knows exactly who I am." Justin sat back in his chair, a knowing grin plastered across his face. He looked like a man who had nothing to lose at this point. "You know, Ginger, maybe we should add Christina to one of the dedication plaques. Maybe the one in the old archive library, below that large portrait. She's quickly becoming as much a part of this city's history as her parents were once upon a time."

The president motioned to Derek and West. "Get her out of here. I'll deal with Justin."

Caine studied me as I passed wordlessly by him. Worry seeped into the deep lines forming across his forehead. "Cricket?"

I paused, and it took everything in me to turn back and meet his probing gaze.

"What did he say to you?"

"You heard President Layne. Nothing but lies."

~~~~~

West, Derek, and I left the city's jail and headed to the command center. Derek led the way. West kept eyeing me sideways, but I refused to meet his stare, as I was still processing everything Justin had just revealed.

244

So much of it didn't make sense. Especially the idea that my own parents were part of the decision to close down the country's borders. They wouldn't have left if they had known there'd be no way back. I'd always thought their reason for traveling was to bring back more bloodstones.

Derek pushed through the command center doors. Guards in gray and emergency personnel in red raced around between computer stations and walls of video screens.

Pushing Justin's conversation to the back of my mind, I focused on the video images flashing across the monitors in front of me. "Are those the outer walls?"

"Yes," West said. "We can monitor every inch of the city—inside and out—from this room."

I thought about the time West and I tried to sneak back into the city. He must have sensed what I was thinking, because he added, "But we haven't actually monitored the outside walls in the last couple of years. Until recently, no one's shown any interest in penetrating them."

I continued to scan the room. A few people glanced our way, but no one approached us. "You said you had an idea how to send Zara and me out."

"Yes." West approached the computer station where Derek was talking with a young woman in light gray. "Any word from Shiloh?" He kept his voice low.

"No, sir. Nothing," the woman said. She glanced up at West, her eyes sad. "I can't even get a location on her. Her PulsePoint isn't turned on."

"Let me know the minute you hear from her."

"Yes, sir."

West's strong fingers slid into mine. He pulled me away from Derek and the woman.

I tugged on his hand, urging him to stop. "West, I have to leave. I can't afford to wait for word from Shiloh. I have to get to Dax before the disease progresses too far." I had no way of knowing how much time the small dose of treatment had bought him.

West tugged me into a small meeting room. He turned, keeping a tight hold on my hand. "What did Justin say to you?"

"He says you knew about my parents and their role in the formation of the city. That you're keeping it from me."

"I just found out. Last night."

"Before you came to me?"

"Yes."

I took a step back, wriggling my hand from his hold.

He immediately slammed a hand through his hair. "Don't pull away. I didn't keep anything from you on purpose. I planned to be completely honest with you, but there wasn't time. Someone had tried to kill you. And I was still trying to wrap my own mind around what Key had told me—and let you recover from the fact that someone tried to kill you."

"How did Key know things that you didn't?"

"She and Ryder both knew more than me."

"Ryder? Mrs. Canary's son?"

"That's right. Apparently, Mrs. Canary told them things about your parents and about you before she died."

"None of this is making sense." But even in the midst of our current debate, I couldn't ignore that Ryder had lost his mother the day before, and I had witnessed it. "How was he doing with his mother's death?"

"Denial is a powerful emotion."

That it was. "So. Do you believe my parents were supposed to be leaders of New Caelum?"

"Maybe. It definitely sounds like they had a lot of power."

"And that power probably threatened other people who wanted it just as badly."

"I know what you're thinking, but I have no reason to believe my mom would've purposely hurt your parents."

"Not purposely, maybe," I said, though I was far from convinced.

"That's not fair."

"You don't think so?" I crossed my arms. I'd never hidden the fact that I held President Layne responsible for my parents getting trapped in Africa. "What about Caine? You think he knew my parents? That he was also responsible for shutting them off from the country?" I blinked hard against uninvited tears. I simply couldn't grasp that a man who was very much a father figure to me might have had a hand in leaving my parents in exile.

West ran a hand down my arm to comfort me. "I don't know."

"Do you think my parents... your mom... and all the other founding members of New Caelum had planned all along for it to be an airtight city for this long?"

"That's what I was taught the past five years."

"Then why are people looking to you to lead them out of here? Why now? How could you get such a following of people who wanted to reenter the outside if the whole idea was to keep New Caelum sealed up from the very beginning?" What had changed? And how did I fit into this?

"You act like I just woke up one day and decided, 'I think I'll lead everyone outside today.'"

"Didn't you?"

West drilled his fingers into his closed eyes, a sure sign of frustration. When he reopened them, I noticed the exhaustion and redness there. "I don't have everything completely worked out." How could he? He hadn't been outside himself until he came looking for me. "Since speaking with Key last night, I've been thinking back to when all this started—when the idea of opening New Caelum's doors was planted in my mind."

"And?"

"I keep coming back to this history class Ryder and I were in a year and a half ago."

"History of what?"

"World civilization. We were studying the many great plagues and pandemics. Before Bad Sam, the Black Death was among the worst. Around half of Europe perished in the span of four years."

"When was that? 1400s?"

"Fourteenth century. Mid-1300s."

"Okay, so what?"

"Well, as often would happen in our classes, we debated politics. We discussed how people were treated inhumanely when they contracted the plague, and that led to the question: Had we been even *more* inhumane with people who contracted Bad Sam? After all, we just left people to fend for themselves. We let the virus spread. We could have opened up clinics, tried to manage the virus, or at least slowed its spread. Some students in the class believed that more of our population would have survived with more aggressive quarantines. We could have stopped the spreading of the virus by keeping the healthy away from the sick, and letting the sick die off."

"So you're saying that some of your classmates thought that if more people had closed themselves up inside a city like New Caelum sooner and turned their backs on sick loved ones when symptoms surfaced, our population wouldn't have suffered so greatly."

"Exactly."

"That's heartless and cruel." The muscles along my neck and shoulders tightened. "We had no idea what we were facing until it was too late. Bad Sam spread too quickly and too easily. You can't possibly compare what happened in the fourteenth century with now. Besides, I never would have turned my back on someone I loved if I thought I could help them." Which was why I was leaving to find Dax.

"Exactly. I agree with you. And I made my opinion very well known in class, going as far as to say I'd rather die than be the reason others suffered and died. I just couldn't imagine turning my back on my loved ones' or my friends' suffering. And before you think this was easy for me to say, this was before I knew I was immune to Bad Sam."

"I'm not surprised that you feel that way." I smiled thinking about how West found me when he thought I had been exposed to Bad Sam.

"Well, my mother heard about my strong opinions."

"And she was not pleased."

He chuckled. "No. She warned me that to be a good leader I had to put myself first. She talked to me about how before Bad Sam struck our country, the president of the United States was protected at all costs. That it would have been irresponsible if he had ever put others before himself. He was too important to the safety of the whole nation."

"And how do you feel now? Now that you could become president of this city?"

"No differently. Bad Sam changed everything. We can't compare the world pre-Bad Sam to now. A good leader today needs to have compassion and be willing to take risks."

"So, what happened? Did you go back to class with a different attitude, or did you stand up for what you believed?"

West smiled and angled his head.

"You stuck to your guns."

"I did. And in the next class, we talked about how the people of Europe didn't spend their days trapped inside an airtight city, and that the world recovered from the Black Death and strengthened over time. And that led some students to wonder if the same thing was happening in the world outside New Caelum. Students began asking our teacher if he knew what it was like on the outside..." West's voice trailed off.

"What is it? Are you remembering something?"

"Yeah, World Civilization was taught by Mr. Herod. The historian sector council representative."

"So?"

"One of his responsibilities was to know everything possible about the outside—even after we sealed the doors. So of all people, he should have known that scouts were being sent into the outside world."

"So why didn't he?"

"Justin removed him from the council the same time Mrs. Canary was removed. Right before he sent out the scouts."

"Why wasn't he added back with Mrs. Canary?"

"He was. He's been very quiet, though." West's eyes glazed over as if he was lost in thought.

"What is it?"

"Justin mentioned the old archive library. I thought it was an odd comment—like maybe he was trying to tell you something. And now, well... that library is where Mr. Herod spends most of his time."

"Do you think he would talk to you? Tell you more about the original plans behind New Caelum?"

"If anyone would know, he would." West narrowed his eyes. "Maybe it's time we pay our dear historian a visit. He and Mrs. Canary were quite close, and they took quite the interest in me after those history classes. In fact, I've often wondered if those two were behind much of the following I've amassed. They're both tied to lower sectors. Especially Mrs. Canary."

"According to Shiloh," I said, "it's the people in the lower sectors who have latched on to you as their next leader. Which makes sense, since they have the most reason to want to return to the outside."

"Yes. Their status inside has deteriorated over the years. I've hated it, but according to my mother and members of council, that is just a normal progression of any society."

"Do you believe that?"

"No. I think every contributing member of society is just as important as the next. Except people like Justin," he added. He massaged the back of his neck, his eyes on mine. "I really need Shiloh back. She's been by my side since the very first rumors of citizens wanting to reenter the outside world. She always kept me informed about grumblings in the lower sectors."

I slipped my hand into his. "I'll find her."

Something akin to pain caused West's forehead to wrinkle. "I really don't want you to go without me."

"You've said yourself, you can't leave."

"And you can't stay," he said.

I nodded.

"Well, Derek should be about ready." West pulled me close and slid his hand around my waist to press against my lower back, bringing me closer. Peering into my eyes, he tilted his head to one side then the other. Finally, he lowered his face and touched his lips to mine. The first kiss was soft, gentle. After that, with his fingers spread wide in the middle of my back, he lifted me off my feet and kissed me deeply. We both knew each kiss we shared could be our last.

When he pulled back, his eyes roamed my face, from my forehead down to my chin, as if he was memorizing everything about me. He brushed my hair from my cheeks, tucking it behind my ears, then framed my face with his hands. "I don't want you to risk keeping your PulsePoint on at all times, but can you please check in with me every couple of hours?"

"I'll try."

"I know I have no right to ask this of you..."

"But?" I tried to smile, but I knew it would be difficult to promise West anything at this point. We just didn't know what I would find on the outside. I could well be walking straight into Governor Jackson's trap.

"But if you find out more about your parents or about my mother, please come to me. As of right now, I've told you everything I know. The founders of New Caelum are keeping many secrets, and I'm afraid these secrets are going to cause even more strife among our people. Don't let them tear us apart."

I narrowed my eyes. "West, I don't want to hurt you, but nothing has changed. We're not really together. You're still promised to be matched to someone else, and I'm still never going to live inside New Caelum."

West smiled. "It doesn't hurt me to hear you say that, because I know you don't really believe any of it."

....

chapter thirty-two

West

Derek and Zara joined us in the meeting room. I had always thought Zara had only two moods: irritable and mean. But today she wrung her hands and watched the monitors as if she was afraid the outsiders might jump straight through them. And her twitchiness was doing nothing to relax me as I prepared to send my number two guard and the love of my life into the outside world. I was hoping to count on Zara as a second level of protection for Cricket. Not that Cricket couldn't take care of herself. She'd done a pretty good job so far.

"You're going to need to hide your PulsePoints," I said to the three of them.

Cricket held her hands out to her side and glanced the length of her body. "Where do you suppose I put it?"

I held up a roll of surgical tape. "Turn around."

With a furrowed brow, she did as I asked. I instructed Derek to avert his eyes, then I proceeded to lift Cricket's shirt. Her skin was pale and soft. A single mole sat just below her bra strap. I placed the PulsePoint in the center of her back and stretched tape across the device, securing it to her back between her shoulder blades.

"You don't think they'll search me?"

"They'll search you, but in all my training, I've never known anyone to pat someone's back. So unless they do a strip search—and I truly hope they don't even consider that or I *will* have to roll some heads—you should be fine."

With Cricket's PulsePoint secured, she turned to do the same for Zara.

"Do you really think they'll let us waltz right through the gate?" Zara asked.

"That's my hope," Cricket said. "Governor Jackson is expecting me. I've got to assume that anyone out there has been ordered not to harm me. Or anyone with me."

"I hope you're right." Zara adjusted her sweater back into place.

"West." Derek tapped my arm. When I turned to him, he thumbed over his shoulder toward the window into the neighboring command center. Councilman Gatewood had entered and appeared to be giving orders.

"We have to go," I said. "I'll distract Gatewood. The three of you will slip out." I framed Cricket's face again. "Be careful." She nodded, and I leaned in and brushed my lips across hers. "And please come back to me."

I exited the room and came face to face with the councilman.

"Hello, West. What are you doing in here?"

I rotated my shoulders. "I would think it was obvious, Councilman Gatewood. I'm just as concerned about the presence on our outer walls as anyone."

Zara and Cricket stood to my side.

"Really?" he asked. "And what brings our two guests in here?"

Cricket stiffened beside me.

"I thought they might recognize someone in the video surveillance."

"And did they?"

"No, sir," Cricket answered. She stared straight at the leader of the emergency sector. "These people are not from our settlement. We've never associated with members of the western settlements, which is where these people are from."

"And how would you know that? If you've never associated with them."

Cricket crossed her arms. "Because Zara and I don't recognize anyone."

"So you said." Mr. Gatewood continued to stare at Cricket. She shifted under his scrutiny.

"Councilman Gatewood," a woman called from across the room. She sat in front of a row of monitors. "You need to see this, sir."

I followed Mr. Gatewood, as did Cricket, Derek, and Zara.

"This is not good," Cricket whispered.

"No, it isn't," I agreed.

The monitors showed three army tanks, each parked at a separate gate. Although the tanks' tracks were pointed at the city entrances, the gun turrets were pointed to the side.

Up until now, the outsiders had posed no real threat to our city. There wasn't much they could do to penetrate the inner walls. Our windows were protected with bulletproof glass. Our buildings were built to withstand hurricane-force winds. But no structure in the history of the world could withstand the destructive force of an artillery round fired from a tank.

Zara moved closer. "Of course," she said, as if any idiot should have predicted this. "Equipment from the armed forces had to have been stored on just about every army base. All it took was people who knew how to operate them."

Zara seemed almost pleased. Or maybe she just admired the intelligence of it.

"You think they'll bomb New Caelum?" Cricket had scooted close to me. So close that I could feel the heat of her body against mine.

"I don't know. It depends on how angry they truly are."

"Have we received any messages from the outside?" Mr. Gatewood asked the woman who had called us over.

"No, sir. Nothing."

"Not even from Governor Jackson?"

Cricket's head jerked toward Councilman Gatewood. "You know him?"

"Of course. It's my business to know who the main players are on the outside."

How would he have expected to hear anything from the governor? The only way to hear word from the outside was from someone with a PulsePoint, which the outsiders didn't have—unless they'd first been inside, like Cricket, Zara, and Caine. Right now, the only PulsePoint outside the walls of New Caelum, to my knowledge, was Shiloh's, and I knew she wouldn't be contacting Gatewood. Besides, even I hadn't heard from her in days.

I glanced at Cricket over my shoulder. The fear in her eyes told me she was having similar thoughts.

Mr. Gatewood turned to me. "West, if you're going to be leader of this city, perhaps you should give the order." By this time, several emergency guardsmen and guardswomen dressed in red had gathered around.

The muscles along my spine tightened until it was uncomfortable just standing there. Cricket's hand went to my elbow. She had to know nothing good was about to happen.

"West," Mr. Gatewood urged.

I'd have to find another way to get Cricket out of the city. "Put up the steel walls," I ordered.

Zara's head snapped in my direction. She knew. She remembered from her own time inside New Caelum—or that of her parents'—what the steel walls meant. "You can't," Zara said.

"We can," Mr. Gatewood said. He turned to his people. "Do it."

"What does this mean?" Cricket asked. And when I didn't look at her, she turned to Zara.

"It means we're not leaving the city," Zara said. "The steel walls will prevent anyone from entering or exiting. It's a level of protection that even the tanks will have trouble penetrating."

Cricket's head snapped in my direction. "No!" She wrapped her hand tightly around my arm and whispered, "You have to let me leave first."

"There's no time," I said, but I couldn't look at her. Her wall of trust in me had just crashed. Yet I'd had no choice. The citizens of New Caelum needed to be protected. And if I hadn't given the orders, Gatewood would have.

"What's next?" Mr. Gatewood prompted me. A smirk touched his lips. Emergency personnel were already raising the steel walls. Others were awaiting my next orders.

"All emergency personnel trained in artillery should get in place and stand by for further instructions," I said.

"That's right," Mr. Gatewood agreed. "And prepare to defend. Get the weapons and tear gas ready."

With those words, Cricket turned on her heel and bolted out of the command center.

....

chapter thirty-three

Cricket

I blew through the door to the apartment. Thankfully, Caine wasn't there. I wasn't ready to face him about what had happened years ago when this city formed, or why he had never told me about his involvement in my parents' plans. I stormed over to the panoramic windows and looked out at my mountains I missed so much. "Please hang on, Dax," I whispered. "I'll find a way."

Zara and Derek entered the apartment behind me. Both were much calmer than I.

I let my eyes drift from the trees to the area just outside the city walls. "How much damage can they do to New Caelum with that tank?" I asked without looking at them.

"Quite a bit," Derek answered. "But our emergency sector won't let it get that far. If the gun turrets so much as rotate one inch toward our city, New Caelum will respond. We are prepared to hit the people outside with tear gas, fire large-caliber artillery, and even launch grenades and missiles."

"Missiles? New Caelum will kill the outsiders?"

"Bringing those tanks right to our gates is practically a declaration of war. If they fire at us with those tanks, we will fight back. They won't have a chance."

Derek's words made me think of a similar claim made by Steve and Cade, the young men who had come to my parents' house. They had said that Governor Jackson and the people of the western settlements saw New Caelum's act of sending out scouts infected with the virus as a declaration of war. Both sides, it seemed, felt that war had been declared by the other. No matter how we looked at it, a battle was inevitable. And once it began, it wouldn't matter who started it; people would suffer and die.

"How could West give the orders to raise those walls?" I asked. "If he had let me go—if I could take the cure to Governor Jackson—maybe I could head off all of this."

"West had no choice," Derek answered. "Mr. Gatewood would have given the orders if West hadn't, and West would have lost all credibility inside that room. This is what everyone in that room has prepared for."

Maybe, but... "How will I ever reach Dax and Shiloh now?"

"Maybe we can help."

I turned to find Ryder and Key standing just inside the door to the apartment.

Derek crossed the room and shook Ryder's hand. "It's good to see you, man. I had heard that they gave you both the all clear." He looked back and forth between them. "What about Willow?"

"She's no longer contagious," Key said, "but she's still very weak. She's been relocated to her own bedroom inside the Presidential Suite." She pulled her royal blue cardigan tighter around her baby blue scrubs. She had lost a lot of weight while she was sick.

"That's good to hear," Derek said. "Very good to hear."

"You said you might be able to help?" I stepped closer.

Key walked closer and touched my arm. "Thank you for saving our lives. We owe you everything." Her voice cracked.

"You're welcome," I said. I took a deep breath. "But now, one of my best friends is sick, on the outside. I've got to get to him."

"We have a way."

"I'm not going to like this, am I?" Derek asked.

"No," Key answered.

"Look, man," Ryder started. He'd also shed quite a few pounds thanks to the illness. His dark gray slacks and his black sweater hung loosely and did little to hide his slim build. He was armed with his Taser and a PulsePoint. "It might be safer if you pretend Cricket ditched you. That way when the council asks, you can honestly tell them you have no idea how she got out."

"You can get me out of New Caelum and past the outer wall?" I asked.

Key nodded.

"But you need to decide now," Ryder told Derek. "We need to leave before West returns. He'll never let Cricket leave now that war is imminent."

Like West could stop me, I thought. But why take the chance?

Derek studied our faces. "No, I'm in. If it weren't for Cricket, Willow and both of you would be dead. I owe her. I've received the same compound protein you have." He locked eyes with me. "If I get sick, you can cure me, right?"

I could feel the color draining from my face. So many people were looking to me to provide a cure, even though it was Caine who had taken over the actual production of a treatment. "I will try my best."

"That's all I can ask."

"Now what?" Zara asked.

"Now," said Key, "you get to meet the Underground Initiative."

~~~~~

"Where are we going?" I asked. Key and Ryder were leading us down yet another flight of stairs. We'd come down a long way, and hadn't taken any elevators. The stairwells were dark and made of concrete, not at all like the colorful interior stairs of the city that Rinala Canary had led me down just before she was murdered. Our footsteps echoed off the gray, drab walls.

"The Underground Initiative started a couple years ago." Key was slightly out of breath. "But the Initiative's mission was more clearly defined after Ryder's mom, Rinala, and Mr. Herod were removed from the council."

"And what is that mission?" I asked.

"To bring equality back to all people inside New Caelum," Key answered.

"And to find the original plans for the city that somehow went missing shortly after the doors to the city were sealed," Ryder added.

"Equality," I repeated.

Key looked over her shoulder at me. "Yes. Don't you believe all people within a post-Bad Sam world deserve equal rights and a voice in how they and those around them live?"

"People *outside* of New Caelum *do* have equal rights," I countered. "They get to choose where they live, and they always have a say when decisions are made that affect them. At least, that's the way it is in Boone Blackston."

Ryder and Key traded a glance.

"What?" I asked. "What does that look mean?"

"We're almost there," Key said, ignoring my question. We reached the bottom of the stairwell, and she pushed open a door. Ryder and Key were bone thin and weakened from the ravages of the virus, but there was also strength in the way they carried themselves and the way they looked at each other. Ryder held the door open for Derek, Zara, and me to pass through. He studied me as I did. Ever since I'd entered New Caelum, I'd been watched and analyzed.

We entered a long hallway; the happy colors of the city were missing here, too. In their place was more gray concrete and exposed metal pipes running overhead. Fluorescent lights flickered, and I breathed in a musty smell similar to the one in the unfinished basement of my childhood home.

"So, when you said 'Underground' Initiative, you truly meant *underground*?"

No response. We rounded a corner. My patience was starting to wear thin.

"Okay, we're here," Key said.

We stood before a set of double doors. After an uncomfortable pause, I asked, "Are you going to show me where 'here' is?" What I really wanted to know was: What could this faraway place in the dungeons of New Caelum have to do with how Ryder and Key were going to help me get to Dax?

Ryder opened the door and let me enter first. I stopped in my tracks just inside the door. Standing in front of a large wall map was a familiar figure.

Rinala Canary.

~~~~~

"But—I watched you die," I said.

Ryder stood expressionless to my left. He obviously knew his mother wasn't dead, which explained why West had said he was acting strange and in denial.

Rinala smiled. "Hello, Christina."

"Does West know you're alive?" I asked.

"Not yet. But he will soon."

"I don't understand. Why fake your death, and why not trust West? I thought you were his friend on the council."

"Your questions will be answered. Come in." She gestured to a sofa. "Have a seat."

"I don't want to sit. Do you realize that New Caelum is under attack?" I threw a panicked look at Key. "You said you could help me get out of New Caelum to reach Dax." I didn't have time to find out what this Underground Initiative was all about. Or what West knew, if anything, about it. Or why Rinala wasn't dead. I needed to get to Dax.

"Yes, we are aware of Governor Jackson's advance on our city. And we are prepared to get you out of the city."

About a dozen people emerged from the door behind Rinala. They were dressed in the many different colors of New Caelum, no one color dominating. They stared at me like they were expecting me to say something brilliant. "What is this?" I said.

"This is the Underground Initiative. Part of it, anyway." Rinala gestured to those who had gathered. "We are a group of people who are committed to taking our country to a much better place. But we need your help."

My PulsePoint buzzed at my back where West had secured it. He had switched it to vibrate, so no one heard the alert. "Zara, please grab my PulsePoint."

Zara reached into my shirt and ripped the surgical tape and the PulsePoint from my back.

I grunted in pain. "Enjoy that?"

She smiled. "A little." It was the first time I'd seen her smile in days.

The PulsePoint held a message from West: *Where are you? Your PulsePoint led me to the medical wing, but I see no signs of you there.*

I met Rinala's stare. "West tracked me to the medical wing."

"I scrambled your signal." Rinala typed something into her own PulsePoint. "He can't trace your whereabouts."

I clipped my PulsePoint to my waist. "What do you want from me?"

"Like I told you the night of the gala, we need your help to take down the current leaders of New Caelum."

"That was you?" So Rinala Canary was the one texting me, encouraging me to attend the gala, and then later informing me that New Caelum needed me. "You made sure I had the dress and everything I needed?"

"With Key's and Willow's help."

"How?" I asked. "Willow, Key, and Ryder were still sick and under quarantine."

"Our network of supporters is extensive," Key said.

"Willow is part of this too?"

"Recently, yes. You know that the leaders of New Caelum purposely infected Willow to get to you. They used her. That didn't exactly make her want to side with them." Key's voice grew louder as she spoke. Ryder placed a calming hand at the small of her back. "Besides, Willow might be young, but she's very much in tune with the people of this city. She has even gone as far as to disguise herself in the varying colors of the city in order to understand how each of the sectors are really treated."

I thought of the huge container of clothes I had discovered under Willow's bed when I initially returned to New Caelum with West. She had collected outfits representing the colors of every sector inside New Caelum. She was younger than me, but she was no longer the young child I remembered from when I was only twelve. "The leaders of New Caelum, including President Layne, weren't happy to see me that night. Especially in that dress. Why?"

Rinala snickered. "Oh, how I wish I could have seen the look on Ginger's face when you entered the gala in your mother's dress."

"My *mother's* dress?"

"Didn't West tell you?" Rinala glanced at Key, who looked down at her hands. "That was your mother's dress. She planned to wear it the night of our very first gala to celebrate the closing of New Caelum's doors. It's the same dress she wore for the portrait hanging in the archives in the government sector of the city."

I squeezed the bridge of my nose and closed my eyes while I processed this. That was probably what Justin had been hint-ing at when he mentioned the archives. I'd had no idea that I was wrapped in clothes last worn by my mother. I would have savored that feeling if I had known. I opened my eyes again. "So, she wore that dress inside this city?"

"She also wore it to the inaugural ball honoring the last president of the United States."

That didn't even make sense. "I had no idea my parents were involved in national politics."

"Of course they were. They knew more about the virus that would destroy our nation than anyone, and were on the president's team of experts," Rinala said. "The Samael Strain was already spreading in the United States, but the inaugural ball occurred before the president had contracted it. And before anyone was taking it seriously. It was at the inaugural ball that Ginger Layne was asked privately by the president to serve as secretary of state. She agreed, and as her first order of business, she tried to convince the president to close off all American borders and ground all flights in and out of the country."

"Two days later, the president came down with Bad Sam," Key explained. "The vice president followed a day after that."

Ryder leaned a hip into a nearby table. "The Speaker of the House resigned from his position when his family became ill. And the president pro tempore of the Senate committed suicide after watching his entire family die from the virus."

"And when both the president and the vice president died a couple of weeks later..." Rinala's voice trailed off.

"Ginger Layne became president of the United States," I finished.

"That's right," Rinala said. "As secretary of state, she was next in line for succession."

"And as president, she had the authority to ground all airplanes and close the borders." I walk over to the hand-drawn wall map Rinala had been examining when I walked in. Boone Blackston was labeled on the right side of the map, to the east of New Caelum, and to the west were the settlements led by Governor Jackson. "But how did Ms. Layne become president of New Caelum?" I asked.

Rinala sidled up to me. "New Caelum was built for the most powerful, influential, and intelligent people in the world. Of course that included anyone left within the current administration. Remember what I told you on our walk through the lower sector, about your parents' positions?"

I turned my head toward her. "They were supposed to lead New Caelum's medical sector…"

"And your father was slated to be president."

"I remember. But I still don't understand."

"Your parents were already friends with Ginger Layne, Dr. Caine Quinton, and many of the people who would become our city leaders."

"Including you," I said.

"And Howard Gatewood," Rinala added. "But your parents claimed they needed to make one last trip to get the supplies they needed for a cure for Bad Sam."

"And they left me in the care of Ginger Layne."

"They also left Ginger, Caine, and Howard Gatewood in charge of New Caelum. At the time, that decision was believed to be mostly about maintaining order and answering questions, not a declaration of complete trust, which is why they chose all three—a built-in system of checks and balances, or so they thought. Your parents had every intention of returning to New Caelum."

"Of course they did." They wouldn't have knowingly left me forever. They had planned to fly to Africa, obtain additional bloodstones, and get back before New Caelum was sealed for good. They had trusted the people who would become the leaders of New Caelum—and as soon as my parents were gone, those leaders shut down air travel and sealed the doors.

"So," I said, "Ginger Layne, as acting president, *was* responsible for killing my parents." But something still didn't add up. I faced Rinala again. She seemed to be having some sort of silent exchange with Key. "You said my parents helped build New Caelum. That it was their money and their vision that created an enclosed city that would withstand a rapidly spreading virus."

"That's right. And they invited as many people as they could find who had not yet contracted the virus. In the initial plans, your parents were afraid they would have to limit access because the city simply wasn't big enough, but the virus spread faster than anyone had expected, and that winnowed down the candidate pool considerably."

"You still haven't explained what you want from me. How can I help New Caelum?" I wasn't even positive I *wanted* to help this city, but I was curious all the same.

"We're going to show you a way out of New Caelum so that you can reach your sick friend. In return, we need you to find your parents' initial architectural plans for New Caelum."

"Architectural plans? Why? What do they matter now?"

"You'll see when you find the plans."

I narrowed my eyes. "What makes you think I'll be able to find them?"

"Because we know where they are."

As I processed what Rinala was telling me, Derek, Key, and Ryder were huddled around Derek's PulsePoint. Derek looked up. "The vials of the Samael Strain are no longer missing."

"Who took them?" I asked.

"Annalise Gatewood has just ordered her emergency guards to prepare projectiles. She's going to launch the Bad Sam virus at the outsiders."

"What?"

Ryder nodded. "She's going to infect everyone out there."

No one would be able to leave the city after that. Not until it was proven that the air outside the city was clean again.

I marched toward the door.

"Where are you going?" Rinala asked.

"I have to find West."

"West already knows," Derek said.

My spine stiffened. I turned. "He knows what? He knows Annalise is a thief? He knows she's a serial killer? What?"

"He knows everything. He's in the command center with Annalise."

chapter thirty-four

West

"Have you lost your mind?" My hands clenched into tight fists, and I suppressed the strong desire to rearrange Councilman Gatewood's face. I'd messaged my mother several times, but had so far gotten nothing in return.

Annalise and Howard Gatewood had stolen the virus and created weapons of mass destruction. If they released Bad Sam into the outside world, I'd have no choice but to take them both down.

"Annalise, give the order." Mr. Gatewood stood behind his daughter. His arms were crossed, his stance wide.

Without thinking, I pulled my Taser from my belt and charged toward Mr. Gatewood. Two of his personal guards—Daniels and Foster—grabbed me and held me back. I grunted and struggled against their hold. Reece and Thomas, two of my own guards, placed hands on their weapons and awaited my command. The other security personnel stationed in the command center traded uneasy and conflicted looks.

"You can't do this," I said. "Annalise does not have the authority. And my mother and I did not approve this action."

"It's about time you learn who really runs this city, and who doesn't, young man. I am in charge of the emergency sector, and I'm giving Annalise the authority to make the call—since you lack the fortitude to do it yourself." He nodded toward his daughter.

Annalise looked at me. I couldn't decide what emotion I was seeing in the crease across her forehead: worry, fear, uncertainty. For a moment I thought I was witnessing some flash of humanity, but then her lips lifted ever so slightly. "I'm sorry, West, but if you're going to lead New Caelum, you have to be willing to make the difficult decisions." Her words sounded like memorized garble she'd been programmed to recite by her father.

A grin spread across Mr. Gatewood's face—a look of pride that his daughter was becoming the ruthless leader he had raised.

"The difficult decisions?" I asked her. "To become a mass murderer?"

"Would you rather they use those tanks to destroy New Caelum?" Mr. Gatewood asked. "This is war, West."

Several emergency sector personnel averted their gazes when I looked at them. I had no idea how many of them were on my side in this argument, but no one appeared ready to take a stand quite yet.

Annalise stretched her fingers out to her side, then let them relax.

"Don't do this, Annalise." I struggled in the guards' hold. "Please. How can you give this order and still want to be matched with me? I will never marry you if you do this." I was grasping at straws now.

"Do you realize how weak you sound right now?" She turned and faced the monitors, which showed the guards that had been positioned around the interior walls of New Caelum. "Listen up! Emergency guards positioned at all stations," she said. An authority I didn't recognize filled her voice. "You will fire in three, two—"

"Stop!" I tried to yank myself free of the guards again. Annalise's head jerked toward me, and she stopped just short of giving the final order. "Reece, Thomas," I said, "place Mr. Gatewood and his daughter under arrest."

Reece and Thomas approached them slowly. Neither looked confident in my orders at first, but when several other members of the emergency sector stood from their stations and faced the situation, Reece and Thomas stood taller and approached the councilman and his daughter with their Tasers drawn.

"You have no authority to arrest us." Mr. Gatewood laughed. "I'm in command of the emergency sector. I give the orders."

I smiled at Mr. Gatewood. "You're not being arrested for doing your job. You're being arrested for stealing the vials of virus from the medical sector, and for lying to the president and vice president of New Caelum, as well as to the rest of the council. In case you and Annalise have forgotten, I'm in charge of the medical sector and the investigation into the missing virus. The virus cannot be used as a weapon unless I say it can." Daniels and Foster loosened their hold on me. I nodded at my guards to continue.

Mr. Gatewood smiled. "You're only delaying the inevitable. If we don't strike the outside first, they will fire on us, and they will compromise our airtight city."

"The two of you are making decisions without the consent of the president. And you certainly don't have mine."

"When those people strike, and our citizens' lives are lost, that will be on your head."

Some people around the command center shifted uncomfortably, while others continued to stand tall. Councilman Gatewood scanned the room, and his gaze seemed to stop on each person standing.

"I'm willing to shoulder that." I faced Daniels. "The two of you will let me go, or I will have you placed in custody with them."

Daniels and Foster looked confused and uncertain, but they immediately released their hold. "We're sorry, sir," Daniels said. "We were just following orders."

Reece and Thomas handcuffed Mr. Gatewood and Annalise. The whole time, Annalise didn't take her eyes off me. I stepped closer and looked down into her eyes while addressing my next command to my guards. "If either of them speaks again, Taser them."

Annalise swallowed hard. All color vanished from her face.

"To think I might have been forced to spend any part of my life with you," I said.

I stepped back, and Reece and Thomas led the Gatewoods toward the exit and out of the command center.

I ran to the microphone and began speaking to the emergency sector down below. "Listen up. This is Vice President Layne speaking. You will stand down." Emergency and government guards circled around me. "Councilman Gatewood and his daughter have been removed from their positions. You will now follow my orders." I swore I heard several quiet cheers from the other end of the microphone. "Stand down while we assess the situation."

After a series of *yes sirs* from the various stations, I turned to the monitors and began studying the hostiles outside the city.

Daniels stood to my left. "What are they doing?"

"They're moving into attack position." I tapped the shoulder of one of the computer techs. "Zoom in on that area there." I pointed at the screen.

"What are they wearing?" Foster asked.

"Those are gas masks," I said.

Of course they knew we would fight by infecting them with the virus. We'd already proven that we were willing to infect outsiders with Bad Sam.

"Why aren't they *all* wearing gas masks?" Daniels asked. "If they thought we might release Bad Sam..."

"Maybe some of them know they're immune?" I answered.

"Mr. Layne," a girl called across the room. "Someone with an RPG is approaching the south door."

I bent down to a microphone. "Who's in command at the south entrance?"

"Commander Anthony, sir."

"Commander, you have a rocket coming your way. Do you have a sniper on hand?"

"Several, sir."

"Good. If that person engages that missile launcher, shoot him in the shoulder."

"The shoulder, sir?"

"Yes, New Caelum will not kill first."

"What is going on here?"

I turned at the sound of my mother's voice. She, along with a team of guards, entered the command center, her heels clicking against the tiled floor.

"What is going on," I said, "is that Councilman Gatewood almost unleashed the stolen Samael Strain onto the outsiders swarming our city."

"Where is Howard now?"

"I had him and Annalise locked up."

Mother pursed her lips while scanning the room of emergency guards and other government personnel. "Westlin, I'd like to speak to you in private." She turned and walked into a meeting room.

As I followed her into the room, I witnessed a number of guards trading raised brow glances. With my wrist PulsePoint, I sent a quick message to Derek: *Where are you and Cricket? Bad shit is going down.*

Mother closed the door after I passed through. "West, we can't leave Howard and Annalise locked up."

"Of course we can. They tried to use the Samael Strain as a weapon on the outsiders."

"I know."

"What do you mean, you know? You knew they stole the virus from the labs? You knew they planned to use it on people on the outside? What, exactly, did you know?"

"All of it. And I told them to do what they had to do to protect our city."

I stumbled backward as if I'd been punched in the gut. "Tell me that is not true." I could feel the sweat beading along the edge of my hairline. "Tell me you aren't prepared to infect those people without at least trying to talk with them."

"Of course I am. They're camped outside my city with tanks."

"Infecting them with Bad Sam will not stop them from launching heavy artillery at us."

"No, which is why we're prepared to launch missiles at their tanks."

"Have we even attempted to communicate with anyone outside? What about Caine? Has he communicated with his daughter since he arrived?" Maybe she could shed some light on what was happening beyond the walls.

"Caine and his daughter are not my concern."

"And what about Cricket? Caine and Nina are her family. Dax is her best friend. Cricket made a deal with Governor Jackson that if she returned with a cure for Bad Sam, he'd release Dax to her. Cricket could negotiate with Mr. Jackson for a way for his communities and our city to work together. We could finally find a way to re-enter the outside."

"West, I know you care for these people, but as president of New Caelum, I cannot be concerned with Cricket or her friend. And there is no 'future' for us on the outside. Those people have gathered around my city and threatened my walls. I will not negotiate with terrorists and allow them to suck our resources dry."

I shook my head. I couldn't stop the laugh that escaped. "Who *are* you?"

"Who am I?" Mother raised her voice. "Who are *you*? You were raised in this harsh world. You know that we have limited resources, and those people threaten our very existence."

"You never planned to re-enter the outside world, did you?"

She stepped closer to me and placed a palm on my cheek. "My dear Westlin. You've always seen the world through rose-colored glasses. I think Cricket has blurred your vision. She's going to have to find a way to fit into our structure, or she's going to have to leave."

"Leave?"

"She's rebellious, West, just like her parents. And she has softened you to the point where you've lost your edge—and your ability to make the tough calls that will keep your citizens safe."

"If by tough calls you mean sentencing other human beings to death by infecting them with a lethal virus, then you're right. I will never support that decision, and I will fight you on it."

She placed a hand on her PulsePoint. "I'm sorry to hear you say that."

The door behind me opened, and before I knew what was happening, two men entered. One pinned my arms behind my back and the other stuck a needle in my neck. My world darkened, but not before I heard my mother speak.

"Find Christina Black. Put her and my son in the dungeon, well away from the other prisoners."

....

chapter thirty-five

Cricket

"**D**id he try to stop them? What's happening?" I pleaded with Derek and Rinala. "West stopped them from unleashing the virus on those people, right? He wouldn't attack them like that. I thought the steel walls were designed to ward off their attack. He wouldn't attack first." I was rambling. I knew it. But no one was answering me.

Derek and Rinala were both watching their own Pulse-Points. We were still standing in the small room in the basement of one of the New Caelum buildings. Everyone else had dispersed, including Ryder and Key.

Rinala was first to tuck her PulsePoint back into her waistband.

"Please, tell me what happened," I pleaded. "Was the virus released?"

"No. West stopped it."

My shoulders slouched forward as I let out a sigh of relief.

"We're running out of time," she said. "It's time for you to go."

"Go where?" I asked.

"I'm going to show you the way out of our city."

"I'm ready." I was more than ready to find Dax, but I glanced nervously at Zara and Derek. Neither one of them was immune to Bad Sam. "What about the virus? Will West be able to keep it from being released?"

Regret and tension swam in the trenches across Rinala's forehead. "Yes." There was zero conviction in her answer.

I took a deep breath then let it out slowly. I squared my shoulders and faced Derek and Zara. "You two can't come with me," I said, regret in my voice. "It's too dangerous."

"Not this again." Zara leaned her head back and stared at the ceiling. "In case you haven't noticed, this city is going to shit. Those people on the outside are on the verge of attacking. The people in here will fight back. I'll take my chances helping you save Dax."

"And I've got my own promises to keep," Derek declared, looking up from his PulsePoint. His voice was strained, but there was fight behind his words. "I aim to see to it that you get out safely and make it back in one piece. I promised West."

I crossed my arms. "You didn't promise him that."

"But I would have if he'd asked. With Shiloh on the outside, I'm his number one guard, and my primary duty is to help him the best way I can. At the moment, that is by protecting you."

"Great! That's settled." Rinala walked over to a wooden structure against the wall. "I have more cold weather gear for you. Coats. Gloves. All you need. It's getting down to twenty degrees at night. You're going to need a way to stay warm."

I glanced down at my PulsePoint one last time. I thought about sending West a message, but I didn't want him to come looking for me. He had his own problems. I handed Zara my PulsePoint, which still had the surgical tape attached to it. She secured it to my back again, and I donned a heavy coat and a set of gloves. I stuffed extra socks and a pair of thermal pants in my backpack. I couldn't carry much more, not with the heavy load of Bad Sam treatments—both real and fake.

Just when we were suited up and ready, the door burst open. Key stood in the doorway, out of breath. "Oh," she said, her eyes wide. "I thought you'd be gone by now."

"What's happened?" I asked.

Key breathed hard, the heel of her palm pressed over her heart, while eyeing Rinala over my shoulder. "Nothing." She patted her chest. "I'm just still trying to regain my strength."

Zara gave me a look that told me she didn't believe Key either.

"Did you take care of that errand?" Rinala asked Key.

She nodded.

"Was everything okay?"

"Yes," Key answered in a low voice. "But barely." She waved a hand like it was no big deal, but the look on Rinala's face told another story.

Zara and I traded confused looks, but Rinala touched my back and gestured toward the doorway. "We need to get going."

I backed up a step and crossed my arms. "You are entitled to your secrets and lies. I get it. But please tell me if it's West. Is he okay?"

Key smiled and laid a hand on my arm. "He's fine. We're not going to let anything happen to him."

Why did I not feel reassured? I turned to Rinala and caught her looking down at her PulsePoint again. When her eyes met mine, she said, "All council members have been called to the command center. We don't have much time."

"How are you still receiving messages?" I asked. "You're supposed to be dead."

"The same way I temporarily scrambled your GPS, and the same way I was able to send you those anonymous messages."

She practically shoved us out the door and down the hallway. Fluorescent lights flickered overhead. The musty smell made me want to breathe through my mouth.

"For the past eighteen months," Rinala said, "the Underground Initiative has been secretly building an underground tunnel. The tunnel will take you under the city and half a mile beyond the outer walls. Do you know how to locate your friend?"

I moved at a fast clip to keep up with Rinala. Zara was on my heels. Derek and Key followed behind us. "Before these people showed up outside New Caelum, I had hoped to drive one of the city vehicles to the western settlements. Now I guess it's going to be a long hike, unless we can find someone who can take us there."

Rinala suddenly stopped. She turned, placed a finger across her lips, and listened. A door slammed in the distance. She motioned for us to turn around.

We tried to keep our steps light as we backtracked. When we reached an open doorway, Rinala hustled us into a dark room. We backed against a wall, out of the light of the hallway.

Voices approached.

"Man, what do you think he did?"

"I don't know, but it must have been something bad to be knocked out and banished to the dungeon jail by his own mother."

Two men in gray walked by, neither turning in our direction. They were dragging a third man between them.

West.

Without thinking, I moved to step into the hallway. I was about to call out to them when Derek grabbed me from behind, placed a hand over my mouth, and dragged me backward. I shook uncontrollably beneath his hold. My heart ached beneath my own hand pressed against my chest.

When the two guards were gone, and their voices faded, Rinala turned to me. "You must go now." Key stood to the right of Rinala.

I shook my head, meeting Key's gaze. "You lied. You said he was fine."

"He was. I don't know what happened."

"Christina," Rinala said firmly. "I need you to listen. West is going to be fine. I will see to it. But in order for him to take over as president and give our citizens any hope for a better future, you need to find the plans your parents had for New Caelum and the supply of bloodstones. That's the only way we can lead our people beyond these walls and give them freedom."

I didn't understand. "He was unconscious."

"He has a city of supporters who will see to it that he's fine. More than fine. The plans you're going after will give him— *us*—what we need to take down the current leadership structure."

Zara grabbed me and turned me to face her. "We have to go. You need to trust West's people to take care of him. The best way you can help him is by finding these plans Rinala keeps speaking of." She breathed heavily.

I studied her eyes. "West wouldn't leave me. How can I desert him?"

"He's got people helping him. And right now, Dax needs your help more than West does. You can come back for West."

I nodded, repeating her words in my head.

"Actually, West needs your help too," Rinala said. "But what he needs from you, you can only give to him by leaving. West needs you to bring back the things hidden behind the supply shelves in your parents' basement."

I spun around. "How did you—"

Rinala's face was calm, and she gave a reassuring nod. "Know? There is much more to your parents' story. We will talk when you return."

A door slammed in the distance.

"But you must go. Now."

~~~~~

The tunnel was long and narrow, and the roof was so low that we had to crawl on our hands and knees. The only light was from a small flashlight Derek held in his mouth. When Derek, Zara, and I climbed out of the hole at the end of the tunnel, we were met with a blast of frigid air and the welcome light of the moon.

I collapsed on the cold, wet ground and stared up, breathing hard and attempting to calm an anxiously beating heart. I'd never suffered from claustrophobia, but that tunnel had given me visions of old, buckling coal-mining shafts I'd seen pictures of in history lessons.

As my heart slowed, I stared up at the trees overhead. The branches clicked together in the wind. With each intake of breath, my chest ached at the drastic change in temperature.

Zara rolled over beside me and climbed to her feet. She helped Derek up, and then they both helped me.

"What do you think?" Zara asked. "Do we start hiking?"

We could start heading in the general direction of the western settlements, but I had no idea where specifically Governor Jackson might have taken Dax by now. And Shiloh had stopped answering her PulsePoint after the first message to West that they had safely arrived at Morgan Creek.

"I think we head back toward the city and see if we can discover any information about the army camped around the perimeter."

The others agreed, and we began the trek back. As we got closer, I breathed in the smell of campfires, and wondered if we could pass ourselves off as members of one of their communities. Or we could just state that we were members of Boone Blackston with a desire to join their cause.

Derek tapped me on the shoulder, then motioned for Zara and me to follow him. We kept the outsiders and their campground to our right as we weaved around trees and dodged low-hanging foliage, navigating forward until we were within sight of a large group of campers. We ducked behind a couple of large trees to spy on them.

They were dressed in long, heavy coats. Various kinds of winter hats covered their heads and ears. It was almost impossible to tell the men from the women.

"The city has been quiet for a couple of hours now," a woman said. "What do you think they're doing?"

A guy stood from a log in front of a crackling fire and stretched. "I think *they're* wondering what *we're* doing."

The woman chuckled in response. "You think that girl was telling the truth? That some of the city wants to rebel and join us outside?"

I looked at Derek and mouthed Shiloh's name at him in question. He shrugged.

"Who knows?" the man answered. "I don't trust any of them. It's a cruel world when any group of human beings is willing to inflict a deadly virus on their own kind."

My teeth began to chatter as I looked on. I wasn't used to the winter temperatures yet. I knew that Derek would be even less conditioned to acclimate to the drastic cold. We would have to find a way to build a fire in order to survive the night.

I glanced up the mountain to my left. I could take Derek and Zara to the spot where West and I had camped the night before he took me to New Caelum for the first time, but even there the outsiders might see our fire—and besides, we'd be even farther from the western settlements.

Before I could reach a decision, I felt cold metal touch my face.

"Well, hello," a voice said. "The governor knew you'd show up eventually."

I turned and stared down at the barrel of a shotgun pointed at my chest. I held my hands out to the side. "Hi, Cade. We're unarmed. We only want to help anyone who has contracted Bad Sam."

"Let's go." He nudged me ahead with the barrel of his gun. He cast a look at Derek and Zara, and they fell into step beside me.

"Where to, little boy?" Zara asked with a certain edge. I wanted to poke her for chastising Cade, but he beat me to it when he shoved her forward.

"You'd do well to shut up."

I eyed her sideways, my expression pleading with her to keep her mouth shut.

Cade directed us right through the middle of the camp. The other campers stared at us as we passed, but none said anything. Finally, Cade stopped us in front of a brown tent. As if he'd known we were coming, General Jackson opened the flap and stepped out.

Zara and Derek stood on either side of me; Derek's hand touched my arm protectively. Governor Jackson faced us while picking at his teeth with his finger. We'd obviously just caught him finishing up dinner.

"Hi, g-governor," Cade stuttered. "I—I f-found the scarred g-girl like I said I would." His hands shook against the grip of the shotgun, his fingers not even close to the trigger. This told me two things: the gun was loaded and he was terrified to shoot it.

"Well, well, well. So you did." The governor wiped his hands on a towel, then tossed it inside the tent, still sucking on his teeth from whatever he'd just eaten. Then he turned to me. "I honestly didn't think you had any intention of keeping your word."

"Why is that?" I asked. "You thought I would leave my friend to die of Bad Sam?"

He angled his head, studying me. Something in the way he smiled and hesitated made my knees buckle slightly—like he had a huge secret.

"Did you bring the cure you promised?" he asked.

My backpack weighed heavily on my shoulders. "Why else would I be here?" By now, several people had gathered around to watch our conversation; I looked around at their faces.

"Will it work?" he asked.

"Yes." I couldn't let myself, or the governor, believe any differently.

"Cade," the governor said, "please remove Miss Black's pack from her shoulders. She must be tired from carrying such a load."

Cade lifted my bag. Zara's eyes stayed glued to the governor's. All conversation around us had ceased. And though I saw it coming, I could do nothing when the governor took two quick steps and backhanded me across the face with a closed fist.

I heard Derek call my name and Zara curse loudly before I hit the ground and lost consciousness.

chapter thirty-six

West

I woke to a sharp stabbing pain over both eyes. A groan billowed up and out of my throat. I rolled over, and before I realized where I was, I fell out of the tiny bed I was in and hit the hard, cold ground.

"What the..." I was on concrete. Where the hell was I?

I rolled over onto my back. My eyes focused in the dim light, and memories flooded my mind—a needle's pinch to my neck and my own mother ordering that Cricket and I be placed in the dungeon jail.

As far as I knew, the dungeon jail had never been used. It was there in case we'd ever had a real crime issue, according to the New Caelum teachers. I had tried to send Key's assailant to the dungeon jail—attempted murder being a "real crime issue"—but Mr. Gatewood had stopped it.

"Cricket." I moaned. I rolled back over, pushed myself to my knees and then to my feet, holding on to a metal bed frame for balance. I staggered toward a door where a small window revealed flickering light.

When I peered through, I discovered a gray hallway with flashing fluorescent lighting. "Hello?" I yelled. "Mother?" My voice turned from a concerned call to an actual growl. I curled my fingers into tight fists.

"Hello, West."

I whipped around to find Mother's picture projected on the opposite wall.

"I'm sorry it had to come to this, but you left me with no choice."

Looking up at the ceiling, I studied the light coming from a small machine in the ceiling. I returned my gaze to my mother. "You expect me to believe that?" A tiny red light flashed high in one corner of the room—video surveillance. "What exactly are you sorry for?" I asked. What would make my mother throw me in a jail that hadn't been used since New Caelum was built?

Mother pursed her lips. She shook her head at someone standing out of view of the video.

"Who's there with you, Mother? Councilman Gatewood?"

"Where is Christina, West? You tell us where she is right now, and we'll let you out of that cell to talk things over."

I swallowed hard and tried to show no reaction. I didn't know how much she could see of me. Could she see my shaking hands, or my unstable legs? Would she see through the hard exterior of my face and know that I had no idea where Cricket was? I hadn't seen Cricket since she left me in the command center. And the fact that Mother hadn't found her both excited me and terrified me. "I would assume she's in the medical labs helping Caine." I lifted a hand and began biting on a hangnail. Anything to keep my fingers busy and let Mother know I wouldn't be helping her.

"Has she told you where the bloodstones are?"

I narrowed my eyes. "I assume Caine has them inside the lab."

A door slammed out in the hallway. I looked through the small window to see a pair of guards dragging a severely beaten Caine Quinton.

"Caine didn't know the location of the bloodstones," Mother said.

"You *beat him up*?" I stormed toward the picture of her. "What the hell is going on?"

She examined one of her manicured fingernails. "Like you've been pointing out, West, the people in our country have been getting restless. We'd like to show them what life must be like in order for our country to prosper."

"You mean inside our city. You said country, but you meant the city of New Caelum, right? They want freedom."

"New Caelum is the future of our country. If people want to survive, they will do so inside New Caelum, or not at all."

"You knew Annalise and Councilman Gatewood were planning to infect the people on the outside. You threw me in here because I disagreed with them and had them arrested." It was all coming back to me.

Mother's facial expression remained unflinching, hard. She didn't even attempt to deny my accusations.

"Why would you allow them to use Bad Sam like that?" Not only was it inhumane, it put everyone inside the city at risk too. We had already seen how difficult it was to contain the virus.

"Now that we have a way to cure the illness, the people of New Caelum would survive just fine if the virus spread inside our city. And by infecting everyone who isn't already immune, and then treating them, we'll never have to worry about the Samael Strain again. Because anyone who survives the illness will be immune. And by saving those on the outside, everyone would then be under our rule."

"That's what this is about? Bringing everyone in the country under your power?" She was no better than Justin, who wanted to keep everyone closed up in an airtight city.

I couldn't believe what I was hearing from my own mother's mouth. Had she been drugged again? "This cure hasn't even been tested completely. The virus *is* still deadly, you know. Even with the treatment, not everyone will survive."

"Don't be so dramatic. Only one person has died after receiving the treatment. And Caine assured me that Cricket's friend had simply received the treatment too late."

"But you don't have the treatment. You haven't located enough bloodstones. There might never be enough bloodstones to cure a large number."

Mother looked away in an unusual show of irritation. "Caine lied to me."

"How?"

"He told me that Cricket had gone to her childhood home and gathered the supply of bloodstones her parents had brought back from Africa."

"When did Caine tell you this?"

"When he brought Cricket's blood to us for testing."

"Okay, and so what? The Blacks' supply of bloodstones was too small for what you're planning. That was the whole reason they returned to Africa. Right?"

Mother looked away from the camera.

"Mother?"

She faced the camera again, the look in her eyes frigid. "West, tell me where Christina is. Now!"

She was refusing to answer the question. I moved directly into the middle of the room and stared up into the camera in the corner. "Cricket's parents returned to Africa for more bloodstones. But they never made it back. Right?"

The red light on the camera blinked five times while I processed what my mother *wasn't* saying. Was she saying that the Blacks *already* had a large supply of bloodstones from earlier trips? If that was the case, and the Blacks didn't need to return to Africa for additional bloodstones...

I turned my head and searched my mother's eyes. "Are you telling me that the Blacks didn't go to Africa for more stones at the time New Caelum's doors were sealed?"

What was that emotion that darkened Mother's face? Sadness? Regret? Guilt? She remained silent.

I ran a hand through my hair then clasped both hands behind my neck, attempting to steady my head in a room that was spinning out of control. Had Mother killed the Blacks? Were they outside the city somewhere? No—if that were true, they would have found their daughter. "What happened to them?" I asked.

"West, if you just tell me where Christina is, we can work this all out. I know there's a way for us all to work together. Howard and I would still like to have you and Annalise next in line to lead New Caelum."

I laughed. How in the hell did she see that happening, after I'd been drugged and thrown in a concrete jail cell? Did she really think I was after power like she, Justin, and Howard Gatewood had been? "I hope Annalise is there in the room with you to hear me when I tell you: It will be a cold day in hell before I agree to marry that cold-hearted witch." I walked closer to the video camera so that I was sure Mother could see my eyes. "And I will never stand by your side again. You might think you're in control of your city, but you're not. When I get out of here—and I *will* get out of here—I will come for you. Family or not, you and I are done."

I walked over to the bed and pushed it to the corner. When I stood on it, I could just reach the camera in the corner. I grabbed hold and ripped it from the wall. Then I pushed the bed to the center of the room, yanked the projector from the ceiling, and slammed it to the floor.

I stared at the pile of plastic and wiring and wondered what had possessed me to react that way. How would I ever get out of this dungeon jail?

Hands clapped behind me. I hadn't even heard the door open. I jumped off the bed and faced my best friend.

Ryder leaned against the doorjamb, his arms crossed and his lips lifted in a smug curve.

"What are you smirking at?" I snapped.

"Relax. I'm here to help."

I ran a hand through my hair. "They were going to fire grenades of Bad Sam on the people along our walls."

"They still might. Probably will."

Footsteps sounded in the distance. Ryder jerked his head toward the sound. "I'll be back." He shut the door and disappeared.

Seconds later, someone else unlocked my door. Two large guards pushed it open, and Annalise appeared in the doorway, dressed head to toe in royal blue. She slithered into the room and strolled up to me, sliding her hand around my waist and down to my butt. She latched on and brought me closer.

The guards in gray behind her remained stoic.

I looked down into her eyes. "I have no idea why you think this would turn me on, but, quite frankly, Annalise, nothing about you is my type."

Flames practically erupted from her cat-like green eyes, and she pursed her creamy crimson lips. "You want to stay down here forever? That's what your future looks like right now. But you have a possible out... with me."

"Oh yeah?" I let my eyes roam the length of her royal blue outfit. "And I suppose being matched to you is part of the agreement."

"Part of it."

"And the other part?"

"Well, you have to agree to send Christina away, for one."

"Send her away," I deadpanned.

"Yes." Annalise's face morphed into a pout as she stuck out her lip. "Christina simply doesn't have the best interests of our city in mind. She doesn't even wish to be inside New Caelum. So she must go. I know that we can be good together, West. I will make you happy, and we will lead this city into the next generation."

I stared into her emerald eyes, which seemed electric against the backdrop of her deep red hair and sapphire blouse. She believed what she was saying. And she had lost her mind.

I angled my head. "There's more to this, isn't there?"

She held up her thumb and forefinger. "Just a smidgen," she mocked. She leaned in close to my ear so that I could feel the heat of her breath against my neck, and she whispered, "If you don't fall in line, I will infect every single person in the lower sectors of our city with the Samael Strain."

Instinctively, I gripped her throat and lifted. She made a choking sound. Her guards quickly shoved me away, and two Tasers drilled into my side. Arching my back, I fell to the floor, striking my head on the metal frame of the bed. The guards gathered Annalise up; one of them held her closer than a guard should have.

Annalise paused in the doorway and turned back to me. "We could have had something good, Westlin."

I tilted my forehead against the stone and concentrated on taking several deep breaths, then I lifted my hand and flashed Annalise Gatewood a one-fingered gesture.

chapter thirty-seven

Cricket

I woke to pain and swelling in my face and lip. The bulging flesh of my cheek obstructed the vision in my right eye. My hands were tied together behind me, and my legs were bound at the ankles. Derek faced me, his body shaking from the cold and his teeth chattering. His limbs were also bound.

"Zara?" I mouthed.

He angled his head to indicate that Zara was behind me.

I lifted my head and took in my surroundings. We were in a tent. The front flaps were open, and I could just see the flickering of a campfire, which had probably prevented me from suffering hypothermia. Though I was worried for Derek.

Beyond the campfire, I could see that a low fog had moved in overnight, and the moisture of the air had settled into my chest, making my throat hurt. I could see it was early morning based on the minimal light. And someone sat just outside our tent.

I tried to move my hands, with no success, and my legs were tied so tightly that my ankles throbbed.

"Dane, bring her out here," Governor Jackson ordered.

A man close to my age entered the tent. He bent over me, and with a knife, he sliced through the bonds cutting against my wrists. When he had freed my feet, he grabbed me by my coat and pulled me to an upright position, holding me so that our faces were so close I could smell spearmint on his breath. His eyes were a dark midnight, and his voice was soft when he said, "Just tell him the truth, and I'll do my best to help you."

I angled my head, studying him. It wasn't what I had expected to hear from one of Governor Jackson's cronies. I looked down at Derek. He had stopped shivering, and his eyes were closed.

"I will provide as much information to the governor as I can," I said, "but I need a favor."

"What might that be, princess?"

"Can you please untie my friends and let Zara help Derek? He's not used to the cold, and I'm afraid he's suffering hypothermia."

The man set me on my feet, and after massaging his light beard for a few beats, he glanced at Derek and Zara, then back at me with a mischievous smile. "You want me to let your friends warm each other up?"

Dane was getting enjoyment out of the fact that the quickest way to heal hypothermia was skin-to-skin contact. "Yes, please," I said simply.

"Fine, but the flaps stay open." He smiled again. "So we can watch."

Closing my eyes, I nodded. What had started out as a hint of kindness had quickly morphed into something quite the opposite.

He bent down and cut through Zara's and Derek's bindings. I squatted before Zara; her eyes were wary. "I'm sorry," I said, "but Derek is suffering from hypothermia. He needs help, or it's going to get much worse."

Before Zara could react, Dane yanked me to my feet and pulled me out of the tent. I could only hope that Zara took me seriously and helped Derek.

Outside the tent, Dane set me in front of Governor Jackson. The governor tried to brush his fingers along my bruised cheekbone, but I flinched away from his touch.

"So, Christina Black," he said. "It appears you brought quite a bit of Bad Sam treatment with you, and no written instructions on how much to inject or how to administer it."

I pointed to my temple. "I know exactly how much and which vials hold the cure."

His jaw tightened. "What do you mean by 'which vials'?"

"Did you think I would just hand the cure over? How could that possibly ensure that I get what I want, or that I would be treated kindly?" I licked my swollen lip, tasting the blood there.

Just over the governor's right shoulder, Dane's lips lifted slightly. Then he met my eyes and altered his expression to a hard stare.

"How much of the treatment did you bring?" the governor asked.

"How much do you need?" I didn't want to tell him that the treatment was limited until I found more of the bloodstones.

He grabbed my chin, his fingers squeezing my already bruised cheek, bringing tears to my eyes. "You better have enough." The warning behind his words was clear, yet the amount of cure needed was not. Then, he yelled over his shoulder, "My crew is moving out in ten."

chapter thirty-eight

West

My cell door opened again, and I jumped up from the bed quickly. When I saw who had entered, I nearly lost my balance backing away from what I thought was a ghost.

"Hi, Westlin."

"You're dead," I said. "I saw the pictures. Someone killed you."

Ryder and Key entered the room behind Rinala. She was dressed from head to toe in winter white, and her clothes reminded me of what Cricket wore on the outside—except cleaner.

"Someone did try to kill me, but a guard stopped him, and I convinced that guard to keep it a secret and to later help stage my death."

"Why would you do that?"

"I had all the proof I needed that your mother and Councilman Gatewood were planning to do what they could to shut our city off from the outside forever. It was time for me to go underground, literally and figuratively, and work with people who could stop it."

"Why didn't you tell me?" I asked her. I faced Key and Ryder. "And you two. You said nothing when I was in your hospital room. I thought Ryder was in denial about his mother's death."

"We had enough doubt about you... we just didn't know for sure," Key said. "And then you seemed to entertain the idea of being matched to Annalise... Like that would be good for the future of the city."

"But we talked that night after the gala. You knew I wanted nothing to do with Annalise."

"I wasn't convinced you were ready," Rinala said. "And I wasn't ready for you, either. So, don't blame Key."

"Ready for me how?"

Rinala walked farther into the room. She placed a hand on the side of my face. "West, darling, we live in a broken world. You know that." She dropped her hand. "It's going to take real sacrifice to lead the people of New Caelum into the next phase."

"What are you talking about?"

"You love this city. You were raised to lead this city. Your time to lead has come. And you're going to be asked to sacrifice a great deal in order to do so."

"Meaning?" I asked.

"You might not like the decisions your mother and the council members have made, but what are you willing to do to them to get them out of leadership?"

They'll suffer for drugging me and locking me away, I thought. And there was no way I would let them get away with infecting our citizens or the outsiders with a deadly disease. But I didn't think Rinala was looking for an answer, so I kept quiet while she continued.

"We have more to tell you before you decide. To show you, actually."

Rinala, Key, and Ryder led me from my room and down a dark hallway. As we walked, Rinala gave me a short explanation of something called the Underground Initiative. She told me that Shiloh was part of the original following, and that it had slowly grown to become a secret society. Members later came to include Councilman Herod, Dr. Hempel until he was murdered, and—to my surprise—my own sister.

"Willow?" I asked.

"Yes. Willow knows more about the different sectors and the layout of this city than any person inside New Caelum. It's amazing what you can learn in secret when most of the city's attention is placed on your big brother."

Huh, I thought. I guessed that made sense. Still, I'd had no idea my sister had it in her to betray my mother.

"Ryder and Key joined the Initiative just before being sent out of the city to look for Christina Black, but they didn't know enough about the movement at that point, only that it was a group of concerned citizens formed to look out for your best interests."

I glanced at my best friends. Ryder hooked his thumbs on his belt loops. "You always knew I was loyal to you, though."

Rinala continued. "The New Caelum council needed to find Christina because she was the key to ridding the world of Bad Sam. The Underground Initiative was excited to meet her for the same reason. She not only had the antibodies to the Samael Strain, but she probably knew where her parents' bloodstones and important papers had been hidden. Not to mention, she was exactly the weapon the Underground Initiative needed to force the leadership to be honest with their people.

"Your mother was the only person who knew where Christina was hiding—until Justin figured it out somehow and began blackmailing your mother. When Willow was infected with Bad Sam, your mother was forced to reveal Christina's whereabouts."

"If Christina was so valuable, why did my mother protect her for so long? Why not bring her to the city sooner?"

"Because Christina is a living reminder of your mother's oldest, deepest secret."

Rinala gestured toward the door we stood before. A light shone through the small window. I walked up and peered through the window. On the other side of the door were two people: a man and a woman. Their room was fully furnished and decorated, unlike my gray room with a single metal cot.

The woman pushed blond hair behind her ear while reading a book. The man was writing on some sort of tablet. They looked content, as if they'd been in that room for...

"Oh my God." I stared at the woman's blond hair, willing her to look at me, wondering if I would see sapphire blue eyes staring back. "Is that..."

"I didn't know when I first met them," Key said. "Dr. Hempel brought me here. He didn't tell me who they were, only that my life depended on keeping their existence a secret. Catherine Black was sick. Dr. Hempel and I treated her."

I watched Key, saw tears in her eyes, then looked back to the couple on the other side of the door: Catherine and Henry

Black. My fears were confirmed. They hadn't returned to Africa; they'd been here all along.

"My mother did this," I said.

"As did Howard Gatewood, Justin Rhodes, and Caine Quinton," Rinala said. "They all knew. Only Caine had an attack of conscience. He fled the city with Cricket in tow."

"And he never said anything?"

"Howard Gatewood threatened to kill Caine's daughter if he did. And to prove that he would, he injected Christina with Bad Sam."

"So Caine took Cricket far away. And saved her life. And my mother kept the Blacks alive... for what? For bloodstones?"

"I guess. Who knows, really?" She shrugged.

I placed a hand on the doorjamb and leaned into it. Christina had no idea that her parents were alive. I had to tell her. I turned to the three of them. "You said you know where Christina is now. Where?"

"She's on a mission to carry out her parents' wishes," Rinala said.

"She saw them? She knows they're alive?"

Rinala shook her head. "Do you think she would have left if she'd known? She's carrying out her mission to save her friend, and then she will try to honor her parents by finding the original plans for the city, which the Blacks hid safely away."

"Where is she? I have to find her."

"If you leave, there's no telling what your mother and Gatewood will do. No one will be safe."

I eyed Key, realization dawning. "Dr. Hempel was killed because he knew. And someone attempted to smother you." Someone had even tried to kill Cricket.

Ryder slid a hand into Key's.

"What am I supposed to do? Staying locked up in this dungeon isn't going to do me or anyone else any good. And there's no way they'd believe my change of heart if I suddenly acted like the doting match to Annalise." I sighed. "You said so yourself. I have to decide what I'm willing to give up. I will not stay locked up in this dungeon while my mother and Councilman Gatewood destroy this city. And I'm not willing to give up Cricket. So please tell me you have a plan. One that involves me helping Cricket, and then returning to take down my mother and the current leadership."

"I have a plan," Rinala said. "But it's not without flaws."

"As long as it gets me out of here, I'll regroup, and we can work out the kinks." I looked from Rinala to Key and Ryder.

"Follow me." Ryder led me down this hallway of jail cells. He stopped beside an open doorway. Inside the cell were some mounds covered by canvas tarps.

"This dungeon has been unused, except for the Blacks," Rinala said. "Someone on your mother's staff comes down twice a day with food. And sometimes your mother visits. But no one really ventures past the Blacks' cell. So we started hoarding weapons and other necessities here—as well as in other spots around the city."

Ryder lifted one of the tarps, revealing a stack of guns, knives, blowguns, and more.

"She visits them?" I said. My mother was one cold woman.

"Yes. She's been trying to talk them into giving up the bloodstones for years. They've refused. Your mother has also asked the Blacks about a copy of the original architectural plans for New Caelum. That's what Christina is planning to look for after she delivers the treatment to Governor Jackson and her friend."

"How did Cricket get outside? Who went with her?"

"Derek and Zara," Key said.

"And Zara could scare anyone away," Ryder joked. I glared at him. "Okay. Not funny." He picked up a blowgun from the stack and handed it to me. I twisted and turned it in my hands, examining it. I'd never used a blowgun before.

Rinala picked up something as well. When she turned and handed it to me, I realized it was a wrist PulsePoint. "To replace the one the guards took when they brought you down here," she explained. "It's programmed just like yours, except it's untraceable and untrackable. When you send a message to one of us, we'll know it's from you, but if you were to send a message to anyone not a part of the Underground Initiative, it will come across as 'anonymous.' And they can't locate you from its signal."

"Rinala," Key said, a warning in her voice. "It's time."

Rinala nodded, then turned back to me. "A guard will be bringing breakfast any time now. You must return to your room. When they're gone, we'll show you the way out."

....

chapter thirty-nine

Cricket

D ane retied Derek's and Zara's hands, this time in front of their bodies. When Dane walked away from them and toward me, I heard Zara ask Derek, "You feeling better?" Her voice was soft, and surprisingly sweet.

Derek nodded wordlessly. He was no longer shaking from cold, and we had been fed some sort of mushy oatmeal, which had helped.

"Hands," Dane ordered me. He smirked, but it stopped short of his eyes.

I angled my head, confused, and held out my hands. There was no use fighting. Not yet. I had to assume the governor was taking us to Dax and to his other sick citizens. I was worried about how bad off his infected were. The treatment's effectiveness would depend a great deal on how far Bad Sam had progressed, and what sort of treatment they'd received thus far.

"How long have you worked for the governor?" I asked Dane.

He wrapped twine around my hands. I was surprised he didn't make it tighter. "Long enough to know he's ruthless, and he disposes of anyone who threatens his people or betrays him." His eyes lifted, meeting mine. "Or when he no longer has a use for that person."

I swallowed. "Is that supposed to be some sort of threat?"

"No." He brushed his thumb across my hands once they were tied, and it took everything in me not to flinch. "More of a warning."

The activity around the camp sped up from there. Men and women broke down tents and carried supplies to two large trucks, one of which I recognized as the one the governor stole from New Caelum after capturing Dax.

Dane directed Derek and Zara to one truck, and me to another. There was an apology in Derek's expression, though he had to know I didn't hold him responsible for not being able to protect me at this point. Our main objective was to get to Dax and Shiloh. I still held the leverage to get us all out of our current situation.

Dane helped me climb into the back of the truck. He had just climbed up after me when an explosion blasted through the morning silence. The truck shook, and it took a steadying hand from Dane not to fall.

I spun around just as a puff of smoke ascended into the air, and someone yelled, "Gas masks on!"

Dane's eyes widened at me. He pushed me down, scrambled over me, and then pulled two masks from under some tarp. "Here. Put this on."

I did as he ordered, though it was difficult with my hands tied. When I looked across to Derek and Zara, I saw that they had masks covering their faces too. My heart raced. Had New Caelum just fired canisters filled with Bad Sam at the outside? Were the leaders of New Caelum really that cruel?

I already knew the answer to that.

Moments later, the New Caelum alarm sounded—the same alarm I'd heard when West and I dropped inside the walls of New Caelum and the two scouts had returned, infected with Bad Sam. It was the alarm that alerted New Caelum that something or someone had penetrated the city's outer walls.

Looking around, I saw what had set off the alarm: two tanks were in motion, and one had knocked a tank-sized hole in the outer wall. The second looked like it was about to add another one.

From what I'd overheard inside the city, I knew the outsiders had at least six tanks, positioned strategically around the perimeter. I could only assume the others were moving on New Caelum as well. Would the steel walls that encased the city stop the destruction that the tanks could cause?

The governor climbed into the passenger side of the truck I was in. "Let's move out!" The two trucks started moving away from the city, and my panic grew. Where was West? Still in the lower dungeon?

Dane stumbled over to sit next to me. His eyes also appeared panicked.

"What does this mean?" I asked, my voice muffled through the mask.

"It means we're at war. It will take a miracle to bring the two sides together now."

As a tear slipped down my face, I knew one thing for sure: this would not end well.

~~~~~

Explosion after explosion sounded in the distance as the two trucks moved west from New Caelum. With each loud boom, I cringed and my eyes tightened. I could only imagine what those explosions meant for both the outsiders and the innocent people inside New Caelum.

If New Caelum was sending Bad Sam into the air outside their city, and if bombs were being fired at the base of the city, would the virus penetrate their air circulation system inside the city? It seemed no one was safe.

"You can take off your gas mask now," Dane told me twenty minutes later. "We're far enough away."

I lifted the mask off my head. I was leaning against the side of the truck and wrapped in the oversized down coat that Rinala had given me. I hugged my legs close to my body with my bound hands draped against my ankles.

With my scarred face resting against my knees, I asked Dane, "What does your master hope to accomplish by putting all those people just outside the walls? By the number of gas masks I just saw, he knew the city would resort to firing Bad Sam into the outside." By the hard glare Dane flashed me, calling the governor his master had hit a nerve—as I had intended. "Doesn't he realize that I don't have enough of the treatment to help everyone?"

"The people camped outside New Caelum volunteered to be there."

My brows shot toward the sky. "Really?" I guess I kind of understood. I'd had such a level of mistrust for New Caelum for so long that I had resorted to camping in the mountains just to see if they were running their incinerators at night.

However, I never would have risked contracting Bad Sam just to keep the city folk on their side of the walls.

"They want the city people to know they're not welcome outside. And most of those people either know they're immune, or they were fully prepared to wear masks until they were far enough away from the city."

"You do realize that by firing on them, you could eventually hit something important enough to force them to flee the city. If you don't want them to leave the city, that's not exactly the best plan."

Dane smiled and rested his right arm against one of his bent knees. "You act like I have some say in the governor's strategy to attack New Caelum."

"No, I can clearly see that you're just a pawn. But since you're so close to his majesty, I thought maybe you could give me some insight into what he's thinking."

Another explosion sounded in the distance. I looked back toward New Caelum and saw a new plume of smoke joined the remnants of seven or eight others.

"The citizens of New Caelum will not be exiting their city anytime soon," Dane said.

"What are you talking about?"

"You'll find out soon enough." His smile grew, and a low chuckle escaped his lips.

"You find this funny?" The nerve of this guy to laugh at innocent lives being lost.

"Dax said you were pretty feisty."

I closed my fingers into fists, causing the rope around my wrists to tighten. "When did you talk to Dax?" I couldn't hide the fear from my voice.

The truck hit a dip in the road, jostling us about and causing me to fall over. Dane pulled me back up.

"Thank you," I said, unable to take my eyes off his. "Is Dax still alive?"

He stared at the back of Governor Jackson's head, separated from us by a glass window. "Yes, Dax is alive. The governor doesn't want you to know that yet."

Why would the governor keep that from me? "Is he okay?" I whispered.

Dane's eyes moved from the governor to me. "He's more than okay. Dax is already one hundred percent free of the virus."

....

chapter forty

West

At the sound of the explosions, I sprang from my bed, my heart thumping hard in my chest. Within seconds, Ryder showed up at my door. After messing with the lock, he swung the door open. "The tanks have pushed through our outer walls." He turned and headed quickly down the hallway toward the supplies he'd shown me earlier.

"Did they fire on the city?" I followed closely.

Ryder began handing me supplies: a heavy coat, weapons to attach to my belt, a knife to strap to my ankle, and a backpack consisting of who knew what.

The sound of the main door to the dungeon jail opened and shut. Ryder stiffened, but then relaxed when Key came around the corner.

"The city has moved into Red Zone Lockdown." Her voice came out in a panic.

"Where is Rinala?" I asked.

"I'm right here." She entered behind Key.

Red Zone Lockdown was the highest security lockdown that the red emergency sector could issue. It meant that the steel doors between sectors were locked, and there was no hope for citizens to pass through to other areas of the city until the lockdown was lifted. Each sector would have to survive on whatever resources they had, until the emergency sector could verify that the air ventilation systems were functioning properly and the air space within each sector was safe.

"I heard the explosions," I said. "Did the outside fire first?"

Ryder shook his head. "No. The outside never fired."

Now that Ryder was cleared of Bad Sam, he was back to receiving all correspondence and news through his PulsePoint. As far as we knew, no one had suspected him of having contact with me yet. What would Mother or Gatewood do when they discovered Ryder and Key were helping me? That thought pissed me off and scared me, but I had to push it away for now.

"But they did send the tanks rolling through our outer walls," Ryder continued. "And we aimed our own tank-buster rocket launchers at their machines and obliterated them."

"But they didn't fire? Why would the outsiders send tanks at us then?"

"To provoke us," Rinala said in a low voice. "They wanted us to fire first. I'm willing to bet they set the tanks in motion with no one inside them. But our people watched us fire first, and news of that will spread fast."

"Not only did we fire first," I said, "we were the *only* ones to fire." Anxiety built in my chest as realization set in.

"And we launched canisters of Bad Sam at them," Key said.

I closed my eyes and let my head tilt forward, ashamed of the city I'd served—the city I'd been prepared to give my whole life to. After a few seconds, I looked at the three of them. "Do we know where Cricket is now?"

No one answered.

I grabbed Ryder and shook him. "Come on, man! Tell me. Where is she?"

"Her PulsePoint was right outside the city when we first launched missiles from the launchers. But the signal is now heading away from New Caelum at a rapid pace."

"So she has to be on one of their trucks."

"Heading toward the western settlements," Rinala said, somewhat hopeful. "As planned," she added.

"I have to go after her. You said she was going to find the original city plans after she got Dax?" If I had any hope of saving the innocent people of New Caelum, I needed those plans. I wasn't sure why, but something in those plans had made my mother and Howard Gatewood lock the Blacks in a dungeon prison forever.

"And the rest of the supply of bloodstones," Rinala said. Her voice turned grim. "And when she does, she'll know."

"She'll know what?"

"She has enough information already to know her parents weren't planning to leave the States again. She just hasn't put it together yet. But when she finds the large stockpile of bloodstones—"

"She'll know that her parents had no reason to get on a plane to Africa." I narrowed my eyes at Rinala. I couldn't imagine the rage that Cricket would feel when she found out that her parents were alive and locked inside this city. I had to be there for her when that happened. "I'm going after her," I said.

Rinala's eyes darkened. "Are you sure you want to do this, West? No one would blame you for trying to fight your mother and Gatewood from within."

"No. I will not pretend for one more second to stand beside any of them. I'll find another way." *With Cricket.*

"I'm going with you," Ryder announced.

Key stepped to Ryder's side, sliding her hands around one of his arms. "Ryder, you can't."

"She's right," I agreed. "You're not strong enough yet."

Ryder placed his palms on Key's cheeks and leaned in to brush his lips across hers. He pulled back and stared into her eyes. "You know I have to." They stayed like that, their eyes focused on each other's, a silent conversation passing back and forth between them.

"You're right." Key nodded with a meek smile, but then grabbed his hands and squeezed them in a show of solidarity.

Right about what? I studied them, saw the love radiating off of them. Finally, Key pulled away, and they began gathering supplies and weapons.

"What the hell just happened?" I asked. Would I ever have the kind of relationship with a woman where I could have an entire conversation with a single look?

It was Key who explained. "The people inside New Caelum are responsible for trying to kill Ryder and me. Cricket risked her life and her own future to cure us. We owe New Caelum nothing; we owe Cricket everything. We're both going with you."

"I'll do my best to keep up communication with the Underground Initiative," Rinala said, sounding pleased. "We're spread all over the different sectors. That's a good thing as long as our PulsePoints continue to function while under lockdown."

I considered whether Ryder and Key would slow me down or be of some help. "Fine. But first, has there been any indication that the Renaissance Ball will still go on?"

"Your mother insisted that the Founders' Day gala continue despite my murder," Rinala said.

"Mostly for political reasons," I added.

"Something tells me that once the smoke settles on the outside, and our walls are proved secure, the lockdown will be lifted and the Renaissance Ball will continue as planned," Rinala said. "Your mother and the council know they need to maintain the appearance that they are still completely in control."

"I don't disagree. In that case, I need you all to do something for me. Unlock your PulsePoint for me," I ordered Ryder.

He handed me his device, and I pulled up a map on the screen and zoomed in until I found the Blacks' home. I typed a private note and shared the note and the map with Key. "This is a list of the things I need and a map to Cricket's childhood home. I want you to gather these items, then meet me at that house in seventy-two hours."

Key, Ryder, and Rinala looked over the list. Rinala smiled. "I knew you would come up with a plan."

"We've got five days until the ball. I'll need people on the inside to be ready."

"Oh, they will be," Rinala said.

I turned to Ryder and Key. "And I'll need you to meet me in three days."

"We'll be there."

....

chapter forty-one

Cricket

The truck slowed. I stretched my neck to see over the sides just as we pulled between two stone walls and then into what looked like some sort of courtyard with brick buildings all around us.

"Where are we?"

"Our settlement's hospital." Dane grabbed my bound hands and pulled me to my feet just as the truck came to a complete stop. I stumbled slightly, but Dane steadied me.

A small woman came flying down the stairs of a building to my right. "Governor!" she yelled. "I'm glad you're here."

"Are we too late?"

"No, but she's not doing well at all. Her breathing has worsened in the past twenty-four hours, and she hasn't re-gained consciousness in forty-eight."

"Who are they talking about?" I whispered to Dane.

The governor looked up at us. "Bring her and her pack of medicines." He appeared more deflated than angry.

Dane jerked my arms, but I resisted. He stepped close, his face only inches from mine. "Look, I'm doing everything I can to help you. But if the governor's daughter dies after he's already lost his son, I won't be able to save you from his anger."

"His daughter? *She* has Bad Sam?"

"Just don't do anything stupid." Dane cut through my bindings and helped me climb down out of the truck. That was when I noticed that the other truck hadn't joined us.

"Where's the other truck?"

"They went on to the settlement."

I stopped walking.

"Relax. I know this is hard to believe, but the governor is only acting this way because he's desperate for your help. He'll be fair if you'll just help his daughter. Hurting you was never the plan."

I pointed at the bruising and swelling of my face. "You're right. That *is* hard to believe."

Dane angled his head. "There was a reason for that, too." He lifted my backpack onto his shoulder and gestured for me to walk ahead of him to the brick building. "He feels betrayed by you."

Because I injected Dax with a treatment?

After climbing one flight of stairs, we entered a dimly lit hallway. The distant sound of a running generator got louder as we followed the governor. We rounded a corner and came face to face with a host of makeshift isolation rooms, sealed off by floor-to-ceiling plastic. A tube ran into the top of each unit, I assumed to pump fresh air into each room. There were seven sterilized units altogether, four of them occupied. I immediately wondered what had happened to the other three. Then I saw the bloodstains, and I knew the others weren't so lucky.

I studied the sunken faces of the infected. They'd suffered at least a week of illness. But not one of them was Dax. Dane had said Dax was one hundred percent free of the virus. I couldn't imagine how that could be so.

The governor slipped into protective gear—a precaution, I assumed, since the rooms were completely sealed. Then he slipped a hand into a plastic arm built into one of the isolation units and gripped the hand of one of the female patients. His face transitioned between sorrow and hopelessness, then turned stone cold.

"Governor Jackson," I whispered, walking slowly toward him. "I'm sorry that you're suffering. No one should have to watch one of their own get sick and die, but..."

The governor stood from the metal chair, and in the blink of an eye, he backhanded me for the second time. The hit sent my entire body flying sideways into Dane, and I slumped to the floor.

"Mr. Jackson!" The small woman who had greeted us grabbed the governor's arm.

Fire erupted in my head and across my face. The cut to my cheek opened up, and the warmth of the blood quickly turned cold and sticky.

Dane knelt beside me. "How about you don't stand so close to him?"

I pushed to my feet and faced the governor. "You can hit me all day long," I said through gritted teeth. "But you have no idea which of the vials in my backpack will cure your daughter, and which ones will kill her. Only I know the difference."

Governor Jackson's chest rose and fell at a rapid rate.

"Governor," the woman pleaded. "Let her treat her." The woman turned to me and approached slowly. She scooped up one of my hands into both of hers. "Will you help our Brooklyn? She's everything to the governor. And to me."

I pulled my hand away from the woman and stared at the other three patients. "What about the others? Don't they mean anything to anyone?"

The woman flinched as if she'd been slapped. "Of course they do."

I looked from the woman back to the governor. "Where's Dax?"

The governor took a step toward me, and I instinctively moved backward. He paused.

I squared my shoulders and looked him straight in the eye. Blood still ran down my face, and I could feel it clotting and becoming sticky against my skin. "You can tie me up, hit me, hurt my friends..." I said, "but I will still do what I can to help your daughter and the other three patients lying here."

"You will?" the woman asked, excitement in her voice.

I blinked at the woman, then glared at Governor Jackson. "As soon as I see Dax and verify that he is, in fact, alive and well. And not your prisoner."

"I find it quite interesting," the governor said, "that you have no idea that the treatment you snuck him worked."

I angled my head. "Like completely?" Was it possible that Dax recovered that quickly from that small dose of treatment? I smiled, relief ran through me in an instant, but was then replaced with doubt. "How am I supposed to believe that? We haven't heard from Shiloh in days."

"I don't care if you believe it or not. But you made a deal with me."

"Is that how you remember it? I remember you kidnapping Dax and threatening to hold him hostage until I appeared with a cure for your citizens." I crossed my arms. "So produce Dax, and I'll produce the cure."

The governor's face reddened. In a fury, he rushed me. He slid his fingers around the front of my neck until he had a tight grasp. He closed off my airflow. I clawed at his hand.

The woman yelled for him to let me go. Dane shifted uncomfortably but made no movement to stop the governor.

"Put her in the hole until she's decided to help my daughter. No food. No water. Nothing until she falls in line."

"Sir," the woman said. "Are you sure you want to do that?"

"Yes. And tie up her friends in the city center so she can watch them slowly freeze to death."

chapter forty-two

West

I left the city through the tunnel Rinala showed me, shocked that such a path could have been built right under our noses. It had to have taken years to build, and yet somehow they'd done it without alerting anyone from the security sector.

As soon as I was on the outside, the cold shocked my senses. The musty smell of the tunnel was replaced by the scent of distant campfires. And I was acutely aware that there were people all around me. I barely made it behind a tree before a group of four passed by wearing gas masks and carrying backpacks.

Had the masks been enough to protect the people surrounding the New Caelum walls from Bad Sam? How did they know to have masks?

More groups of people followed the first. It appeared they were all moving out. I listened in on their conversations.

"We can't return to Morgan Creek until we're sure all traces of the virus are removed from our clothing and gear," one of them said.

Others followed up with words of agreement and plans to camp away from the city tonight. Tomorrow they would spray each other with a dry disinfectant before traveling home to Morgan Creek.

None of these travelers seemed the least bit worried about a deadly virus having been spewed all over them.

Could it be that all these people were immune to Bad Sam? It would make sense that the survivors on the outside would be people with increased immunity to the virus. That could be why they never contracted the virus six years ago.

"I heard the girl showed up with the treatments," I heard a woman say. "You know, the one who was supposed to cure the governor's daughter."

"Yeah, but didn't you hear? Her boyfriend split as soon as his fever broke. That girl ain't gonna cure nobody when the governor's got no proof that her boyfriend is even alive."

"How did that guy get better so quickly?"

"I don't know, but the governor was pissed when he went missing. That girl better hope she has a cure for his daughter. You know he likes to knock people around when he doesn't get his way."

Their voices faded as the distance between us grew. I stepped from behind the tree and stared at the campers' backs until the last one was out of sight. Then I turned and bolted in the opposite direction. How fast was I going to be able to reach Morgan Creek? And where the hell was Dax?

chapter forty-three

Cricket

D ane didn't hurt me, but he did place me in a concrete bunker in the center of what must have been Morgan Creek. And, in keeping with Governor Jackson's orders, some of his cronies tied Derek and Zara to a pair of posts high up on some platform wearing nothing but their underwear. I could see them clearly from the hole I now stood in.

Dane made eye contact with me as he closed a rusted metal grate over my head.

I curled my fingers around the grate and lifted my body up so that our eyes were close. Well, my one good eye met both of his; my other eye was swollen shut. "Governor Jackson is no different from the leaders of New Caelum. They're all just evil bullies. You don't have to blindly follow his orders."

"All you had to do was give his daughter the treatment."

"Yeah? And the governor was just going to let me go after that? How do I know that he hasn't already killed Dax? How do I know he's not planning to kill me and my friends as soon as I provide the treatment? How do I know you're not a liar?" I breathed heavily through each question. "All *he* has to do is produce Dax. Then I'll treat his daughter, and I'll be on my way."

"He would produce Dax if he could," Dane said. "Your friends escaped. I told you that he's completely cured. Well, he was apparently feeling well enough to slip past our guards."

Could Dane and the governor be telling me the truth? Or was this just a trick to keep me from Dax?

Dane found my eyes. "How long would it take to notice a difference in Brooke?" he asked. "Once she has the treatment."

"It might already be too late." I thought of Dylan. "But even if she does survive, she won't recover quickly. She's too sick." I backed down from the grate, studying the intense look on Dane's face. "Who is Brooke to you?"

He didn't answer, but I knew. He was in love with the girl lying in that isolation unit.

"Dane," I said. "I am not the enemy. I brought your settlement a treatment for Bad Sam, like I promised I would. I did it with every intention of curing your friends. But I also came to save my best friend, a man your governor took from me when he was very sick. And as much as I'd like to believe you that Dax is already cured and away from here..." I pointed at my swollen face, then gestured at the walls around me. "Your actions don't exactly inspire trust."

Loud yelling erupted close by. Dane's head jerked up, then he looked back at me. "There's bread on the floor behind you." He turned and left.

My eyes darted to Zara and Derek. Zara was struggling against the restraints. Her face was red with fiery anger. Derek remained perfectly still, his eyes closed like he'd disappeared to some realm deep within himself.

I turned in my hole and found the bread, wrapped in a towel. The walls were so close around me I could barely squat down to reach it. I ate it quickly; anything to give me some strength.

The hole wasn't even big enough for me to sit in, which was by design. I was forced to stand and stare at the two people who had insisted on coming with me. The two people who now suffered *because* of me. Zara was now shaking uncontrollably. Derek looked limp on the pole.

I ran through my very few choices. And my thoughts continuously turned to West. I had no idea if the explosions at New Caelum had crippled the city, or how many people had been hurt. If West had been injured, or worse...

No. I had to stop thinking about things I couldn't control.

For now, I needed to find a way to free my friends and complete my mission.

~~~~~

Though the cloud cover was thick that day, I still caught glimpses of brightness as the sun passed overhead and began its decline on another day. The temperature would fall even further as the sun fell lower in the sky.

My legs and feet cramped. My cheekbone throbbed. And my heart ached each time I looked up at Derek and Zara.

They were so still. Their heads dangled. Every once in a while, a shiver would move through one of them, letting me know they were alive. But I knew I had to do something.

They had come here as added protection for me. Zara had wanted to help save Dax, but she also had come for me. I couldn't let them suffer a minute longer.

And I was starting to worry what the governor would do to the three of us if his daughter died while we were still here.

"Dane!" I yelled, my voice slightly hoarse. "Anyone! I want to talk to the governor."

Dane suddenly appeared as if he'd been close but just out of sight the whole time.

"Tell the governor to let Derek and Zara go, and I'll help his patients."

~~~~~

"Well, that didn't take long," the governor said as I approached. He sat at his daughter's bedside, and he didn't look up at me or at Dane.

Dane had given me a moment with Derek and Zara before some guys led them away from town. It gave me enough time to give them some instructions, but not without argument from both at first. They were to go to my house and find the plans and bloodstones that Rinala had spoken of. If they succeeded, Derek could hopefully make it back to the city before President Layne had even missed him. And Zara could return to Boone Blackston and make sure Nina was okay.

Either way, they'd be out of Governor Jackson's clutches, and Rinala and West would have what they needed.

"I trust that Miss Black's friends are on their way back to New Caelum?" the governor asked Dane.

"Yes, sir. We dropped them halfway back to the city. They would have a difficult time finding the settlement again. Not quickly anyway. And they're far enough away that—"

"That's it for now, Dane. You may wait outside."

334

Dane looked nervously from the governor to me. Then his worried eyes drifted in the direction of Brooke, who lay very still.

When Dane was gone, the governor stood and walked over to a long table where my backpack sat. He opened a small refrigerator, pulled out the case of treatments I'd brought with me,, and set it down beside the backpack. "I assumed since the treatments were packed in dry ice that they needed refrigeration."

I wrung my hands, rubbing my fingers over the red welts around my wrist where the bindings had cut through my skin. Slowly, I stepped forward, trying to see if the other contents of my backpack had been left untouched. When the governor moved again, I flinched.

"I'm not a monster, Christina," he said, towering over me; he was well over six feet tall. "I shouldn't have hurt you." He reached out his hand as if to examine my injured cheekbone, but I quickly leaned away. He pulled his hand back, closing his fingers into his palm. Not only did I despise the man, the idea of him touching me in any capacity sent a chill through me that started at the base of my neck and shot down my spine.

Also, I didn't believe him. I had a lovely bruised cheekbone and a swollen black eye to prove what kind of man he was.

"You know my name," I said.

"What?" he asked.

I stood close enough that I knew he could hit me again. I was also close enough that I caught a whiff of whiskey on his breath.

"Oh, right," he said. "I know who you are. I've known Caine for a long time. I put it together when we found Cade and he went on and on about a girl he'd met who had survived Bad Sam."

"Cade said Steve was your son."

Jackson walked back to the chair beside his daughter. He picked up a glass from beside the chair and took a generous sip of dark amber liquid. He swallowed, then sucked in a sharp breath through clenched teeth.

I felt for the man. Losing his son, and his daughter was near death.

"I can't lose Brooke." He rubbed his beard back and forth, and his voice broke slightly with emotion. "Will you please tell me which vial to inject her with?"

I glanced toward the case of treatments. He had opened the lid, exposing the twelve vials inside—six containing viable treatments and six with placebos, all topped with different colors.

"Do I get to leave when I've treated your daughter?"

He swished the drink around in his glass. "Of course." He didn't look at me.

"Fine." I walked over to the table and pulled out the supplies I needed: alcohol wipes, syringes, and needles. I ran my fingers along the multicolored vials, contemplating an escape plan.

That's when I noticed a corner of the bright orange biohazard bag sticking out of the small pocket in the side of my backpack. Tucked inside that bag were the syringe and needle Caine and I had used to treat Dax outside New Caelum, just before Jackson took him from us. Would the needle still contain traces of Bad Sam? It had been several days since we'd treated Dax.

I spotted a box of surgical gloves and grabbed a couple. The governor just watched.

"What are you doing?" he asked when I was back in front of my supplies.

"I assume you want me to treat all four patients," I said, keeping my back to him.

"You can fix up four treatments, but we'll treat Brooke first."

Of course we would. I grabbed the biohazard bag and ripped it open, carefully placing the used syringe and needle aside and stuffing the orange bag back inside the pocket. Then I unpackaged one of the fresh syringes, and after attaching a needle, I pulled medicine from one of the vials. I repeated the process four more times, careful to line up the treatments strategically across the table.

I heard the governor's footsteps behind me. I grabbed the used syringe and hid it in my closed palm before facing him.

"What are you doing?" He shoved me aside. "Why are there five treatments here?"

"One of them is a placebo." I clenched the syringe, bracing for another backhand. My other hand shook at my side. "Who will be giving the patients the treatments?"

"I'll do it." The small plump woman from earlier had appeared in the doorway. "I know the proper procedures on how to enter and exit the units." She walked over to the table and stared down at the syringes.

"They're not all treatments," I said. "Use the wrong one, and someone dies." I circled the table and started packing up the rest of the vials, stuffing my supplies in the backpack while still grasping the possibly infected syringe in my palm.

"What do you think you're doing?" Governor Jackson asked.

"I gave you what you wanted. And as soon as Dane leads me a mile from your settlement, I'll tell him which of the vials hold viable treatments."

The governor smiled, though I couldn't imagine which part of this situation was even close to humorous. "You think I'm just going to let you leave?"

"If you want your daughter to have a chance to survive." I backed away, but his face reddened, and he stormed toward me.

The governor circled a hand around my neck and pushed me against the wall. "Who do you think you are? You will tell me which of those treatments will cure my baby girl." There was a crazed look in his eyes.

"Governor, if you hurt her, she might never tell us how to help Brooke." The small lady had already slipped into protective gear and was holding the mask that would cover her head. "Please, Eli."

"You've... already... hurt... me..." I spat.

The governor squeezed harder, cutting off my air supply. The room started to blur and darken. I heard screams, and I was close to passing out when the pressure was relieved and I fell to the hard floor. On my hands and knees, I coughed and gagged.

"Do you want Brooke to die?" Dane asked, his voice breaking.

"She's already dead!" the governor yelled. "Look at her. If she recovers, she's going to be scarred, just like this girl. And she'll have who knows how many medical conditions. She'll never be my little girl again."

I coughed again. Miraculously, I still gripped the needle in my hand.

"Throw that city trash back in the hole," Jackson barked. "Maybe another day in there will convince her to give us what we need."

I stood slowly and quietly. "Another day, and your daughter will be dead," I hissed.

The governor had turned his back on me. I flicked the lid of the needle off. Dane's eyes went wide, and his hand went to his waist as he pulled a knife, but I was quicker. I leaped onto the governor's back and stuck the needle directly into his neck. He instinctively whipped around, throwing me several feet across the room.

Dane yanked me from the ground and placed the knife at my throat. He whispered in my ear so softly that I thought I misheard him: "Trust me."

The governor pulled the syringe from his neck and held it out to the side. "What is this?" he boomed.

My cheek was bleeding again; the wound must have been reopened in the struggle. My entire body ached. But I smiled at this evil man who refused to keep his side of the bargain we had made. "I knew you'd turn out to be a dishonorable man," I said. My throat burned as I spoke. "That's the needle I used to treat Dax before you took him from me."

The woman had been sobbing in a chair, but now she looked up and gasped. Her eyes were red, and her face was streaked with tears. "Are you saying you just infected him with Bad Sam?"

"Hard to tell," I answered, my neck pressing against the blade of Dane's knife with each word. "The virus *might* have survived on that needle. Then again, maybe it didn't. But you're going to want to watch him closely."

The governor's fingers curled into tight fists, and he growled. Then he swallowed hard and approached me slowly. "What do you want?"

"I already told you. Dane escorts me away from this settlement; I tell him which syringes contain the treatment."

The whiskey on his breath threatened to suffocate me. "Why shouldn't I just snap your neck?"

"Because then your daughter will die, and you'll be close behind her."

"We need another treatment," the woman cried. "For the governor."

"I'll provide Dane with another treatment once I'm far enough away from the settlement. That simple."

"Fine," he puffed out.

Dane's grip on me relaxed just enough for me to push his arm out of the way and drop kick the governor exactly where he deserved. He fell forward on his knees, grunting in pain. I bent down near his ear. "And if you ever touch me again, I will kill you."

···

chapter forty-four

West

"How's it possible that you healed that quickly?" I asked Dax.

"No idea," Dax replied. "Maybe because I received the treatment so soon after showing symptoms?"

I had stopped by Boone Blackston in search of a vehicle to take me to the western settlements, and to my great relief had found Shiloh and Dax there. Shiloh had been thrilled to see me; Dax, not so much. After I had filled them in on Cricket's plan, the three of us, plus Nina, immediately set out to find her.

"I'm scared, Dax," Nina said. "The stories you told me about that man... What if he hurts Cricket?"

"What stories?" I asked. I held tight to a strap above the door as Dax navigated over bumps.

Dax reached over and grabbed Nina's hand and squeezed, then draped an arm over Shiloh, pulling her in close. Had something romantic ignited between them? Perhaps they had simply shared a traumatic experience. Or maybe both.

"Governor Jackson is a violent man," Dax said. "There's not a kind or rational bone in his body."

"He threw me in this hole in the ground when I wouldn't tell him things about the city," Shiloh said. Dax white-knuckled the steering wheel with one hand and squeezed Shiloh closer with his other arm. "He tried to starve me."

"The people who live there are so frightened of leaving and trying to survive on their own," Dax said. "They simply stick it out and do whatever he asks."

I dug the fingers of my free hand into my leg thinking about how he and his people had beaten Zara. "You think he'll hurt Cricket even though she brought them a treatment?" I asked.

Dax's jaw tightened. He didn't say the answer I already knew. Instead he pulled over to the side of the road. "We'll have to walk from here." He shut off the truck, released Shiloh, then reached into the glove compartment and pulled out a small handgun. "We'll want to go in quietly. Hopefully our truck will still be here when we return."

chapter forty-five

Cricket

"I'll give you one thing," Dane said. "You've got guts."

The sun had disappeared behind us as we walked away from the settlement. "Some would argue insanity," I muttered under my breath.

Dane and I were almost a mile from the settlement.

I knew my way home from here. But first, I'd have to lose the two men who had tailed us from the settlement.

"Dane," I whispered. "Don't react to what I'm about to say."

He moved closer, keeping my pace.

"Two men followed us from Morgan Creek."

"How do you know?"

I angled my head slightly. "How did you *not* notice them?" I gave my head a little shake. "Anyway, I assume they mean to kill me once I give you the information."

"Maybe they just want to make sure you don't escape first," Dane said, but he didn't sound convinced.

"I'm assuming that *you* don't wish to kill me, too?" I asked.

"I just want the treatment for our patients. That's all."

"And I'm going to give you that. And then I'm going to disappear." I took a look around. The forest to our left was thickening. I was going to need to head more north as soon as I ditched Dane and our two followers.

The two men had gained on us. With the light disappearing, they were following closer.

Dane pulled something from his waistband. "Take this." He handed me a knife in a leather sheath.

"Thank you." I grabbed it, then leaned in closer to Dane. "All five of the syringes hold treatments."

His eyes widened and he drew back, obviously surprised.

"I wish you and Brooke all the best," I said. "She's got a long recovery ahead of her." Without warning, I shoved Dane backward and darted into the trees. I didn't think he meant me harm, and I figured he'd be in a hurry to get back to Brooke, but I wanted to give myself at least a small head start.

I ran at full speed.

Voices rang out. "She gave us the slip!"

"That way! She went that way!"

My eyes adjusted to the dim light, and I leapt over tree roots and ducked beneath low-hanging limbs. The thick, fallen leaves were wet from the latest melted snow, and there were patches of ice here and there. I knew that at any second I would probably either fall over an obstacle or slip in the foliage. But I kept running.

Just when I thought I had lost them, someone darted from behind a tree. Strong arms circled around me, and a hand covered my mouth before I'd even had the chance to scream.

....

chapter forty-six

West

I heard the voices, all of them male.

I held out my arm to silence the others. Dax was already on high alert, his gun drawn. Shiloh and Nina traded fearful glances.

The sound of footsteps running along the saturated forest bed grew closer. That's when I saw the flash of blond hair running past us.

I darted right, then I lost her. I followed the sound of her feet.

The voices yelled, not all that far behind us. I ran at full speed along the path until I was sure I'd gotten a little ahead of her.

I heard her footsteps coming closer, each one like my own heartbeat—proof she was still alive.

Just as she rounded a tree, I stepped in front of her and scooped her into my arms. I knew she hadn't recognized me. Not yet. I covered her mouth before she could let out a scream. "Shhh. Don't scream," I whispered close to her ear.

Her body tightened in my arms. Even beneath the heavy down coat I could sense her pounding heart, both from the running and from the fear of whoever was chasing her.

She turned, her eyes as wide as I'd ever seen them, including one that was nearly swollen shut. "West." My name passed through her lips in a hushed whisper.

"Shhh." I tucked her head into my chest, hugging her close, as I dragged her off the path and behind a tree.

"Where did she go?" a man yelled less than twenty feet from us.

Cricket trembled. I held her tighter. I'd kill the man with my bare hands if I had to.

"She's gone, man."

"How could that little girl disappear that quickly?"

"I don't know, but Dane got what he needed. He's heading back to the settlement. We'll just tell the governor that we wounded her bad enough that there was no way she'd ever make it out of the woods alive."

I listened closely to their retreating footsteps. If I hadn't been holding so tightly to Cricket, I would have asked Dax to help me teach them a lesson.

"They're gone," I whispered.

Cricket looked up. Our eyes met, and I gently brushed her hair away from her face. Her cheekbone was bruised, and the area around her right eye was swollen.

"How did you find me?"

I smiled. "I'll always find you."

"The explosions. They bombed the city."

I shook my head. "No. They didn't bomb us. We blew up their tanks."

"Hey, Crick," Nina said behind Cricket.

Cricket turned. "Nina?" She ran at her and threw her arms around her best friend. Then she saw Dax. She stepped out of Nina's arms and latched on to Dax. "You're okay."

"I am," Dax whispered. "Thanks to you."

Shiloh sidled up beside me. "I love happy endings."

"It's not a happy ending yet." I moved toward Cricket, and when she let go of Dax, I slipped my hand into hers. "It's getting cold quickly. Let's get back to the truck and get to your house."

Cricket nodded and snuggled into my side when I put an arm around her. I knew I still had a fight ahead of me back inside New Caelum, but I wasn't sure I'd ever be able to let go of Cricket again.

....

chapter forty-seven

Cricket

Without even opening my eyes, I recognized West's scent, the slight hint of pine. Burning wood crackled nearby, and I felt... warm. Warmer than I'd felt in days.

The brush of fingers along my arm brought a smile to my face. Only a thin layer of cotton separated the pads of his fingertips from my skin. I didn't recognize the heavenly surface I was lying in, and I was afraid to look—afraid that West had taken me back to New Caelum instead of to my house like he had said before I'd passed out from exhaustion.

"Good morning." His breath tickled my nose.

"If I open my eyes, does everything I'm smelling, feeling, hearing go away?" My voice was hoarse, and my throat still burned from the previous day's strenuous activities.

"Try it."

I opened my eyes to find West fully dressed, lying on top of the covers I was buried beneath. "What time is it?"

"Early."

"Why are you up?" I sat up and looked around. It was my parents' old bedroom, but it was completely different.

"I'm expecting Ryder and Key."

I shook away my confusion about the room temporarily. "Ryder and Key? Why..." I looked back at him. "Wait a minute." Details of the previous day were flooding back. "Derek and Zara—" Panic entered my voice.

West placed a hand on one of mine. "It's okay. They're here. They found what you sent them for. They were so relieved when we showed up with you. They're coming back once they've secured weapons."

I scanned the room again. A fire burned in the fireplace at the foot of the bed. I didn't recognize the down comforter. Where there had been cobwebs the last time I was here, the room was now clean. It even smelled like lemons. "What's going on? Who did this to my house?" When West didn't answer, I turned my head and raised both brows.

He lay, smiling, with his head propped up by a bent elbow. "Soon after we left here and re-entered the city, I sent a crew of my best construction workers and maintenance staff here to see what they could do."

"You what?" I turned more toward him, my knee bent in front of me, so that I could stare at the dimple on the right side of his mouth.

"I had them fix your solar panels, the water pump, and that fireplace." He pointed to the roaring fire. "And a few other things. I also had someone clean and replace the sheets and blankets and pack the bathroom closet with fresh towels."

"Why would you do all that? How did you even know we would come back here?"

"I wasn't sure I would. I knew my place was inside New Caelum. But I saw the look on your face when you left here.

This is your home. And no matter where you go or what you decide to do in your life, it always will be. I wanted you to have this house."

I gazed into the fire. Was he telling me that he thought my place was outside, and his was inside?

West sat up, and touching my cheek, he brought my eyes back to his. "I didn't do this because I was pushing you away."

"Are you a mind reader now?"

"I wish. If I were, I'd know what you were thinking."

"Why are Ryder and Key coming here?"

"They're bringing supplies. And information."

"Tell me what happened. I saw guards carrying you in the basement of New Caelum. I didn't want to leave, but Rinala—"

He placed a finger over my lips. "It's okay. You had to leave." His eyes darkened, and his lips thinned. "I was thrown in the dungeon jail before I discovered you were gone. My mother imprisoned me and threatened to keep me there if I didn't agree to marry Annalise and get in line."

"New Caelum is your life, West. What are you going to do?"

"New Caelum is *not* my life. My place is not beside my mother or Annalise. But I do feel that the people of New Caelum are my responsibility. I'm going to take down the council and the current leadership of New Caelum, Cricket." He paused. "But I have more I have to tell you. I would have told you the minute I found you last night, but you needed sleep before I told you what I discovered in the dungeon."

"What you discovered? You're scaring me."

"I'm sorry. I need you to get dressed and come downstairs with me."

I glanced around at the rumpled down comforter, the crackling fire in the fireplace, and the flickering candles on a small table across the room. "I knew this was too good to last."

West placed his hands on my cheeks, being gentle with the bruised one. He leaned in and brushed his lips across mine. "All of this is real. And it is yours. But I swore I would never keep anything from you. As much as I want to get under these covers and sleep all morning with you in my arms, I can't. Not while you don't know everything."

I placed my hands over his and brought them down in front of me. Since seeing him dragged through the hallways in the basement of New Caelum, my heart had ached for him. "I don't want any of this if I can't have you," I said. "I thought there was no future for you and me, that we simply wouldn't work when we wanted such different things, but..." I pushed back the covers and slipped out of bed. I grabbed my sweater off of a nearby chair.

West turned me around. "But we *don't* want different things."

"No. I think we both want what's best for the innocent people all around us—both inside New Caelum..."

"... and out," he finished.

"Since when did we start finishing each other's sentences?"

He smiled. "I'm not sure, but I like it."

Still dressed in my olive cargo pants and thermal cotton shirt from the day before, I pulled my heavy wool sweater over my head. "Let's go downstairs. You can tell me everything, and we can decide what to do. A lot changed for me when I met Governor Jackson." I shivered instinctively when I said his name. "The other settlements aren't like Boone Blackston.

There are people on the outside that need change just as much as those on the inside do."

West smiled at me, but it stopped short of his eyes.

"What's this look for?" I rubbed my fingers along his small dimple.

"I don't know. You seem different."

"I got the crap beat out of me yesterday. I *am* different."

He cringed when I mentioned Governor Jackson's abuse. "No, you seem more sure of what you want." He wrapped his arms around me and pulled me close. "Maybe you'll tell me exactly what that is soon."

chapter forty-eight

West

Derek and Zara hugged Cricket when she entered the kitchen. They hadn't told me what had happened at Morgan Creek, but I could tell it had been significant.

"Did you find it?" Cricket asked Derek and Zara.

They both nodded, and then they glanced at me.

"You've already seen it?" Cricket asked me. "Then maybe you can explain what's the big deal about a set of architectural plans?"

Shiloh, Dax, and Nina sat around the kitchen table, doom and gloom on their faces. I'd already filled them in, and they knew Cricket was going to need all the support she could get.

I walked over to the large rolls of paper spread out on the table, nudging Shiloh in the process, letting her know with a hard glare that I needed help. "They're not just architectural plans," I said. "They're a complete detailed blueprint for organizing New Caelum in three separate phases over three years."

Shiloh stood and leaned against the kitchen sink. She had erased the mournful look on her face, which was an improvement.

"Three years? I don't understand," Cricket said.

"Your parents—creators of the blueprint—wrote a detailed analysis of how long it would take for the Samael Strain to run its course and die out." I linked a finger with one of Cricket's. "It was never your parents' intention to keep the people of New Caelum locked inside. Once it was deemed safe to leave the city—which your parents predicted would only take six months to a year, based on how fast the virus was spreading and killing its victims—your parents planned to help the remaining citizens move to a nearby town already equipped to handle the fuel crisis, electric, food and water, medical needs, everything they'd need." I shook my head, still having a hard time believing such a plan could have worked, but the Blacks' analyses were convincing.

"And what? They never told anyone about the plans before they were trapped in another country?"

Nina let out a quiet sob. Dax reached over and rubbed her back.

"Nina? What's wrong?" Fear filled the trenches along Cricket's forehead.

"I'm sorry," Nina said.

Cricket's eyes jumped from person to person until she focused on me. "When we were upstairs, you said you'd discovered something in the dungeon. Did Rinala tell you something about my parents?"

I didn't want to tell her with an audience. "Do you guys mind excusing Cricket and me? Just give us a few minutes. You don't have to go far."

One by one, they left the room. But Dax hung back. "Cricket, I didn't get the chance to tell you last night, but I'm sorry I blamed you for Dylan. I know you did everything you could.

I'm still here for you." He leaned in and kissed Cricket's forehead, an indication of just how close they were. Then, after a touch to my shoulder, he exited.

"Should I sit?"

I pulled out a chair for her, then took the seat beside her, but sat facing her. I leaned close, our knees touching. I took her hands in mine, rubbing my thumb across her skin as if I could rub away the pain I was about to cause. "I can't imagine there will be another time in our lives that will be harder than this moment."

"Just say it, West, because I'm flipping out here."

"Your parents..." I swallowed hard, then managed to meet Cricket's frightened gaze.

"What about them?" Tears pooled in her eyes, threatening to spill over.

"They're alive, Cricket. They're inside New Caelum."

A single tear escaped and streamed down her cheek. "What?" She sat back in the chair, taking her hands from mine and leaving my skin cold from their absence. "Could you say that again?"

"Your parents are alive. They're in the dungeon jail beneath a building in New Caelum."

She stood and walked over to the kitchen sink. She stared out the small window.

I approached her. Raising my hands, I let them hover just above her shoulders, scared to touch her at first for fear that I would break her. When I did, her body began to shake. I circled my arms around her, and she grabbed hold of them like her life depended on it. Her body collapsed against me. "They're alive," she said through hoarse sobs.

She turned, put her arms around me, and buried her face in the crook of my neck. And she cried, letting go of six years of mourning she'd been saving for the news of her parents' deaths. News that would never come.

~~~~~

I held her for twenty minutes. She had stopped crying and was drawing figure eights on my arm, but she'd yet to say anything.

The sounds of voices outside the house made us both sit up. "Stay here," I said. I helped her climb out of my lap, then I reached for the blowgun lying across the kitchen table, staying low so as not to be seen through the windows.

But instead of staying put, like I had asked, Cricket produced a kitchen knife from somewhere behind me.

Dax met me at the kitchen door. His back was glued to the wall, as he was also trying to stay out of the view of windows.

Following the voices, I darted around the corner and hurried to Dr. Black's office. I peeked through the window of the side door.

All of the air I'd been holding rushed out when I saw my two best friends approaching the house. "It's okay. It's Ryder and Key." I opened the door to greet them.

"Nice place," Ryder said as he climbed the steps and entered the house. He leaned in and gave me a one-arm hug. Key followed him in.

"Did you have any trouble? See anyone unusual on your way here?" I asked.

Key shook her head. "All of Governor Jackson's people dispersed after the city blew up their tanks and fired the virus on them."

We all walked into the living room, and Ryder greeted Derek and Shiloh with fist bumps.

Dax and Nina backed away a bit, but if they felt any anger, they appeared to be swallowing it. I thought they were starting to realize who the bad guys were in all this.

"Cricket?" Key asked.

"I'm right here," Cricket said from the doorway while placing her knife on a shelf. She had dried her face, and I couldn't really tell if her eyes were swollen from crying or from the hits from the governor.

"He told you?" Key asked, as if she could see into Cricket's mind.

"That my parents are alive and imprisoned in your city? Yes."

I stiffened at her words, but she was right. New Caelum was *my* city. In many ways, I was responsible for what was happening there. If I had hope of leading the people who counted on strong leadership—hope of taking them into a newer, more hopeful reality—I had to be willing to accept the darkness I'd overlooked in the past.

"We're here to help." Key shrugged out of her winter coat and laid it over the back of a chair. "Rinala and the rest of the Underground Initiative sent us with a plan. But we don't have much time. The Renaissance Ball has been moved up. It's tomorrow night. Who's in for—"

"Wait." Cricket interrupted Key. "I realize that you and Rinala and this Underground Initiative want to take down the leaders of New Caelum, which includes West's mother." She eyed me, a determined look replacing the sadness that had been there just moments ago. "But there are some things I need to know before I join you in this fight."

chapter forty-nine

Cricket

"**A**sk me anything." West sat in one of the wingback chairs. He leaned forward, resting his elbows on his knees and clasping his hands in front of him.

Dax threw another log on the fire. Everyone had gathered in the living room to stay as warm as possible. All eyes were on me. I was sure they were wondering what could possibly be going through my mind after finding out that my parents, whom I'd thought were gone from my life forever, were really only seven miles away, locked in a jail cell in the basement of New Caelum, where they'd been languishing for six excruciating years.

I sat in a neighboring chair, my legs tucked beneath me, and faced West. "What do you think the people of New Caelum truly want?"

"They want a leader who will listen to them—to their needs. They want to be allowed to leave the city, and to be welcomed back if they find the outside too difficult or not what they expected."

"And what kind of leader do you want to be?"

"That's a trick question." When I didn't return his smile—an attempt to soften the atmosphere—he continued. "I want to be chosen by the people I lead. But assuming the people of New Caelum want me, I want to be the kind of leader who makes his people realize that they don't need my permission to leave or return to the city, but who will listen when problems arise." West stood and paced. "I won't have all the answers, but I don't think the people of New Caelum expect me to. They just want a leader who will be honest with them."

"What do you think it will take to empower your citizens to start living their lives again? To realize they don't answer to a few people at the top, but to each other?" I asked.

"It will take a leadership that can keep order without dictating each citizen's entire life. If a person doesn't want to garden or maintain the elevators of the city, then he or she can choose something else. It will also take citizens who are willing to see that they still have an active role in achieving success in their lives, and in contributing to the success of our city. If they choose to do nothing, then they'll get nothing out of life. If they choose not to help others, they might find themselves without help." West tilted his head from side to side. "Or they might get help anyway, because of the kindness of others. That's what I want for our city."

I smiled. I remembered my mother's statement to me: Always be willing to help others, even when they don't deserve it. I always wanted to amend that statement to include helping people when they don't even realize they need it or won't ask for it. My way was more complicated, but that was life: complicated. And my way required people to anticipate the needs of others and be willing to go the distance for people they might not even know.

West knelt in front of me, and when his warm hazel eyes pierced mine, I forgot that anyone else was in the room. "There's one other thing I think the people of New Caelum need."

"What's that?" I asked. My eyes locked on to his.

"You."

"The people need me," I repeated. It was more a question than a statement.

"Yes. They do. And not just the people. *I* need you. I need you standing beside me."

I squirmed under his gaze. Did he really think I could make a difference to what happened next? I'd been so angry at the entire city of New Caelum for so long. How could I possibly be the right person to bring order and peace to the very city that had imprisoned my parents?

"He's right," Key said from her spot beside the fireplace.

Ryder nodded beside her.

Shiloh squeezed a throw pillow against her chest from her spot on the sofa. "I told you once that West would be chosen by the people of New Caelum to be their next leader. I also told you that we didn't need you, but that West wanted you. I was wrong—so wrong. The city—no. This *country*—needs both of you. And I still think West wants you..." She winked at West. "... but I also think you are the perfect person to show the people how to live in the outside world."

"I've met your parents," Key said, her voice soft. "I didn't know who they were at the time, but after hearing about their plan—what Rinala told us about it—I know that their vision for the country was solid. Though it's been a few years, I still think that plan can work. And I think people want it."

I looked at West again, still kneeling in front of me. "Do *you* want this plan to work? Do you want to finally open the doors to New Caelum?"

He nodded. "I want us to show people a new future. I want to show them they have choices."

Several heartbeats passed. "What do you guys think?" For the first time, I noticed Dax holding and caressing Shiloh's hand. Nina sat comfortably beside them like it was no big deal.

Zara hopped up from a cushion on the floor. "On behalf of the Boone Blackston crew, we're in."

"So, what's it going to be, Cricket?" West brushed a loose strand of hair off my face and tucked it behind my ear. "Can we take control of New Caelum together?"

I eyed each face around the room. "Together."

chapter fifty

West

"Why haven't you asked her?"

Shiloh and I were setting up Cricket's homemade booby traps, despite the fact that I'd had my construction crew reinforce all the windows and doors. No one was getting inside this house without bombing one of the entrances. Of course, now they'd have to get past Cricket's booby traps to even *reach* the doors.

"Asked who what?" I tugged on a rope to one of Cricket's deterrents. None of the traps would seriously injure trespassers, but they would make them think twice about continuing toward the house.

Shiloh crossed her arms and leaned against the side of the house. We both knew I understood her question.

When I had finished tying up the skunk bomb that would explode all over anyone who tripped the line as they stepped onto the front porch, I stuffed my hands in my pockets and faced my number one government guard, who was growing impatient with my lack of acknowledgment. "And exactly what do you want me to ask her, Shiloh? To be matched to me? Is that it? She doesn't believe in any of our city's bullshit. She's agreed to stand by me as we take down my mother and her administration, but we're not even close to being ready to deal with more than that."

Shiloh actually guffawed. "You're kidding, right? Did you even see the way she looked at you in there?"

I chanced a look over my shoulder to make sure no one was eavesdropping on our conversation. "I just don't want to scare her away. This might not go well. My mother didn't hesitate to poison me—her own son—and throw me in a dungeon jail cell. When my dear ol' mom discovers that I've left the city, she's liable to put a hit out on everyone she thinks is involved."

"That's already happened." Key came around the corner of the porch. "The message went out to everyone within the government sector first thing this morning."

"See?" I said to Shiloh, ignoring for now the ramifications of what Key had just said. "What can I offer Cricket? I can't even promise she'll see her parents again before someone in the current regime does something to hurt them. We still don't know who killed Dr. Hempel and tried to kill Key and Rinala."

"And Cricket, in case you've forgotten," Key added.

"I haven't forgotten." Though I had tried.

"I agree with Shiloh," Key said. "You should make it clear what your intentions are with Cricket before—"

"Before what?" I threw my hands up. "Before I put her and all of your lives in danger? Before she meets her parents and sees what our city did to them for the last six years? Before she has the chance to really think about what our plan really means?"

"You're scared. We get that." The fire had returned to Key's eyes.

"How about we focus on what's ahead of us today," I said. "Has anyone checked in with Rinala this morning?"

"Yes." Shiloh pushed away form the porch railing with a heavy sigh. "She says they're ready for a true uprising."

"How are our numbers?"

"She claims that if anything goes wrong, she'll be able to get us back out."

"But she can't guarantee how much of the city will take up arms against my mother, Gatewood, and whoever else they control on the council?"

Shiloh and Key both shook their heads, regret obvious in the lines between their furrowed brows.

"Derek and I will be right beside you the entire time," Shiloh said.

"Ryder and I will be close as well," Key added.

"If the city rises against us in support of Mother and Gatewood, I want all four of you to get out," I said. "Get to the basement tunnel and exit the city."

They both nodded, but I could tell they didn't mean it. They'd be loyal to the end.

chapter fifty-one

Cricket

I found Zara in the kitchen, playing with one of the scrambled PulsePoints. The large box of bloodstones—enough to vaccinate the known population in and around New Caelum—sat on the kitchen table, mocking me. I fingered a few of the beautiful red-speckled green stones. "If I'd seen this box of stones sooner, I might have known my parents hadn't returned to Africa—that Ginger Layne had lied to me. Lied to everyone."

"Maybe. Or maybe you would have just had more questions that still wouldn't have gotten honest answers."

"Maybe." I climbed up and sat on the table, letting my legs dangle off the edge. "Zara, I need you to do something for me."

She looked up from the PulsePoint.

"I need you to talk Nina and Dax into going back to Boone Blackston."

She chuckled. "They'll never go. They're tougher than they look." She set the PulsePoint on the table. "I mean, look at you. Who would have thought *you'd* become this tough?"

I angled my head and smiled at her attempt at sarcasm. "I'm not saying they're not tough, but tonight could go very badly. And this isn't their fight. Or yours either, for that matter."

She picked up the PulsePoint again and began sticking some sort of pin into one of the controls. "You don't think so? West says Caine is locked up in their jail below the city. And Nina doesn't want to believe her father had anything to do with locking up your parents; she deserves to confront him. After we break him free, of course."

I placed my hand on top of hers, stopping her from fiddling with the device. "I just don't want to put the three of you in danger again. West and I, with the others' help, will get Caine out." I had questions of my own for the man who'd taken me from that city.

She stood and glared at me. "I understand your concerns, but you don't get to choose for us. Isn't that what this whole operation is all about? We all get to choose our own path?" Her lips twitched. "Besides, I'm in the mood to kick some ass. I was in the city. I saw how they're treating their lower sector."

I chewed on my lower lip. "I guess you're right."

"We each have our own reasons for wanting to be a part of this takedown. I, for one, want to free a city of people who have no idea what they're missing on the outside. And I want to see the city that destroyed my parents go up in smoke. Figuratively speaking."

I wanted to ask Zara more about what had happened to her parents, but West interrupted us. "Everybody's ready." He stepped between my dangling legs and put his arms around me, kissing the top of my head.

"I'll see you guys outside," Zara said as she slipped through the doorway.

I peered up at West. "You're going to be a wonderful leader."

He brushed a thumb over my lip. "So are you." He leaned down and, tilting his head right then left, pressed his lips against mine.

I brought my arms up around his back. He deepened the kiss and pressed my body closer. We stayed like that for several heartbeats before he pulled back just a little.

I smiled. "Will there ever be a time when we can finally get to know each other without carrying the worries of everyone else around us?"

He cocked his head. "I'm going to hold off on answering that for now." The look on his face was confusing and strange, but I knew I had asked a question that would take a lot longer to answer than the time we had right now.

"Okay, then answer me this: When will I get to see my parents?"

"I'm going to do everything in my power to free them as soon as possible."

I bit my lower lip. "It just seems so surreal. What if they don't recognize me?"

"What?" He scoffed. "Of course they'll recognize you."

"You didn't."

He seemed to think about that. "Yeah, but I was a fool. I see Christina Black's sapphire blue eyes so clearly now. So what that your hair is a different color? And you're slightly bigger than you were when you were twelve."

I hit him playfully. "Bigger? What are you saying?"

He nuzzled my neck. "That you've filled out in all the right places." He kissed me along my neck and shoulders. "Your parents are going to recognize you the moment they lay their eyes on you."

My heart sped up just thinking about the prospect of freeing my parents from the prison they'd known for the past six years. "West, I don't know how to deal with the anger I feel for your mother or Caine. Justin was easier because he had never pretended to be anything to me other than cruel."

"Trust me, I know exactly how you feel." There was regret and sadness in West's voice, but also rage. "They're all going to get what's coming to them. Speaking of which, I spoke with Willow."

"Was she okay with our plan?"

"Not at first, but she said she trusts the person who saved her life." He touched a finger to my nose. "And she understands that our mother is responsible for some horrible things. She deserves to be held accountable."

"Then let's get going. We have a ball to get ready for."

....

chapter fifty-two

West

Everything was just as Rinala said it would be. All nine of us—Shiloh, Derek, Ryder, Key, Dax, Nina, Zara, Cricket, and me—slipped back through the same tunnel we'd used to exit the city. Cricket had attempted to get Zara, Nina, and Dax to return to Boone Blackston, but they had refused. They each had a vested interest in some part of our plan, and they wanted to help Cricket and me try to build a better country.

I still had no idea how we were going to pull everything off without getting caught by the wrong guard or the wrong council member. How would we even know friend from foe? But I knew we had to try.

At the end of the tunnel, we stopped below the entrance that would lead us up into the New Caelum dungeon. The same dungeon where my mother had imprisoned me. I forced myself to keep remembering the look in Mother's eyes when she finally and completely turned on me—the look that said her thirst for power was greater than her love for me.

Beside me, Cricket wrung her hands nervously as we waited for Rinala to open the entrance. "You think something went wrong?"

I slid my fingers through hers. "No. Everything is going according to plan."

"We're not going to have much time to get ready for the ball," Key said.

Ryder lifted and kissed Key's hand. "You'll be beautiful no matter what."

"What are we even going to wear?" Shiloh asked.

"Willow says she's taken care of everything." When I had spoken to my sister, she had informed me that Mother had been so distracted with my and Cricket's disappearance that she hadn't even noticed Willow had recovered fully from Bad Sam.

Cricket tugged at my hand. "Why do you look nervous? Are you afraid she found you a powder blue tux?"

I mirrored her grin. She had it completely wrong though. I wasn't nervous about my attire, but about hers. When I couldn't sleep the previous night, I had sent Willow a sketch of what I wanted Cricket to wear. I'd never had any interest in women's fashion before, but a vision had come to me as I watched her sleep. I could already see her deep blue eyes against the city's royal blue fabric. Willow had immediately told me she would make it happen. She was maybe a little too happy to comply with my wishes.

In addition to figuring out what we would all wear to the ball, Ryder, Key, Derek, Shiloh, and I had conferenced with Rinala and decided how the takedown should go and how we should appear before the city.

I probably should have run it all by Cricket before I okayed everything.

....

chapter fifty-three

Cricket

"**N**o boys allowed," Key yelled out the door. "We only have one hour to get ready." She leaned into the crack in the door, and all I could hear were hushed whispers on the other side. "Fine, I'll have her ready in thirty minutes, but if you mess up her makeup after that, you'll answer to me."

Key acted like we were going to a high school prom—some dance I had learned about from reading teen fiction. I had always enjoyed escaping into such fantasy books about the pre-Bad Sam world. I could never tell fact from fiction in those stories, but they always seemed too good to be true.

We were all in the suite where Rinala had been running the Underground Initiative. Other members of the resistance were off in their own sectors preparing for the Renaissance Ball—and their own parts in the takedown.

As I stared at the dress Willow had picked out for me, I was teetering on the edge of a full-on panic attack. "I can't wear this," I finally said.

Shiloh and Key looked at each other and shook their heads.

Nina stood beside me and crossed one arm while cupping her chin with the other. "I can see why. It's hideous." Then she shot a sideways look at me. "I'll trade you."

I angled my head and laughed at her sarcasm. I threw my arms around her. "I've missed you. We have a lot of catching up to do." After she nodded and blinked back tears, I turned back.

The form-fitting black velvet bodice promised to cling to my curves and hug my slim waist. Soft layers of midnight blue fabric flowed to the ground and were decorated with intricately detailed royal blue flowers. Each flower was accented with leaves of blue sapphires. The dress was, no doubt, beautiful, but the black and royal blue colors suggested way more than I was ready for.

Or was I? Maybe it wasn't that I wasn't willing to grab hold of the obligation this dress suggested. Maybe it was the simple fact that West hadn't asked me to be a part of what the royal blue symbolized.

"Tell me again the significance of this royal blue? Something about a matching?" Nina asked.

"It's just a dress," Zara said while slipping into a simple scarlet gown that reached all the way to the floor.

Colors would no longer mean anything if we successfully destroyed the hierarchy of New Caelum, but they still meant something tonight. They symbolized everything to the people who had come to count on order and routine inside this city. The question was: What did this dress symbolize to West?

Key stepped in front of me. "Don't look at it as a commitment. Look at it as a power statement. You will be staking your claim of power over that witch, Annalise Gatewood."

She was right. I couldn't look at it as the engagement of marriage that the color symbolized. West hadn't even mentioned this so-called matching to me. He hadn't asked me to be anything more than a co-leader of those who wanted to experience life on the outside. He had asked me to stand by him, but never—not once—had he proposed marriage. We were too young for that. A shiver moved through me, and a cold sweat formed along my neck.

What would I have said if he had?

"Hi, ladies." Everyone turned at the sound of a girl's voice. *Willow.*

My heart practically stopped at the sight of my long lost friend, West's little sister. I stepped over to her and threw my arms around her. "I am so happy to see you," I whispered.

She pulled back, holding me at arm's length. She was so mature. Growing up with Ginger Layne as a mother would do that to you. She gave me a knowing nod, one that said we'd catch up after this night. "We have a job to do." Confidence rolled off of her in waves. "First, we need to get you into this dress."

"I hear you're responsible for this," I said.

"Me?" Willow asked. "No way. I can't take responsibility for this. I was just following orders."

I stared sideways at her. She shrugged. I turned back, and finally defeated, I took a deep breath and pulled the dress off the hanger with shaking fingers.

~~~~~

Willow led me to a room down the hallway within the same suite. "I have to get back to Mother before she gets suspicious."

I grabbed her arm, stopping her. "Is everything in place?"

She nodded, worry etched into the lines between her eyes. "We're ready." She angled her head toward the door. "Now get in there. We're running out of time."

I stepped inside a simple white room. West turned, and all the air was sucked out of me as I took in the sight of him in a black tux and white bow tie. My knees nearly buckled.

"God, you're beautiful," he said.

There hadn't been much time for primping—just quick, barely warm showers at the house before returning to New Caelum—but thankfully, Nina and Key had done my makeup and hair. Small braids pulled some of my hair off of my face, and long blond strands hung down my back in loose waves. Nina had left my bangs long against the side of my face to hide my scars. I thought I had felt pretty on the night of the Founders' Day gala, but tonight, everything was different. The black I wore felt prestigious, and the royal blue intimidated even me. Both colors held a promise of power inside New Caelum.

The air surged with electricity. Doubt had mixed with hope on everyone's faces as I dressed. And now, the look on West's face... His jaw was stiff with confidence, authority, and determination, yet his cheeks softened as he smiled at me. And when he moved closer, his hazel-green eyes sang with desire. I squirmed under his gaze, and was about to back up when he slipped a hand along my waist and around to the small of my back. His other hand traced the line of my bangs down my cheek to my chin.

He leaned in and lightly touched his lips to mine, and I trembled.

He held tighter. "You're terrified."

"Yes," I said, my voice cracking.

"Of my mother?"

"Of all of it: your mother, Howard and Annalise Gatewood, that enough citizens won't accept us crashing the ball, let alone their lives... I thought I was fine living my little life in and around Boone Blackston. You changed everything when you showed up and told me Willow was sick. Do you really think we can give the people of New Caelum a better future?"

"I think we can show them that a better future exists. It will be up to each person to grab it." He kissed me again, another light graze of our lips. "I promised Key I wouldn't ruin your makeup."

I smiled, and the muscles in my back relaxed a little.

"The people of New Caelum are going to love you. You ready to talk business?"

I nodded. He backed away from me just a little, allowing us both to breathe, I think. He still had said nothing about the color I was wearing—or what it meant to him. I refrained from literally shaking the insecurities from my head. Instead, I smiled at him, encouraging him to continue.

"Derek got word that he's on the list of people to be detained. As are Shiloh, you, and me. Ryder, Fin, and Xander will lead us to the ball and protect us the best they can. Shiloh and Derek will stay close and be ready at a moment's notice. But if something goes wrong..."

"Nothing will go wrong." Even I heard no conviction behind my words. "This city has been preparing for the right to live where they want, whether it's inside the city or out. You've said so yourself. And those who aren't ready will welcome the ability to decide for themselves."

"You're right." He grabbed my hands. "But if things go to hell—if something happens to me—I want you to get out of the city. Shiloh and Derek are prepared to get you out, along with Dax and Nina. Dax will be taking Nina to see her dad in the dungeon jail, so they'll be waiting there for word of whether to flee or stay."

"Does that mean Caine will be coming with us?" And my parents.

"As soon as the ball has started, and all emergency and government sector guards are in place in the grand atrium, Rinala will be moving Caine and your parents to a safe spot inside the city."

He wasn't telling me something. If he was warning me to get out of the city along with Dax and Nina, why wouldn't Caine and my parents come with us?

West's PulsePoint pinged, and he glanced down at it. "It's time."

chapter fifty-four

West

I wanted to take Cricket to see her parents before the Renaissance Ball, but I couldn't. Cricket and I had a job to do that would ensure that she would have many future days to spend with her parents, not just a few minutes. Also, I wasn't sure Cricket would be able to focus on the critical task at hand if she witnessed her parents in the dungeon jail. I suspected that was also why she had yet to insist on seeing them. She knew she had to take down my mother and Howard Gatewood first.

And I knew the Blacks would be taken care of. Rinala was moving them to a safe spot—a suite within the medical sector—and Key would be there too, to tend to Catherine Black's and Caine's medical needs. Caine, I'd heard, had been beaten badly.

I looked once again at Cricket beside me. She was beautiful in everything I'd ever seen her in, including her dirty and torn olive and khaki, but seeing her in the black and royal blue dress took my breath away. Though the colors had no significance to her, they held enormous meaning to me, as I was raised to know that when a woman wore royal blue, it meant that she was committing to stand at a man's side, and for him to stand at hers, for the rest of their lives. And the black, the color of the government sector, would tell the city that she was committed to them as a leader. I was sure the lower sector already loved her after seeing her shine in their golden beige at the Founders' Day celebration.

The door opened and Ryder entered. "You ready?"

We nodded and followed him out. I greeted my two new guards, Fin and Xander. They were each armed not only with Tasers, but blowguns and actual guns. The city didn't issue real guns to guards for fear they would puncture our airtight structures.

"You'll be careful where you fire those things, right?" I gestured toward the pistols. "For now, we still need to keep our city airtight."

"We'll be careful, sir. We'll only fire if necessary."

I held tight to Cricket's hand as the five of us traveled through dark corridors and up stairs that were seldom used and were only in place in case of emergency situations. When we had climbed several flights, Xander opened a door and ushered us into the first of many colorful hallways. "Don't worry," he said. "Cameras along our route have been scrambled and replaced with an earlier, looping video. We won't be seen on surveillance."

"What about the people? Couldn't we run into someone?" I asked.

"We might see a few people from the lower sectors as we get closer to the ball," Fin said. "But by now, most everyone is either already at the ball or they're already hidden away safely."

"Why would they need to be hidden away?" Cricket asked.

It was Xander who answered. "After President Layne makes her initial welcome statement, a host of guards will scour the buildings and place anyone who's not at the ball under lockdown, to be punished by the council later."

"All citizens are *required* to attend the ball?" Cricket asked.

"Yes, ma'am," Xander said.

Our city could really be cruel at times.

"We'll be going through the main kitchen, and you'll enter the ball through one of the service entrances," Fin said.

Ryder added, "We'll time it so your grand appearance will appear on the atrium's screens right after your mother welcomes everyone to the ball."

At which time either the Underground Initiative would show themselves, or we'd be taken into custody.

We made our way through more hallways. As Fin had predicted, we encountered few people along the way, and those quickly scurried away.

When we reached the entrance to the kitchen, Ryder turned. "Okay, guys. Are you ready?"

Cricket looked up at me. "I'm ready." The fear was completely gone from her face.

"Let's do this," I said.

chapter fifty-five

....

Cricket

I felt everyone's eyes upon me the second we entered the banquet kitchen. Chefs stopped stirring and chopping. One server dropped an entire tray of champagne, shattering glass and spilling the bubbly beverage everywhere.

West turned up the volume on his PulsePoint. That's when I heard President Layne's voice. "Welcome to the Seventh Annual Renaissance Ball, where we celebrate all of our city's accomplishments. This is a time when we reflect on the past year and make promises to ourselves and others on how we can move forward with a sense of renewal. And at this year's celebration, we have something extra special to celebrate. The union I promised you weeks ago between Justin Rhodes and myself is back on."

The crowd in the ballroom cheered, but it was nothing like the day President Layne had first announced that she and Justin would marry. I looked up at West, our eyes wide with shock. "What is she talking about?"

He shrugged. "I have no idea."

Ms. Layne continued. "Justin has been cleared of all charges and will once again stand by my side as vice president of New Caelum."

All color drained from West's face, and I must have turned three shades of raging red.

"However," President Layne said, and the people quieted, "I also have news that I am sure will trouble you almost as much as it does me. In the course of investigating the charges against Mr. Rhodes, we were able to identify the real perpetrator of those crimes. I am deeply saddened to report to you that the person responsible for sending Bad Sam into the settlements, and thus turning those settlements against us, was my own son. Westlin Layne."

Rumbles and harsh voices erupted around the ballroom and city atrium. The kitchen staff gasped, and hushed whispers spread, but no one moved toward us.

"Westlin set us back six years in negotiations with the outside. As you know, his actions caused the outsiders to declare war on us. We had no choice but to fight back. But now, as a result of these hostilities, we will be forced to keep our city sealed for a little longer."

More rumblings.

"I know you want to venture outside. We have heard your pleas. You *will* get to see the outside again. I promise you that. Justin and I just need your patience a little longer."

My fingers curled into my palms, nearly drawing blood when my fingernails dented the skin. "I am going to stop her. She is lying to her people." I said the last part for the benefit of the audience in the kitchen. I moved toward the doors that would take me into the atrium. Fin stepped forward with me.

But West grabbed my arm. "Wait. We go together."

I was suddenly surrounded by a quick whirlwind of motion. As I took a step back toward West, I saw the doors behind him open, and Derek appeared, Shiloh on his heels. Derek raised a blowgun to his mouth—aimed directly at me. I screamed.

Then Fin threw himself in front of me. His eyes widened and a gasp escaped him as he collapsed against West.

Finally, the rest of us reacted. Shiloh put Derek in a choke-hold while West lowered Fin to the floor. I knelt and took Fin's pulse. When I felt none, I met West's gaze and shook my head.

Xander and Ryder rolled Fin over to reveal a dart in his back. It had pierced straight through his clothing. West and I both raised our heads toward Shiloh and Derek.

"What the hell?" West screamed.

"I'm sorry, I—I don't know," Shiloh answered. "Derek got a message on his PulsePoint, and he left for a brief time. And when he returned, he seemed—I don't know—out of it. Rinala ordered us to join you here, and I didn't think anything more about it."

I touched West's arm. "Didn't you say that the people who carried out the attacks on Key, Rinala, and me seemed like they were in a trance, or drugged?"

West looked from me to Ryder. "Check Derek's PulsePoint. Who was the message from?"

Ryder pressed Derek's finger to his PulsePoint to wake it up. After pushing a few buttons and scrolling across the screen, he looked up. "Annalise."

"What does it say?" I asked, still kneeling beside Fin.

Ryder read the screen. *"If you want to continue to serve your government, and if you want West to live, you'll report to me in Justin's jail cell immediately."*

"Of course," I said. "She still wanted me out of the way. And Justin was working some angle to get back into your mom's good graces." I touched West's cheek. "It's time we stop this government. They are poison to the people of this city."

I stood. It was then that I noticed that the kitchen workers all staring at me. Their faces were fearful, but a sense of hope lit up their eyes.

A cook in a white apron stepped around a couple of women and approached us slowly. He stopped when Ryder placed a hand on his Taser, but spoke anyway. "It's time for all of this to stop. The council has made New Caelum a miserable place to raise our families. No one can speak out without worrying about punishment." His voice was eloquent, poised. He narrowed his eyes on West, who stood to face him. "If you are that leader, then lead. Stop hiding in your mother's shadow." The man then looked to me. "If the outside is a wonderful place to live, then lead us there. We've been forced to fear the unknown for far too long. The people out there..." He gestured to the doors that led to the ballroom. "They need to hear from you."

"He's right," I said.

West grabbed my face. "One of my most trusted guards just tried to put a dart in you. I can't be certain there aren't others."

"We're here to protect you both," Ryder said. Xander stood beside him.

"As am I." Shiloh had used kitchen twine to tie Derek's hands and feet, and a couple of the cooks had moved to stand guard over him.

Another small group of young men and women, dressed as cooks and servers, stepped forward. "And if you'll have us, we will walk with you."

West's lips twitched at the corners. "I cannot promise this will go smoothly," he said.

"We understand."

Ryder produced two small microphones. "You'll need these." I grabbed one of the microphones and clipped it to my dress. West clipped his to his lapel.

Then we looked at each other, took a deep breath, and pushed through the door to the grand ballroom.

Heads turned. Mouths fells open. Little girls tugged on their mothers' dresses. "Mommy, is she the same princess that was here last time?" one girl asked.

Another said, "Daddy, isn't that West? You said he would come. You were right."

The moms and dads hushed their little girls and backed away, clearing a path for the group led by West and me. In addition to Ryder, Shiloh, and Xander, a dozen or so kitchen workers followed us toward the platform where President Layne stood with Justin, Mr. Gatewood, Annalise, and Willow.

Willow's eyes met mine, and she blinked three times. That was the signal we had set, telling me that she'd done her part. I still had mixed feelings about Willow's form of "punishment," as she called it.

President Layne's gaze landed on West and me.

I made a soft curtsy to the president, not once removing my eyes from her. My subtle move was more patronizing than respectful. "Good evening, President Layne," I said. My voice was soft yet confident. Whispers tiptoed through the main ballroom.

"Mother," West said. He made no move to bow or nod, or in any way acknowledge his mother's current title.

"West, Christina. How nice of you to join us this evening." President Layne cast an uncomfortable glance in the direction of her guards, who stood at attention with hands on their weapons. "Christina, I thought you had left us."

"What made you think that?" I asked.

She looked from me to the dignitaries lining the main level. The large screens at all levels of the atrium alternated between images of West and me and images of the president. "You and Caine were so generous to generate a treatment for the Samael Strain and a vaccine against future breakouts. We thought that since you had completed your mission, you would be leaving us."

"Hmm. Right. We were generous, for sure." I shot a sideways look at Willow. "It's so wonderful to see your daughter up and around after her terrible illness."

"Yes. It is."

Several guards in light gray were starting to form a horseshoe around us, still keeping their distance. And just waiting for an order from their president. They would have to get through our guards first.

I fixed my eyes on Ms. Layne. "Your daughter tells me that she shared a celebratory drink with you, Mr. Gatewood, and Annalise tonight." I could feel West's gaze on me.

Ms. Layne grabbed Justin's hand. "Don't forget my vice president. He was there as well. Or maybe you didn't hear—"

"We heard," West said, his voice harsh.

"The drink I'm speaking of didn't affect Mr. Rhodes." I nodded at Justin, who lifted a champagne glass to me. He must have known I would discover that my parents were alive—the secret he had kept from me during our recent visit. I think he had wanted me to figure things out, based on the hints he dropped when I interrogated him. And he knew I would fight back. This was all a game to him, a chess match—and I was about to claim checkmate.

The features of the president's face darkened as she narrowed her eyes at me. "I'm sure I don't know what you mean." She lifted her chin, but her voice cracked slightly.

"Let me explain so everyone will understand." The guards in gray, as well as a few in red, moved closer. "But first, you're going to want to ask your guards to back off."

"I will not," she said. "Guards, take Miss Black and my son into custody."

At Ginger's command, a dozen of the president's elite guards bolted toward West and me, wielding Tasers and shoving shocked partygoers aside. We braced for battle, but a gaggle of kitchen staff formed a protective barrier around us, some wielding knives and cleavers.

Before the guards halved the distance between the opposing factions, the crowd did the opposite of what was expected. Rather than scurry from the determined presidential guards, a mass of humanity surged into the gap in utter defiance. The guards found themselves trying to swim upstream against an ever-increasing swell of citizens.

Still, these were elite guards going up against partygoers, and a couple of guards managed to break through the throng. When they reached West and me, they grabbed us and pulled us in opposite directions. My hand was ripped from West's hold. I stumbled on the hem of my dress and went sprawling to the ground.

"Cricket!" I heard West yell, but I could no longer see him through the crowd—a sea of black, gray, royal blue, and a host of other colors starting to intersperse. Just when I thought I would be trampled on, I felt a firm hand to my upper arm, and I was hoisted to my feet.

"I've got you," West said close to my ear. Beside him, Ryder drilled his Taser into one of President Layne's guards. "Shiloh is going to get you out of here." He nodded to Shiloh, who was standing beside me, bracing for more guards to charge us.

Another of President Layne's frustrated guards ordered the citizens to clear the way. The man closest to the guard, dressed to the nines in a shimmering black tuxedo, stood his ground and belted out a single word in response:

"West!"

Instantly, the people around him took up the call, chanting West's name as one. And with each shout of West's name, the crowd around us began to calm.

"I'll stay." I stood strong. West nodded with a proud smile.

I glanced to President Layne, who was literally stomping her foot in anger while pointing and screaming for her guards to continue.

The guard that had issued the order moments ago raised his Taser at the defiant tuxedoed citizen and blasted him in the neck. One of New Caelum's own people, an unarmed man, had just been attacked by a presidential guard. This was the moment that would dictate whether New Caelum was headed for revolution or a fall to dictatorship.

As the tuxedoed gentleman slumped to the ground, those nearest the assailant paused for the briefest moment—and then they swarmed the guard. His screams were drowned out by an ever-increasing chorus of "West, West" chants. Someone tossed the guard's Taser backward toward the stage, where it clanked to a stop at Ginger Layne's feet.

The entire atrium was overtaken by the chanting of the crowd. Scanning the room, I couldn't find a single face that wasn't shouting West's name. I noted that some of the presidential guards had now disappeared quietly into the crowd, while others scurried back toward the stage. President Layne's carefully coiffed hair had come undone by her tantrum, and she was now shoving guards back toward us—but it was clear the guards wanted nothing to do with further conflict. The atrium buzzed with electricity and literally shook with each exclamation of the name of their vice president, their favored leader, their hope for a better tomorrow...

"Enough!" West's voice boomed into his microphone.

The guards and citizens around us paused. West scooped up my hand and pulled me forward toward the stage, where Willow stood, smiling, next to her mother.

Ryder, Shiloh, and Xander had gathered additional guards and were taking the president, Councilman Gatewood, Annalise, and Justin into custody as West and I stepped up on the platform. President Layne was screaming, but her microphone had been removed. West approached her slowly. I was at his side. He covered his microphone to keep what was said next private. "This is over, Mother. You have managed to oppress an entire society of people who deserved so much more from you. I am ashamed to have ever called you my mother."

"As am I," Willow echoed behind us.

"Willow," Ms. Layne said. "You don't know what you're talking about."

"Don't I?" Willow asked. "West, you're going to want to deliver our mother, Mr. Gatewood, and his daughter to the infectious disease quarantine units."

West shot Willow a sideways glance, and President Layne and Mr. Gatewood jerked against the guards holding them.

Annalise gasped. "What did you do?" Furrowed brows cast a dark shadow over her face, and a look of pure terror shone in her eyes.

"Nothing you've not done as a leader yourself," I said.

"You... *infected* us," President Layne said to me, realization dawning.

"She doesn't have the guts." Mr. Gatewood practically laughed.

"You're only partially right." Willow stepped up beside her brother and spoke softly, without a microphone, so that only those close to us could hear. "You see, I had a little chat with Dr. Pooley the other day. And he told me something interesting."

Ginger Layne's eyes softened as she stared at her daughter—a trick I'd seen before. "He's a liar, honey. You can't listen to him."

"I might have believed you, Mother, had Dr. Pooley not shown me a video of the private meeting where you agreed to have me—your own daughter—infected with the Samael Strain just so West would be convinced to leave the city in search of Christina."

This time it was I who held tightly to West's hand, letting him know I was there to support him.

"So," Willow continued. "While I trust Christina would fairly punish the people who imprisoned her parents—and who most likely infected her with Bad Sam years ago—I felt this was a fitting punishment for the crimes you've committed against me and the people of New Caelum. Christina may not believe in the death penalty, but after what you, Mr. Gatewood, and Annalise have done in your lust for power, trust me, I'll sleep well tonight."

West nodded to the guards, and they led the fallen leaders away. Though the people couldn't hear what had transpired between Willow and her mother, cheers erupted around the atrium.

West and I made our way to the podium. West smiled at me with mixed emotions, then after a deep breath, he turned to his city.

"Ladies and gentlemen, my mother was right when she said that tonight's celebration represented another chance for our city to start over. Only this year, we have something new to celebrate. I, along with the lovely Christina Black..."—he paused long enough to glance sideways at me—"stand before you tonight to carry out the original plan for this city.

"This city was only supposed to stay sealed for six months. Yet we have sealed ourselves away for more than six *years*. Until now. Christina and I stand ready to lead you to a more hopeful place in this world. We want to show you that the outside is safe and thriving with life. If you will give us your support, we will prove it to you."

Murmurs spread through the crowd. One person yelled out, "How do we know you're telling the truth?"

"If you don't want to take their word for it—take mine," a microphoned voice boomed from above.

All heads turned toward a man on the fourth level balcony—the same balcony where President Layne had stood with Justin the day they announced that West and I would be matched. The atrium fell silent.

I gasped and nearly crumpled at the sight of the man with chestnut hair and a full beard.

"Dad," I whispered.

A small woman with long blond hair stepped up beside my father at the microphone. "And you can take my word for it."

My parents were alive. I had known it, but until this moment, a part of me had still struggled to believe what I had yet to see with my own eyes.

My father spoke again. "Citizens of New Caelum, I am Dr. Henry Black, and this is my wife, Dr. Catherine Black. I know that you remember us. We stood here more than six years ago and told you we would protect you during the darkest time our country had ever seen. You were told shortly afterward that we flew to Africa and got cut off when the nation halted air travel. Some of you were even led to believe that we knowingly *abandoned* you. This was not true. For the past six years, your president, and several of your council members, have kept my wife and me imprisoned in the dungeons of this city. And they misled not only you, but our own daughter"—his voice broke— "into believing we were most likely dead." For the first time in six years, my father turned his eyes on me, and even from four levels away, I could see them brimming with tears.

Then, like dominoes, the men around the room bowed, and the women curtsied. Children clung to their parents' legs. It was as if we were royalty standing before them. That was not the role West or I desired, but we understood that their bows and curtsies were not for us, but for the promises we were presenting to them.

My parents moved aside, and Rinala stepped up to the microphone. "Good evening, citizens," she said, and she was met with more gasps and hushed voices. "You know me. I am one of you. I have worked my way from the lower sector, to the gardening and food sectors, to becoming a member of the council. I have watched Westlin Layne grow up. I assure you, he is ready to take over this city. But he brings to you a different sort of plan—one in which you get to decide how, and where, you will live."

West squeezed my hand. "Citizens of New Caelum, I ask... no, I *beg* you to please place your trust in us. We will show you a new life. A rebirth. A true renaissance."

A low rumble of voices moved around the room. Soon, the rumble grew, until, once again, the crowd broke into a chant: *West. West. West. West.*

I smiled up at West, and I was more certain than I'd ever been in my life that I was where I was supposed to be.

....

chapter fifty-six

West

I stood at the entrance to the living room of one of New Caelum's suites, watching Cricket get reacquainted with her parents. I was touched by how forgiving Dr. and Mrs. Black were toward those responsible for keeping them locked up. They understood that the guards who had brought them food, the doctors and nurses who had brought them medical care, and the others who had tended to their needs over the last six years, had done so only because they were certain they'd be killed if they revealed what they had seen.

"My beautiful girl," Mrs. Black said, patting her daughter's hand. They sat on the sofa looking out over the forest Cricket loved so much. "You're all grown up."

"And we heard you took on Governor Jackson," Dr. Black said from a neighboring chair.

"You know the governor?" Cricket asked.

"Oh yes," her dad confirmed. His eyes found mine across the room.

Cricket followed his gaze. "What are you keeping from me?"

"You uncovered so much by finding those plans at our house. But we didn't keep a complete written history of what the world was like when the Samael Strain first broke out all those years ago. Many of the top doctors and scientists who tried to help ended up inside this city, but a few refused. Governor Jackson was one of them."

Cricket's mother patted her knee. "That's a story for another day. I'm tired."

"I'm sorry, Mom. We'll let you rest." Cricket stood, and I joined her, putting my arm around her and letting her ease in close to my body.

"Dr. and Mrs. Black," I began.

"Oh, dear, I think you'd better call us Henry and Catherine. Seeing as—"

"Henry and Catherine it is," I interrupted, and she smiled at her near mistake. "We're going to let you rest. Christina and I have our own rest to catch up on."

"That you do," Henry agreed. "If you're going to run a city, you'll need it."

Cricket leaned over and kissed her parents' foreheads, and I could tell by the way she bit her bottom lip that she was terrified to leave them.

I pulled her in close and placed a kiss of my own on top of her head. Thankfully, Cricket missed the wink her mother gave me just before I turned and led Cricket to the door.

I had thought I would never tear her away from her parents, but thankfully they understood that I had something I needed to do—which was why they had made up the excuse of being tired.

As soon as we were on the other side of the door, Cricket looked up at me. "What are you up to? If you think I bought that my parents were tired, you're crazy. I can sense a scheme a mile away."

....

chapter fifty-seven

Cricket

"**M**y eyes *are* closed," I said for the millionth time as West led me down a long hallway. "I know we haven't left the government sector. You can take me down a thousand hallways, up and down stairs and into elevators—I know the smell of the government sector."

"Okay, we're here." The sound of another door clicked closed behind me.

I could tell by the darkness behind my eyelids that we were in an unlit room. "Can I open my eyes?"

"Yes."

When I did, I thought I was under the night sky, only it was warm, not cold. I tilted my head back and took in the sight of stars all around us. "What is this?"

"It's so cold out tonight—below freezing—that I thought I would bring the night sky indoors to you."

I turned in a circle. We were in a large dark room. The walls were black or midnight blue. And some sort of machine in the middle of the room was projecting the stars, including constellations and planets, on the ceiling above us.

"It's beautiful," I whispered.

West's arms circled around me. I let my head rest against his shoulder as I admired the view of the universe.

"Come on." He pulled me to the other side of the room, where blankets and pillows had been thrown about, much like on the roof weeks ago. He lowered himself to the pillows and reached a hand out to me.

I stared at his hand, then lifted my gaze to his face. "Thank you."

He climbed up on his knees and grabbed my hand to pull me closer. I fell to my knees in front of him.

"Don't thank me. Don't you realize? Everything I do, I do because I love you."

"We have a long road ahead of us, West."

"And we're going to travel it together."

I couldn't help but let a hint of a smile touch my lips.

I wanted to remind him that nothing had changed. He still belonged inside the city, and I still craved a home on the outside. But something stopped me. Every time I reminded him of our obstacles, he found a way to destroy them. Not to mention, here I was again inside his city. And the people here had made me feel more than welcome.

And my parents were here. My smile grew at that thought.

"Cricket," West said, "you're right. We do have a long road ahead of us. Our country has a lot of rebuilding to do. Some people will choose to remain inside, and some will look to start over outside. We knew that when you agreed to stand beside me."

Did I dare tell him that part of why I wanted to help him command this city was because I hoped to take down Governor Jackson? And I would need West's help and the firepower of

New Caelum to do so. The governor had shown me that the settlements on the outside were just as flawed as New Caelum.

"But I had ulterior motives for having you next to me," West said.

I angled my head and studied the scheming look in his eyes.

"I didn't ask you this before the Renaissance Ball, because I wanted to meet your parents and talk to them first."

"Didn't ask me what?"

"And I didn't want this to be some New Caelum ritual. I wanted to ask you this when we were settled between our two worlds."

"Ask me what?" I whispered.

"Will you stand by me? Will you help me lead the people around us... as my partner? As my wife?"

"Your wife? Aren't we too young?"

"Probably. I have no idea. But I know that there will never be anyone for me but you, and I know that this world of ours needs a fresh start. We need a fresh start. Besides..."

I raised a brow. "What?"

"I want a legal promise from you that every time you run off—no matter where you run to—you'll come back to me."

I let my lips lift in a smile as I gave him a playful shove backward onto the pillows. Then I lowered myself to him and let my lips find his.

His hand snaked up through my hair, and he rolled me over onto my back, exploring my mouth slowly. He brushed the side of my face with the back of his hand, and let it travel down the side of my body until it rested at my waist.

When he pulled back, giving us a chance to catch our breath, he said, "Is that a yes?"

Several heartbeats passed as I nearly got lost in the intensity of his gaze, and in those heartbeats I tried to imagine what the rest of my life would look like without him in it. When I couldn't imagine that life, I gave him my answer: "Yes."

"Yes?" He smiled.

"Yes."

He kissed me again, and when we took a break from that, we both stared up at the stars and got lost in the promise of endless possibilities.

Note From the Author

Please visit the retailer's product page if you have enjoyed this story to leave a review. It helps me to know which characters and story lines readers enjoy so I can make future books even better. You are the reason I write these stories and I sincerely appreciate you!

And if you'd like to hear about future releases from me, please visit my website and subscribe to my newsletter.

Thank you for your support,
~ Heather Sunseri

Also by Heather Sunseri

The *Mindspeak* Series

Mindspeak

Mindsiege

Mindsurge

Tracked

The *Emerge* Series

Emerge

Uprising

Renaissance

"The Meeting" (An *Emerge* short story)

Acknowledgements

Luke 8:48

Thank you:

Mike Sunseri. I could not ask for a better first reader, cover designer, father to my children, husband, and best friend.

David Gatewood. So thankful for your ability to take my words, rearrange them, and make them still sound like me, only smoother and with more sense.

Melissa Bybee-Fields and Connie Boyce. For finding those pesky typos. They're like gray hairs. Pluck one, and three more pop up in their place.

Katie Ganshert and Kathleen Brooks. For listening to me when the self-doubt seeps into my world just as I think I'm almost done with the book.

Donna McDonald. For being a superhero when it comes to eBook formatting.

Kathleen Brooks (again), Kris Calvert, J.M. Madden, Donna McDonald (again), and Robyn Peterman. For breakfasts, lunches, long talks about writing, publishing, and other things I can't repeat in a young adult novel.

ABOUT THE AUTHOR

Heather Sunseri was raised on a tiny farm in one of the smallest towns in thoroughbred horse country near Lexington, Kentucky. After high school, she attended Furman University in Greenville, South Carolina, and later graduated from the University of Kentucky with a degree in accounting. Always torn between a passion for fantasy and a mind for the rational, it only made sense to combine her career in accounting with a novel-writing dream.

Heather now lives in a different small town on the other side of Lexington with her two children and her husband, Mike, the biggest Oregon Duck fan in the universe. She is a recovering CPA, and when she's not writing, she spends her time tormenting her daughter's cat, Olivia, and loving on her son's Golden Retriever, Jenny.

Heather loves to hear from readers. Please sign up for her newsletter—*A Piece of My Mind*—to hear when future novels are released by following this link: http://heathersunseri.com/newsletter. You can also connect with her in several other ways:

Heather Sunseri
P.O. Box 1264
Versailles, KY 40383

Web site: http://heathersunseri.com
Email: heather@heathersunseri.com
Facebook: http://www.facebook.com/heathersunseri.writer
Twitter: @HeatherSunseri

Photo by Candace Sword

Made in the USA
Lexington, KY
09 December 2016